About the Author

Mohanalakshmi Rajakumar is a South Asian American who has lived in Qatar since 2005. Moving to the Arabian Desert was fortuitous in many ways since this is where she met her husband, had two sons, and became a writer. After she joined the e-book revolution, Mohana dreams in plotlines. Learn more about her work on her website at www.mohadoha.com or follow her latest on Twitter: @moha_doha.

Also by Mohanalakshmi Rajakumar
Fiction
The Opposite of Hate
An Unlikely Goddess
The Dohmestics (please enjoy the free excerpt included at the end of this book)
Love Comes Later
Saving Peace
Coloured and Other Stories

Nonfiction
From Dunes to Dior
So You Want to Sell a Million Copies
Mommy but Still Me

Receive a free copy of the short story collection, *Coloured and Other Stories*, by signing up for her newsletter: http://www.mohadoha.com/newsletter.

At the end of this novel you will find a free preview of the award winning contemporary romance, *Love Comes Later*, which is also set in the Arabian Gulf.

No Place for Women

Mohanalakshmi Rajakumar

Mohanalakshmi Rajakumar
July 2016

No Place for Women
Copyright © **2016 Mohanalakshmi Rajakumar**

For Lauren, Jennifer, and all expat women who never make it home

Prologue

Droplets gushed like hundreds of living, writhing beings, scurrying from the tip of the stainless steel faucet to the far end of the bathtub. Finding no escape, they banded together and rose, climbing the curved sides.

She lit a candle, breathing in the floral scent and shaking the crick out of her neck, shedding the complaints that rang in her ears. *He's not sharing. She's tattletaling.*

The singsong tones of nursery rhymes played on repeat in her mind. *Forcefully exhale. Inhale through the nose. Focus on the present.*

She flicked the tap closed. No, the sound remained. Musical notes called her to the front door. Her phone's blank screen said it couldn't be an emergency. Whoever it was could come back.

The notes persisted.

Drawing on a robe, she stalked to the door.

Dark eyes darted up, down, and around in a now familiar circle of servitude, taking in the concrete stairwell, the doormat made from recycled rubber, anywhere but her face.

"Sorry, I'm bothering."

"About to take a bath." She leaned against the jamb. "You okay?"

"I—I want to talk."

Of course. Her reputation as the listening post was cemented.

"Not take long. Five minute?"

"Alright. Come in." She pasted on a smile that went no further than the corners of her mouth. *Don't be too nice, don't go out of your way, people take advantage* – her mother's dictums were for another place, another culture. *Delayed,* she consoled herself. *I wasn't in the tub yet.* This is a slight *delay* in having a bath. Not exactly bending over backward. If modifying your evening was the price for being a listening ear, then she could afford it.

But tonight, the price of being a decent human being, which was how she thought of herself, now, after moving to the desert and retaining her conscience, tonight the cost would be much, much higher.

Chapter One

Ali brushed at the front of his *thobe*. Triangular sliver cufflinks winked in the mirror, wider than anything he would choose, but his sisters would be offended if he didn't wear them, tonight of all nights. On the hook in the bathroom hung the black *bisht*; a gauzy robe lined with gold cord, normally worn by ministers and bridegrooms.

On the surface, Ali made a respectable bridegroom: no smoking, or drinking, no girls. Prayer—he could do that more publicly. But he couldn't change his deformity or the fact he clung to the last rung of respectability in his profession. Last year's demotion challenged Ali's reputation as a shrewd policeman but so far he managed to keep his professional difficulties from his immediate family. Only his mother knew about his childhood deformity; the illness that claimed one of his testicles and half his manhood.

"You look so handsome," Aisha gushed from the doorway. Her girlish voice broke through his assessment.

Ali turned with a start. "Don't sneak up on people."

She showed no signs of having seen his practice smiles, lips together, forcing warmth into his eyes. No one told Aisha that the night ahead would be awkward, not festive. At the glow in her pre-teen eyes, his mood lightened. *Let someone have fun.* A pink bow cinched her white lace dress at the waist. Children enjoyed themselves most at these things.

Since their father's death, Ali skipped social niceties such as weddings and funerals. He was the only son, and most of his cousins enjoyed the bachelor's lifestyle. Aisha twirled, letting the bell of her skirt swirl. The fabric settled around her knees. She stood on her tiptoes to gaze in the mirror. "Do I look fat?"

He scrunched his face, pretending to scrutinize her. "I see muscle," Ali said, pleased to be telling the truth. The lingering pounds on Aisha's frame were disappearing thanks to the afterschool activities he'd enrolled her in at the international school. Basketball would help her for a few more years until university, when playing sports in a head covering would become more complicated and she would no longer consider being muscular a positive attribute. He squeezed her arm and she flexed, curling her bicep and beaming at him.

"Ready?"

"Yes." Because no other answer would do. His heart thudded as if he had run a 5K, not been primping like a woman. First in the barbershop, trimming his beard, resisting the Turk's recommendation of a shadow and opting for a clean shave. The man rubbed his hands through Ali's hair, shampooing it.

This is a new beginning, his mother said as she read Qu'ranic verses over him when he announced his intent to propose to Maryam, the university student instrumental in finding the labor smugglers. Her beauty—and singularity as the first woman Ali spent time with other than his sisters—didn't hurt. A wife meant certain future happiness for Ali's widowed mother. *Grand-children* all but beamed from her eyes. But a wife also meant brothers, uncles, and a father who would want to check the groom's reputation. Ali's secret would be discovered. Being half a man wouldn't sit well with most local fathers. Honor dictated he should reveal this to Maryam's family. Jaber could take any excuse to send his daughter to the extended family living in Saudi. Exile would be an unfair return for the girl who helped solve his first case and also, if he were honest, captured his interest. He could provide a note, should provide evidence of the English doctor's assurances that his deformity would not affect anything—even the ability to have children.

"Some *oud?*" Maha, his other sister, held out a beveled glass bottle the size of her palm. The deep purple of her dress reminded him of a bruise, her hair cascading in waves down to her waist.

Ali flexed his hands. His engagement meant as much to them as it did to Maryam's family—maybe more. With him married off, the door opened to suitors for his sisters. The haste with which Jaber arranged things left little time for anyone to object. They were family, after all, though Ali's side from a less prominent branch. Same tribe, steady job, out at night with his daughter—the sheikh wrote the contract without the reputation checks most grooms endured good-naturedly. He moistened the tip of his finger with oil-rich fragrance and wiped it on his neck.

"Ah this night, finally this night, *inshallah kheir,*" his mother said under the breath. Gold glinted from her ears, neck, and wrists, for the first time since her husband's death, almost a decade ago. She emanated happiness, in a long-sleeve, blue suede gown, with a wide necklace against her throat.

Unexpectedly, Ali's vision clouded. She didn't dress up, not even to attend weddings. Unlike many local women, she shrank from social obligations, pressed into the home by her widowhood and her son's deformity. He would never know what his father would have made of his soon-to-be wife. Yusuf died with Ali still a boy, around Aisha's age, oblivious to the demands the world made on men.

"Ali?" Maha snapped her fingers in front of him. Aisha giggled.

"Yes." He started, his attention snapping back to his sisters.

"If we are going—"

"The truck is outside."

They trooped through the house, their heels clicking on the marble. He glanced in the mirror in the entryway as his sisters pulled on their *abayas*. Maha turned to help her mother. Aisha pirouetted in the foyer. A few more months, weeks, years—Ali didn't want to ask, but the signs of puberty were on Aisha's rounding hips and chest—and she would also cover herself in black to leave the house. If she continued playing sports, it would be while tugging at a scarf with one hand and dribbling with the other. This was the way of things; his mother wouldn't have it otherwise.

He went out the side door before them, unlocked the truck, and brought out the step. Ali swung into the driver's seat, but the lack of running board would make it tricky for the ladies to get in. He helped each of them into the back cab, waving off Nareena, the driver who came running from his room at the side of the house. "I'm taking them, but you may have to bring them back."

Nareena smiled. He rushed to Ali at the driver's side and pressed a box into his hands. "Congratulations, Sir." His thin face split in half with a wide smile. "*Mabrook*, I am meaning."

"Uh." Ali clutched the square box.

"Many happy returns," Nareena said.

"Yes," Ali said.

Nareena tapped his chest twice. "You are calling me when ready for Madam to come home?"

Ali set the box on the seat and climbed into the truck. The engine jumped to life with a metallic roar. "Thank you," he mumbled. Ali waved to the still-smiling family driver, outlined by the light in the courtyard.

"Did Nareena give you a present?" Aisha reached for the box wrapped in yellow and white stripes.

"Leave it." Maha swatted at her sister's fingers.

"No, it's fine. Open it," Ali said. "Let's see what's inside."

"He's a nice boy." His mother fanned herself. "But not very smart."

"He's older than me," Ali muttered, watching his mirrors as the car slid out of the boundary gate surrounding the house.

"It's a wallet!" Aisha passed the brown faux leather wallet over Ali's shoulder.

He took it, placing it in the gap between the cup-holders. Ali swung through the neighborhood, raising his hand in greeting at the men gathered on the wooden benches outside their boundary wall, leaning on their upright knees. "*Salaam alaikum*," he answered, using the car's speakers.

The blare of his phone startled him. "Why aren't you here yet?" His cousin's breathless voice filled the cabin. "The sheikh is waiting, and I'm sitting in the car outside the house."

Ali switched the audio to the phone's speakers. "We're five minutes away."

"Okay, hurry up because her dad looks like he's still—"

"Coming." Ali disconnected the call in case Hassan said anything else about how Jaber felt about his future son-in-law. His own family assumed he met Maryam through work; an idea he encouraged, and technically true. Ali said nothing about the investigation into labor malpractice that brought them together in the industrial area on the fringes of the city. He glanced in the rearview mirror. Maha used her phone, sending selfies and Snapchats of her make-up and jewelry to friends. Aisha hummed along to the innocuous pop song on the radio, her favorite. His mother stared out the window, her lips moving rapidly, reciting the Qu'ran. The crease in her brow belied nervousness.

True to his word, Ali pulled up in front of Maryam's house a few minutes later. Hassan gave him a thumbs-up from inside his Nissan SUV. Ali gave his cousin a nod. He nosed the truck through the gate in the boundary wall of Maryam's family house and parked in front of the main part of the building, letting out his sisters and mother, who paused to squeeze his arm tightly. The women gathered the folds of their robes and made their way up the three steps of the veranda.

"It's happening," his mother whispered.

"*Enshallah*," he said. Sweat beaded his lip.

"Park there." Jaber emerged from the *majlis* and waved at the carport on the left of the house.

Ali nodded. His future father-in-law watched as he reversed and slid the truck under the curved metal covering. His future father-in-law nodded his hellos to the women. Ali climbed down from the truck, jogging back to his cousin outside the perimeter of the house.

"You forgot your *bisht*?" Hassan whispered, as they exchanged nose-bumps.

"It's not required for tonight," Ali said. His cousin knew how much his bride needed this night to go without a hitch.

"Don't forget it for the wedding," Hassan said with a wink.

"I'll see you later. Thanks for coming." Ali's cousin's congratulations would have to do in absence of a father's pride. Only males from the immediate family were allowed at this ceremony that would usher in the next stage of Ali's life.

Ali re-entered the compound, loneliness dispelled by the phone ringing.

"Sir, sir—I need you to come quickly." His undercover agent's voice trembled.

"What is it, Manu?" Ahead of him, Nasser, his soon-to-be brother-in-law joined Jaber in the courtyard. "You're not supposed to call me. I'll ask for an update later."

"No, no, no, no." The protests rose in volume.

"Take a deep breath."

The two waiting men eyed Ali.

Manu's voice shuddered. "You come now."

"Deal with it. I'll call you back." Ali slipped the phone into the pocket of his *thobe,* rubbing his hands to remove the sweat that laced his palms. With everyone watching him, he forced a smile. Not a moment of privacy to call Khalifa, his supervisor, asking for back-up; or to text Manu and ask for an explanation. Ali handpicked the Nepali agent after rescuing him from an exploitative company. The man was his responsibility. Ali wanted a promotion and back into the intelligence services, yes. Ali remained stuck on the Missing Persons detail while his boss contemplated his future. One of the safest countries in the world, and he assigned to a desk that dealt with ex-pats who got turned around in the desert or stranded in other countries, unable to get back in. His failure of a routine physical landed him in the regular police force, not the specialized one he trained for in England. He needed back in.

They swept him up in an informal receiving line. Ali said his hello to Jaber and then Nasser, who shifted from foot to foot, glancing from Ali to his father. They entered through the male *majlis* and through a connecting door to the interior of the house. Ali breathed in the scent of flowers. They were led to a circular room outfitted with green brocade and tasseled chandeliers. The women's *majlis*. His mother's and sisters' eyes were wide, taking in the trimmed pillows and plush carpet. Nothing so feminine graced their house, not with his mother's restrained tastes. Jaber brought forward the sheikh, who stood at a square marble-topped table with a long piece of parchment that outlined the terms of the marriage. White hair peppered the man's beard, his hands veined.

"Does the girl agree?" he asked, peering around the room.

Maryam popped out from behind a wooden lattice.

Ali's mind snapped to attention, his heartbeat thrumming in his ears; keeping his eyes on the sheikh as Maryam came into view, taking her position next to her father. She wore a plain black *abaya* to cover up her finery, the skirt of her gown swishing into place.

"Yes," she said.

"Conditions?"

All eyes focused on Maryam. Make-up enhanced her heart-shaped features, long lashes screening her eyes. "None," she said.

The sheikh eyed her. "The bride has a right to ask for her conditions."

"There are none," Jaber said.

"So it is." The sheikh passed Ali the pen. "Sign."

Ali signed, steadying himself at the edge of the table so his hand didn't tremble. The pen skidded across the page. He placed it on the table. Maryam picked it up, the silver stark against her painted nails. She signed her name in Arabic with two swooping strokes.

Jaber's breath came out in a small *whoosh*. His lips lifted in a smile that did not crinkle the laugh lines around his eyes.

Ali dipped his chin in acknowledgement.

The sheikh walked with Jaber to the opposite corner of the room to settle payment for his services. Nasser and Hassan signed as witnesses, turning their backs to drum up a conversation and give the couple a moment of privacy.

Maryam, her wide eyes accentuated by black eyeliner that extended upward, gave Ali an arch glance. The tremor in her hand drew him closer.

"You're nervous?" He murmured.

"Is that surprising?" Maryam whispered with a shaky laugh.

"I didn't think anything scared you," Ali said.

She glanced at him and then down at the contract. "I signed myself away to you."

He regarded the contract under her polished manicure. Now they were in the moment, the one he never thought about, a dream that other men took for granted. "I'll be—"

His phone rang, shattering the bubble of privacy. He silenced it. "Manu," Ali said by way of explanation.

"Is he in trouble?" Maryam leaned closer.

Floral scents, jasmine, and a hint of wood assailed Ali. "He's on his first assignment, probably scared." He shrugged with more nonchalance than he felt.

"He doesn't scare easily," she said, worrying at the sleeve of her *abaya*. "They tried to kill him and he didn't complain."

"Dinner." Jaber extended an arm, intending to take Ali further into the house.

"I'll buy you some time," Maryam whispered. "I need to change," she called to Nasser.

"Now?" Nasser asked, exasperated.

"Two minutes," Maryam said. "Wait here for me, please."

Nasser nodded, snapping his fingers. "Make it quick. *Ummi* will faint from the excitement."

"Good thing there's a doctor in the house." Maryam slipped past her brother, giving Ali a wink over her shoulder.

"Doctor in training," Nasser called after her. "I can't actually practice yet unless someone is in dire need."

"I'll make a quick call," Ali mumbled. "Work."

Nasser threw up his hands. "You two are perfect for each other."

Warmth spread across Ali's cheeks at the idea this might be true. Manu's voice in his ear brought him back to reality. "You come now sir, please. Everyone yelling about some lady. American. No one see her for days."

"I'll be there as soon as I can," Ali whispered, hunching his shoulder and hoping Nasser couldn't hear.

"They want me to open the apartment to check," Manu said.

Ali placed Manu as a security guard in an ex-pat compound to ease him into his new identity as an undercover officer. Of all the luck. "Don't touch anything."

Through the open door he saw the tables with tiered flower arrangements set for dinner in his honor. "Don't panic, don't touch anything," he repeated.

"The others who live here," Manu said. "They are insisting on calling the police."

"You are the police!"

"They don't know that," Manu wailed.

Ali pinched the bridge of his nose. "Yes, I see. Give me twenty minutes."

Nasser poked his head back around the door. "They're waiting for you."

"Yes, coming." Ali hung up and joined his brother-in-law, his bride behind him.

"What is going on?" Maryam whispered as they strode across the courtyard. She did double-time to keep up.

"Not now," Ali said.

"Is this what it'll be like to be married to a policeman? Mysterious calls, only it won't be girls? Or I have your word that they aren't."

He squinted at her. "I don't know."

"You won't know if there will be girls?" she asked, deadpan.

"I don't know what it's like to be married," Ali said, laughing despite himself, "or to a policeman. Maybe ask my mother." The levity lightened their mood. She followed him into a foyer, set with a series of circular tables and chairs. He stopped short, taking in the flower arrangements up close, pink hue to the lights, and silverware on both sides of the plates. "Wow," he said. "This must have taken a few days."

She chuckled; a low, warm sound that tickled his ear. "Welcome to my family."

"*Salaam alaikum.*" Fatma came to them, squirming with delight. "Here, here."

They were led to a table in the center of the room, where his mother and sisters sat like still islands in a sea of activity. Waitresses scurried here and there, setting out appetizers.

"*Mabrook,*" his mother said, her upturned face radiating relief.

Ali dropped a few kisses on her forehead in the traditional show of respect between children and their elders. The last one lingered. Ali eyed the place setting. He didn't know forks came in so many sizes. He silenced the vibrating phone in his pocket.

"Now for sure we will get proposals for your sister."

Ali blanched. His mother did not usually bring up women's subjects with him. The floral arrangements must have been getting to her.

"I don't think—"

Hemiyan put a finger to her lips as Maryam swiveled toward them. She tilted her head to the table behind her, where the glee that oozed from his mother glowed in Fatma's eyes. *Another wedding soon,* the women agreed, regardless of what their children might feel.

For her part, Maha sipped at her water glass, shushing Aisha, who kept bopping to the music. An engagement made the perfect occasion for mothers to size up potential brides. A bevy of waitresses, almost one per diner, brought out salad plates. They were like an army, black-haired women half Ali's height, standing to one side until signaled by a woman in white gloves to set the plates down.

Fatma's gaze lingered on the length of Maha's curls. "Why can't my mother sit still and enjoy this moment?" Maryam stammered. "She'll spend the rest of the week trying to convince my brother to skip his residency and settle down."

"Juice, sir?"

Ali grabbed a glass of fresh orange juice from the tray and downed it as quickly as he could.

"The men are waiting for you," his mother-in-law said.

Ali inclined his head, thankful for the reprieve, although being in the room with his father-in-law would be even more awkward than eating in the house of strangers that were now his family.

Aisha reached for a glass full of thick strawberry juice with the consistency of a smoothie.

"Wait until our reception," Maryam muttered. "We may have to build a stage on the grounds at the Ritz. My mother says no ballroom is big enough."

The juice went down the wrong pipe. Ali choked.

"*Asaha.*" Maryam patted near his hand.

Faced with a missing woman or hundreds of women at his own wedding reception, Ali preferred the mystery.

Chapter Two

Maryam bit the black seeds scattered through the kiwi juice. She wanted to douse Ali with it instead, but there were too many watching eyes: her aunts, her mother, and her cousins. The embroidery of her *dura'a* itched at the sleeves. She weighed his wide-eyed profession of ignorance against his level tone.

The remaining four seats at the circular table were taken by his mother and sisters, who said very little. The youngest one smiled at Maryam, forking in bite after bite of pasta in white sauce. Maryam smiled back. Adult events were much more fun when the consequences were waged in someone else's life. "Let her have some more," Maryam said to the waitress hovering behind her.

Aisha's face lit up.

"She's full." Ali's mother pushed Aisha's elbow off the table.

The girl's smile faded, the glow disappearing from her eyes. She sat up straighter.

"There's plenty," Maryam said. "We won't run out. *Ummi* ordered enough food for a hundred people." She beckoned again to the waitress. This is what her life would be reduced to: making pleasantries with her new family, unsure of where the fault-lines were, relying on her husband to do the translating. When she came home from university, these were the people she would be waiting with for Ali's return. Her meal congealed in a pit in her stomach.

She said no when the sheikh, his cloudy eyes resting to the right of her face, asked again for her conditions to the marriage. She said no because of her father. *Take him as he is, or go to live with family in Saudi.* But Maryam did have a condition. One unfamiliar to her mother's generation but all too common nowadays for university-educated brides. *I want my own house.* Many girls were surprising their families and grooms with that request at the signing of the marriage contract. *If only.* The other sister scanned the room, sizing up the dresses and jewelry of every other woman. Her mouth hung slightly ajar at the candelabras towering in the middle of each table, giant ropes of beaded crystal entwined around their stems.

Maryam's mother worked around the clock, making sure that their housemaid, Maria, got up with her, measuring the hang of the tablecloths before anyone laid the first utensil on them. "You may come and have your dessert together," her mother said in a low voice behind them.

Maryam stood up so quickly the silverware rattled. She followed Fatma to the small seating area to the right of the dining room. Her heels sank into the blue-and-cream carpet that covered the alcove. The tree of life pattern. Her father's favorite. Similar-style rugs lay scattered throughout the house in hand-knotted silk and machine-made carpets, vestiges of his own father's start as an entrepreneur, importer of Indian handicrafts. Her mother outdid herself, re-upholstering the armchairs in a deep green fabric, overlaid by a pattern of lace. Normally, plastic covered these chairs and they were stashed in the corner.

Maryam sat at the edge; if she got comfortable, she wouldn't be able to get back up and her mother would have to hoist her out of the chair's deep pockets. A low circular table separated them. Away from an audience, they stood closer together than at the dining table.

Ali re-entered, led by Nasser. Before he turned to leave, allowing them a few moments of privacy, he mimed a thumb sideways. Tedious small talk and long pauses dominated the male meal. Ali sank into the other chair, rubbing his temples. He bumped her knee under the table. A pleasant hum traveled up and down the length of her right side.

"Gently, gently," Fatma hissed to the two waitresses who scuttled forward with china plates, embellished with a mosaic pattern, laden with slices of three-tiered chocolate cake.

They clunked one down in front of Ali and slid one in front of Maryam.

"Enjoy," her mother chirped. She disappeared into the dining room to see to the rest of their guests.

"I asked for carrot cake, but apparently that's not sweet enough," Maryam said to fill the silence. *Uff, small talk.* "Cream cheese icing is my favorite." She bit into the three layers; anything to give her more time to sort out the swirl of emotions competing for a chance to speak. He looked sharp in his *thobe,* his hair curling over the edge of the collar, the *ghutra* at a tilt. Out of uniform, Ali appeared vulnerable, less in charge.

There would be many more meals like this. Or would there? Her parents rarely ate together, only on Fridays when the extended family gathered—including grandparents. There were few intimate moments in their household.

"Couldn't be that bad. *Ubooy* seemed okay during the signing."

Those unions were arranged. She and Ali met accidentally, on opposite ends of a self-appointed mission to bust a labor agency switching contracts for incoming Nepali workers. People like Manu were promised easy work, bringing tea and coffee to expatriate white-collar bosses in swanky glass-fronted office buildings. Instead, the men sweated out their days on unfinished cement structures around the Arabian emirate. Their unconventional beginning would be quashed by social convention. Her unusual engagement would morph into the staid unions of other couples.

"I have to go," he said, leaving the cake untouched

"Excuse me?" Maryam blinked. "Because of the thing with the pasta—"

"I have to return a call," he stammered.

"Liar." She leaned closer, scrutinizing his face. "It's about the missing woman."

He looked away.

"Take me with you."

Ali recoiled in horror as if she suggested they sneak a kiss. "You are not going on assignments with me any more."

Maryam slumped, elbows on the table.

"Don't feel bad about the pasta, my mother thinks Aisha is fat."

"Your little sister?" Maryam glanced at the crowded dining room. "She's a child. Who wasn't chubby at that age?"

"You?"

She blushed as his gaze lingered on her collarbone, the bones of her clavicle sharp above the scoop of her gown. "Stop trying to change the subject. I'm coming."

"Impossible." He gestured to their relatives in the other room. "Your father wouldn't allow it. Where I'm going isn't appropriate."

"Stop listing reasons," she snapped as he counted them on his fingers. Maryam played with the remains of her cake, poking the fork through the icing. "This is going to be married life. Me sitting around, waiting for you."

"That's what most women do," Ali retorted. "But I won't be out with my friends."

"Are you going to let me drive?"

Ali blanched. "You want to drive?" The law said Maryam and any woman, local or foreign, could drive a car or ride a motorcycle. Most local women, however, did little of either. None of the women in Ali's family wanted to drive. *That you know of*, he admitted, eyes skirting over to their table in the main room. Having a relationship with Maryam made it painfully obvious how little he knew about women. Even those he lived with.

"I'm responsible," Maryam said, tapping the back of his hand.

Her touch sent an electric current that shot through his arm to the tips of his toes.

He brought his gaze back to her. She stared back, chin tilted upward.

"It's not you I'm worried about."

"I can handle those teenagers." She waved a hand. "Besides, I have a policeman as a husband; I can call you if any of them get out of hand."

Ali drank some water, to keep from saying the boys who cruised the streets could be her brother or his cousin. God help them if he found out someone harassed his wife. Did anyone follow his sisters around?

"This is what married life will be like," she said. "Waiting at home to ask you a hundred questions."

He drank some more water.

"Or waiting for you to say a word?" She stamped her foot under the table, causing the silverware to jump and the waitress to start forward.

Ali waved her away with a shake of his head. "I won't leave you at home long if I have any choice." The baritone in his voice must have caught her attention because she blushed. "And you won't be alone." He could have bitten his tongue in half. The reference to their shared home broke the spell. The thought of the shared house with his mothers and sisters weighed on them both.

Her shoulders slumped. "At least tell me what happened," she pleaded. "I'm dying in here."

He let out a sigh, rubbing the back of his neck. She leaned forward.

"You can tell no one. Not even your brother."

Maryam nodded again, wondering for the first time what Ali thought of her friendship with her brother. Many siblings grew apart the older they were. She noticed no interaction between him and his oldest sister, Maha.

"Manu called when I got here. They're looking for a woman in his compound."

She leaned closer, bracelet clanging against the rim of the plate. "Dead?" A shiver went down her spine at the memory of the body, the first time they met, face-down in the family's camp for workers.

He rubbed a hand over his face. "I hope not." The table lamp cast shadows under his eyes. "Ex-pat."

"American?" They sat very close and she could see his eyelashes were long, fuller than those of the men in her family.

Ali peered at her. "I told you, no more writing for the university!" He hissed this, hand clenched on the table.

"I'm not writing for them," she shrugged. "Curious. A woman goes missing for the first time in decades. Everyone is going to be talking about it."

Ali folded his napkin into a triangle. "You don't know what you're playing at."

"My playing has been helpful in the past." Maryam whispered as her mother craned her neck to catch a glimpse of them. Maryam smiled, whirling back to Ali when Fatma turned away.

"This is different," Ali said. "This is big time. My boss, my mission—"

"What mission?"

"I can't talk about that." Ali drummed his fingers on the table, his blunt fingernails a contrast to the delicate pattern on the china. "We were watching that compound because—" He broke off and glanced at her, "— we were asked to watch the compound, and the day after my guy shows up, this happens. Could be a warning?"

"Or coincidence." Maryam enumerated the possibilities with her fingers. "Illness, accident, or murder."

They contemplated her pinky finger, jutting into the air.

"If we find her dead," he said, voice a deep rumble.

"So rare," Maryam protested. She leaned on her elbows. "No one would risk a lifetime of jail if they were caught. Or being sent to a Saudi beheading."

"Could be suicide," Ali said. "Westerners don't think that's wrong."

"Not true," she said.

He raised an eyebrow.

"My twelfth grade research paper: suicide in teenagers in America. They make everyone mad—those they leave behind."

"Huh," Ali said. He and his sisters attended government schools in Arabic.

"We are sure she's missing and hasn't just left the country? Maybe dodging some loans."

He ate a bite of cake, chewing instead of answering her question. He added this unconsidered possibility to his list.

"You might as well tell me." She rolled her eyes at the shake of his head. "Who am I going to tell? My mother? I have no real phone; thanks in part to you, remember."

"Thanks also in part to your asking questions like this," Ali countered. "Leaving the country is a possibility."

She took a sip of tea in triumph, burning the edge of her tongue. "Then really not suicide. Women are much less likely to go through with it."

They contemplated each other. His breath stirred the hanging droplets of her earrings. The position of his leg, so close to hers under the table, derailed her train of thought.

"You are beautiful, *masha'allah*," Ali said.

She leaned further towards him. These were the words most girls dreamed of, even those in British novels. Closeted away from men most of their lives, her cousins savored the night of their engagements.

"My mother warned me against you for this reason."

Maryam sat up as if he'd slapped her. "Being pretty is a crime?"

The light refracted in the diamond anchor of her earrings, casting a kaleidoscope of colors across his face.

He gave a small laugh. "I hope you like the *shabka*."

"The set is fine." Maryam waved in the direction of the matching necklace and bracelet in their velvet case on the coffee table.

He raised his eyebrows.

"I mean, it's lovely," she said.

"The jeweler said this is the latest design. From Dubai."

"You went yourself?"

Ali nodded, flushing.

"My brother chose your watch."

"He has good taste," Ali said.

"I didn't know what you would like," she said in a rush in case she hurt his feelings. "I don't really know that much about..." she trailed off.

"Are we really going to do this?" Ali said at the same time.

"What?"

"This marriage."

Maryam's head spun. If Ali felt her less than serious, he could back out. And if he did so before their reception, before they lived together, her family could still marry her off to someone else. "Yes, of course we are."

"Your parents don't know everything," Ali said gruffly. "About me."

She grabbed his hand. His fingers clutched at hers. "It's too late."

"Alright, you know the rules. No touching," her mother *tsk*ed from the landing. They sprang apart and Maryam knocked aside her silverware. She picked up the fork from the floor.

"And don't stay all night," Fatma joked in a loud whisper to Ali, drawing nearer. "She does want to spend time with her friends."

"*Yema.*"

"You two will have plenty of time to talk between now and the wedding." Fatma waved a hand in the air. "So go on." She shooed Ali again. "We ladies would like to see the bride." Her enthusiasm gave Ali the excuse he needed.

He stood, giving her another glance. "*Ma'a salama,*" he said to no one in particular.

She fiddled with the cutlery. Unspoken questions swirled in Maryam's mind like a swarm of locusts. What would their married life be like? Who was this woman Manu called about?

"That all went extremely well." Fatma led Maryam by the arm back to the dining room. "His mother thinks you're beautiful—she hasn't taken her eyes off your hair all night."

"From what I hear, that's not a good thing." Maryam touched the braid coiled around the crown of her head, helped to its height by well-placed mesh squeezed under her real hair.

"What do you mean?" A skittish look appeared in her mother's eyes.

"I'm glad you're happy," Maryam said.

The music grew louder as the waitresses cleared the dessert plates. Through the side window, she saw the taillights of Ali's truck. She worried the tablecloth with her knife at the unexpected sense of abandonment. Maryam was religiously and legally married, though they would have to wait for the wedding reception to move in together.

Fatma took the seat so recently vacated by the man now legally her husband. "Stop frowning," Fatma hissed. "They'll think you don't like him." She beckoned for tea to be served to everyone.

Maryam joined the rest of the table in studying her mother's manicure, working to make her face neutral as her future sister-in-law exclaimed over the color, a deep red.

"Won't that be difficult to remove for prayer?" Maryam's future mother-in-law asked.

Fatma demurred. Maryam heard every word. Men like Ali came from pious families. She hoped they wouldn't ask her if she woke for the dawn prayer. *What if they do all get up for* fajer *together?*

Maryam studied the similarly-cut damask gowns Ali's mother and sister wore, which were without embellishment. Dark traces of eyeliner signified their only make-up. Next to them, Maryam resembled a painted doll.

Oh, Ummi, you may have sent me to Saudi in spirit.

"Where did you do your hair? The style is trying to be traditional," Maha said.

"Oh, she came to the house," Maryam said. *Traditional.* The word hung in the air like an insult. She patted the back of her braid to make sure it stayed in place. "I'll get you the number. She's really cheap."

The rounded 'O' of Maha's mouth said she'd blundered. Maryam's mind raced. What did she say to warrant such shock—that she didn't bother to go the salon? Did they read this as their brother not being worthy of elaborate preparations?

"Cheap is good," her future mother-in-law said. "Considering how many parties and weddings Maha has to go to. She's so busy, everyone wants to invite her."

"Oh, you know Maryam," Fatma chimed in. She stepped on Maryam's foot underneath the table, and her heel dug into Maryam's big toe so that her daughter flinched. "She gets invitations too. But she's very frugal. Lots of business sense."

Glances passed between mothers and daughters.

"I'm not that into parties," Maryam agreed. The point of the heel relented. "I would rather read a book." Her mother's heel jabbed her again, this time higher, on the top of her foot. Maryam scowled.

"Yes, I'm surprised Ali wanted a smart wife." Her mother-in-law's lips twitched downward.

"He's got a mind of his own," Maha said with a grimace.

Maryam accepted the offered tea from the waitress standing at her elbow. Money. Of course that's all anyone ever thought about. A scene from her English class flashed before her. Mrs. Bennett clucking over her daughters. *Someone write me an exit stage left*, Maryam thought. *Oh, Jane Austen, if only this were an Arab version of one of your novels.* Instead it resembled a Ramadan soap opera construed as a comedy of errors.

"All well and fine," Hemiyan said, taking a big bite of the three-tier chocolate cake placed before her by the waitress. "I'll keep a good eye on her, don't worry. Besides, there won't be much time for reading once the babies arrive."

Maryam's mother pounded her on the back as her tea went down the wrong way.

Chapter Three

Manu stared at the four flat-screen monitors that displayed grey images of various sections of the compound. The empty clubhouse and the placid water of the pool sat in the bottom right screen. The empty interior street, missing cars and residents at the height of the day, filled the opposite screen. In the upper right, cars whizzed by in front of the compound, the rear of which shimmered in the morning heat in the top left corner. No sign of the woman they were all searching for.

An audience of ex-pats waited outside the guard booth for Manu's answer. He hung up the phone, wiping his palms on the black company-issued slacks. "Manager said wait." He cleared his throat. *They don't know,* he repeated to himself. *They think you are security.* The terse details of his cover story mirrored the facts. Manu could keep his own name. He blended in like thousands of other twenty-somethings sent here to make money for their families. He worked in security because of his degree and a sister with some connections. These were actual facts of Manu's own life, except that the first time he entered the country, he'd fallen into the hands of a disreputable labor agency that sold his contract to a construction company instead of finding him employment as office help. He spent months sweating away on the fringe of the city, accidentally uncovering an illegal ring of double contract-issuers—the profit taken by the agency owners—and finding himself nearly killed for his efforts.

Among the South Asians in the construction force, he blended right in. Tonight, however, the challenges of posing as a security guard grew. He knew nothing about responding to a resident crisis. The men he worked with were older, better educated than the laborers, and more familiar with the city as many of them lived here for several years. If they discovered the truth, he failed his first assignment.

"That's ridiculous," a chubby man said, his chin wobbling. "You call him back and say all of us have noticed the same thing."

"He will be calling back," Manu said. He hoped his level tone would still the rising turmoil in the guard station.

"Call back—why isn't he on his way here? Where is he? At the movies?" a woman snapped, her eyes narrowing.

"Let's not give this guy a hard time," said another woman, adjusting her headscarf, and sending her polka dots askew. "It's not his fault no-one in this country takes anything seriously."

"Security," the portly man sniggered again. This time his belly did the dance as he stood. "What a joke."

Manu shied away. The rest of the group trudged out the glass door of the security booth. Manu breathed a sigh of relief. His first week on duty and this happened. He sank into the wheeled office chair. Two hours had passed since he called Ali. Two hours in which he kept questions at bay. Like why didn't he have keys to all the apartments? And where was the other guy? Two people on duty at all times. He scratched the inside of the collar of his button-down shirt, also part of the company uniform.

A knock sounded on the glass door.

Manu braced himself for another tirade of questions.

"Hello?" A woman in a black tank top and matching leggings entered. A tail of braided red hair snaked around her neck and over her shoulder.

"Lauren?" Manu asked.

"No, Jenny. I'm sure she'll turn up," Jenny mimed writing. "I need a form."

"Maintenance?" Manu guessed, remembering some of the company briefing. That seemed like ages ago and child's play compared to what he faced.

Jenny sighed. "Yes, wouldn't you know it?"

Manu tried to keep up with her clipped vowels. She spoke more sharply than his sister's employers, as if someone kept cutting off the edge of her words.

"May I borrow a pen?"

"Yes, yes." He procured a blue one from the desk.

She filled the form out.

"How long time?"

"They can come any time today. I'm staying home. Not feeling well."

"Okay, I tell them now." Manu reviewed the form, thankful for something to do other than face a barrage of suggestions.

"The yogurt I dropped off is great for your bones. Calcium."

"Ah, madam, I the new guy."

She tilted her head to one side.

"Oh god, really?" The skin on Jenny's neck turned pink, a narrow trail flowing downward. "I'm sure we met before."

"No problem," Manu said. "No problem."

"Okay, thanks." She left, trailing a stream of perfume in her wake.

He looked familiar to her – he blended in with the thousands of other South Asians wearing guard uniforms in this country. She was unique to him. The sway of her hips stirred an unfamiliar longing in Manu. These were the types of urges that got young men in his village married in their twenties.

"Berries." A short, swarthy man in guard's uniform entered the guard station, breathing in the scent.

"If you're supposed to be on shift," Manu laughed, despite himself, "you're late."

"Ah, my friend. I didn't even say hello. I'm Adhik."

"Manu."

They suffered through an awkward pause in which each pretended they weren't directly sizing each other up. Manu stared. His co-worker wore a black leather belt as opposed to the elastic one they all received from the company.

"You in a hurry this morning? Not tie your tie properly."

"Uh, yes," Manu mumbled, surprised to be on the defensive.

"Still using company belt? You are the new guy." Adhik guffawed. "Don't worry. You save some money, you'll get a new one." The overhead light winked off the silver buckle, as if laughing at Manu's realization that the guards were fashionable.

"And there are many more like her," Adhik said with a low whistle. "This place is full of teachers. Young teachers." His eyebrows wiggled.

Manu sat in the chair across from the monitors. This job couldn't be as bad as he feared. Once they found this Lauren, he could hang out in here all day – looking for clues.

"Sometimes, they come back with their boyfriends. Sitting in their cars, they-" Adhik wrapped his arms around himself, squeezing, making kissing noises.

"They don't," Manu said. These were the scenes Bollywood movies left to the viewer's imagination. No couple ever kissed on screen. His mind ran wild with the images Adhik planted, with Manu as the hero. "No one in my sister's compound does this."

"Your sister is here?"

Manu bit his lip at his hastiness. He barely knew the man yet revealed facts about his true identity. "She's a housemaid," he mumbled. "The compound much smaller. Any way, this bigger, more units, younger people. You said they kiss in their cars?"

"A little," Adhik said, squeezing the air between his thumb and forefinger. "If the man is new. If he is old friend, they go straight inside."

The door swung open. "Sorry guys, but didn't Management say they'd give Maintenance a place to sit?" Jenny stood, arms akimbo, on the top step.

Manu snapped around to the desk. Guilt bent his head toward the newspaper, and the Arabic letters blurred.

"Uh, I don't know, Madam," Adhik stuttered.

Lauren gestured at the compound maintenance crew lined up on the lip of the clubhouse window, passing a two-liter bottle of Pepsi between them. "This isn't okay. They work hard. It's hot out here."

"I'll ask manager again." Adhik's voice gained more confidence.

Jenny gave him a thumbs-up then walked away with a smile for the guys on the ledge. Manu never would've guessed there'd be a woman like this in the cars that drove by him as he sat in the bus, being driven to construction sites.

The crew of men kept their focus on the ground as she walked by but, like a tightrope, the second she passed, their eyes lifted, caressing her behind as though they were hands. Manu gritted his teeth. Those insolent looks would not be tolerated in the village. If a boy looked at his sisters like that, there would be a fight.

"You'll see, night shift is best." Adhik brought him back to the moment. "Villa 2, she leaves her curtain open while changing. Sometimes you can see when walking around the compound. I'll give you the timings."

What else can you see here? Manu wondered. *Who else comes and goes?* He reminded himself to stay focused.

The door swung open. "We got a key." The woman in the headscarf stood in the doorway.

Manu started. "Excuse me?"

"Lauren uses a cleaner who lets herself in. She's on vacation so gave it to one of the maids on the compound." She held up a house key. "We're going in."

"I'll go," he said. One of them needed to wait in the guard station and Ali wouldn't be pleased to find Manu sitting around.

"I wait," Adhik said. "This is what they pay us to do." He threw himself in a chair and swiveled in a circle. "All day." He leaned back in his chair. "We wait for Mr. Eric, he gives us the password for his Internet and we watch movies." His phone landed on the table with a clunk. "Don't tell me." He covered his eyes in mock horror at the look on Manu's face. "You have basic phone."

Manu's fingers itched to take out the Nokia given to him by Ali and laugh in derision. Ironically, his being undercover meant he probably made more than this guy.

A car horn blared.

The shorter man sat up to lean out the window. "No gate pass, you take ID." He ran out the door to the driver's side of the car and handed over a red piece of paper with the number 3 on it.

Their exchange in broken English drifted back in bits and pieces to Manu. The other man came back in with a white plastic card.

"Damn Egyptians. Never want to do as they're told." He tossed the ID onto the desk.

"You always take the ID?"

The other man gave him the once-over. "You never been security guard before?"

"Only in shopping mall," Manu mumbled the line he rehearsed with Ali. His worst trait; always asking questions, wanting to know things down to the last detail.

"We're going to the apartment," the woman harrumphed from outside the door.

Manu followed a few steps behind, sand blowing across the pavement and onto the parked cars that filled the street, outdoor lamps reflected in their windshields. His mind whirred with facts. The missing woman, Lauren, worked as an elementary school teacher. Single, living on her own, her first year in the country.

They ran up the few steps to the apartment block, a beige-colored three-story building. Yellowish light filled the stairwell, casting the brown front doors in a dim glow. Her friend darted up the stairs. Manu trudged up behind her. He tried Ali several times without success. Whatever held his boss must be important. "Uff." Manu put his arms out, brushing against the back of the woman in front of him. She stopped short in the doorway, handing him the key. Manu took it. "Probably staying with a friend," he said.

The tremble in his voice echoed in the stairwell, magnifying his uncertainty. *The gods protect us,* Manu pleaded. His mind drew a blank on which deity his mother relied on most when alive. He snapped on the lights to dispel the shadows. In the living room everything remained in place, as if the furniture were waiting for the occupant to bring it back to life. Blue sofas with yellow fringe trim sat facing each other in a square.

"Lauren?" The missing woman's friend disappeared into the kitchen. The silence emboldened her to open the door to the hallway bathroom. The stillness made Manu uneasy. Everything in its place, not an envelope or book tossed to the side in haste. Bookshelves framed the hallway back to the bedrooms. His sister's employer owned this many books. Which made sense as a university professor.

"Lauren."

Manu went into the hallway, wanting to put distance between himself and the hopeful note he heard behind him. Framed art hung on the walls, black-and-white portraits. He peered at one. The man's broad features and flat nose could be Nepali. A squiggle repeated in each right-hand corner.

"Lauren." The friend's steps slowed. She pressed open the door to one guest room and then the other. Both swung open on their hinges, revealing rooms with marbled floors and twin beds covered by brown comforters and plump pillows. *All this space*, Manu thought, *for one person*. His thoughts skidded to the overcrowded concrete box he shared with ten other men while in the labor camps. They slept like sardines stacked in bunk beds.

Yet another room. He paused in front of the master bedroom, the door closed tight. She faltered, raising her hand to knock, eyes darting to his. He nodded, hand on the doorknob. They pushed in together. Here also, the pristine room waited for an occupant. Four or five decorative pillows sat in the middle of a blue satin bedspread.

"She's not here." The friend's voice came out in a *whoosh*. "She's not here." She spun in a circle to reassure herself.

Manu scrutinized the room, as he did in the others. Nothing out of place, the picture frames with gleaming smiles. The same woman towered in each of the photos, her chin lifted to the left, a smile dancing in her eyes. Here with her arms around a group of children. There with a woman, much larger, same dimples. "Yes," he said turning away. His eyes fell on the door ajar in the room's interior. He approached—to be thorough they should open the wardrobes in each room. And probably the bathrooms as well. He charged into this one. Immaculate white towels hanging on a stainless steel rod, a matching spotless rug in front of the sink. He thrust aside the shower curtain.

"Oh my god."

Manu spun around, dropping the curtain. Too late, the other woman spied the figure of her friend, sprawled nude in an empty bathtub. Her head listed to one side, strands of hair screening her face. She could have been asleep, Manu reflected. Except for the dark fingerprints across her collarbone like a necklace.

"We found her," he stammered into the phone to Ali over the sobs of denial behind him. He shut himself into the bathroom with the dead woman, pulling the shower curtain closed. He wished it would be that easy to avoid her neighbors. Hundreds of people lived here. Not one of them with any idea what happened to a woman right under their noses.

Chapter Four

She turned the corner, toward the playground at the end of the street, with swings and a wrought iron bench, patches of grass worn by dozens of little feet. Two-story adobe-colored houses ringed the small street, two-by-two feet of grass and bushes separating the units, double-paneled glass front doors rendering the interiors inscrutable. On the straightaway, azure water glimmered in the moonlight. The fountain of the shared swimming pool continued to pour an artificial waterfall, without the presence of swimmers. Ex-pats lived clustered together around a set of shared services, forcing a sense of community, even if they were all strangers. Sanjana knew it didn't work.

A maid at the playground without a toddler to watch became a bystander or accessory. Sanjana sat on the iron bench in the gazebo. At night an eerie calm blanketed the same area that children overran in daylight like ants at a picnic. She spent many hours here minding a younger Daniel, sitting on the same pigeon-stained bench while Filipina nannies hunched on the curb, telling stories and backing them up with photos on their phones. Now, with a teenager in the house, Sanjana lacked a segue into the circle of other child-minders on the compound. Though even with an errant child, as a Nepali, she remained in a minority. With Manu taking on a new role in the police force, her yearning for a new responsibility, a boy to push in a stroller or a girl to watch over in the swing, felt insignificant.

Habit led her to the playground in the middle of the night. But what to do with her life remained the bigger mystery. A girl in striped pajamas, her blonde plaits bouncing on either shoulder, darted into the street, making her way into the playground while looking over her shoulder. She stopped at the sight of Sanjana, giving her a wide-eyed stare.

"What are you doing here so late?" Sanjana asked.

"I want water," said the girl.

"Sorry," Sanjana stammered.

The girl's skin was white as cream. Sanjana couldn't place which family lived in the house the girl exited. She didn't keep up with the comings and goings of ex-pat families. Most of the children Daniel once played with were now back in their home countries.

"I'm *thirsty*." The girl stamped her foot.

"Ask your nanny."

"I don't have a nanny."

"Oh." Sanjana scanned the playground, wondering if she should take the girl by the hand back to her house. No nanny, yet the girl demanded water from Sanjana. One good thing about this child—she dispelled Sanjana's ache from growing into a maternal longing.

"Alice? Alice!" The mother arrived in black leggings and a tank top. "It is time for bed."

Alice said nothing, her eyes fixed on Sanjana. "I want her to be my nanny."

"Sorry about this," the mother said to the area above Sanjana's head. She glowered at the top of the girl's head. "Alice, let's get you home. We can read one more story." When this got no reaction, "Don't you want to watch *Peppa Pig* tomorrow?"

The girl whipped her head around. She placed her hand in her mother's outstretched one and they walked away. Sanjana hurried home before any other mother-daughter pairs could make her feel redundant. She slunk into the kitchen through the side door.

Water rushed through the pipes, like the sound of rain. Madam was still awake. Their neighbor Amira's high-pitched laugh reverberated in the living room. Sanjana remained in the yellow-tiled kitchen, the most comfortable room in the house for her, over and above her own room. If in her bedroom, she searched for things to do. Her active mind and energetic body were at sea in front of the television. There were only so many hours she could sleep. In the kitchen, her hands buoyed with purpose. Madam said as much to her friend.

"She's been moping around here," Madam confided to Amira.

Amira *tsk*ed. "What does she have to be upset about? You're a good employer. Daniel is at school all day. He doesn't need looking after. I'd love a job like hers, if you ask me."

Madam sipped at her glass of wine, unaware that Sanjana hung on every word. "I get the feeling she wants to go home."

Amira gave a laugh. "She wants to go home now. Then she'll be calling you in a few weeks, wanting to come right back when she can't pay for her sister's wedding."

Sanjana gripped the dish towel, squeezing it, wishing it were the woman's throat. How could she talk like this about other people's lives?

"Well, I understand being homesick."

Amira groaned. "Don't be too nice to them, I'm always telling you."

"What happened to 'remember the poor'?"

"They're not talking about housemaids in the Bible." Amira grimaced. "Now you sound like Robert."

"That is what the Bible says."

"Says lots of other things he sees fit to ignore."

Sanjana dropped the dishtowel. The nannies on the compound whispered about the American serviceman seen leaving Amira's house in the hours after dawn. Sanjana worried about Madam's sense of loyalty when Robert's friend Jonah began hanging around. Thankfully their short-lived friendship, or Madam's fascination, ended.

"He wants to move in," Amira said.

"Isn't that illegal?"

"Plenty of people do it."

These women with their free time and loose morals. Sanjana bit her lip at the thought. Her thirtieth birthday lurked around the corner, and she with nothing to show for it.

"I'm more worried about Sharif's reaction. He's not taking it well with his father going to Dubai to fly for Emirates."

Sanjana gave up the pretense of working. She braced a hip against the counter, taking in their conversation. Sharif lingered like a thorn in her heel ever since his brush with drugs nearly landed them all in jail.

"Maybe you can send him there for the weekend," Cindy offered.

Ever the problem-solver, Madam sustained the friendship in order to feel useful. And superior about her picturesque life.

"He's not getting one second with my sons," Amira snapped. "Though I do use it as a threat if nothing else is working with Sharif."

Sympathy stirred for the teenager. Trapped between a philandering father and a distant mother, what resources did the boy have? Daniel's presence glowed like a beacon, dependable as the sunrise, in comparison to the adults who surrounded his friend. Turning the lights off in the kitchen, Sanjana made her way to her room, flopping onto her bed. The theme music of her favorite soap opera sounded garish and taunting, the images of the glamorous women judging her, watching from her twin bed in a floor-length cotton nightdress. She flipped through the channels. Cartoon girls, perfect proportions, moaning about when their lives would begin.

She shut it off, staring at the ceiling, pushing away thoughts of how much she shared with a child's movie. Unlike the little mermaid, she would not be meeting a Prince Charming who would first create a series of problems that they could solve together. Nor did she have a father who could give her magical land legs to spend the rest of her life next to the one she loved. Sleep eluded her. The shrill ring of her cellphone interrupted the melancholy. Sanjana cheered up at hearing her young sister Meena's voice chattering on with the mundane details of village life. The cow gave birth to a healthy calf. Two cows meant more milk, manure for fertilizer, a fuller garden.

"Are the twins behaving?" Sanjana plied her sister with questions to avoid answering how things were for her. She couldn't muster false enthusiasm or find neutral phrases. No, nothing was the matter. She was... if she said *tired* that meant the sponsoring family worked her too hard. *Bored* meant she was sad to be away from her real family.

"They're fine. Playing," Meena replied.

"How is school?"

"Today is Saturday."

"Right." Sanjana mentally kicked herself for the oversight.

"*Didi*, we got the salaries. Oh my god, what type of work did *bhai* find?" The excitement in Meena's voice crackled.

"What do you mean?"

Her sister whispered the amount.

Sanjana pictured her, cupping a hand around the phone in the multi-purpose store at the entrance of the village so the other customers and the nosy shopkeeper wouldn't hear.

"What?" Sanjana sat up. "Don't tell anyone else."

"Of course not," Meena huffed. "Auntie is already asking me about when I want to get married."

"Married?" Sanjana's thoughts ran in multiple directions. She couldn't keep up with the information Meena hurled through the phone. Their maternal aunt took the children in, letting the three of them share a room in exchange for Meena's help with housework and a small portion to cover the children's food expenses. The salary transfers still remained in their father's name, so the boys were the only ones eligible to receive it. Meena served as their intermediary guardian until they came of age.

"You're only eighteen," Sanjana sputtered. "Tell her you're going to university."

"I am?" An intake of breath sounded on the other end.

Sanjana worried at the piece of skin hanging from her left forefinger. "Yes, you are. No marriage until you finish." A series of electronic beeps interrupted her.

"I have to go. Someone else wants to use the phone. Plus my time is up."

"Tell no one about the money," Sanjana repeated again. Meena murmured sounds of agreement. The line went dead. From victim to agent, Manu out-earned her. Sanjana despaired of finding her place in the family again.

Chapter Five

As Manu paced the guard station, the static grey-and-black images on the monitors taunted him. All these cameras, with next to no evidence of who or what killed the teacher, Lauren.

"Tell me again," Ali said, his elbows on his knees.

Manu wiped the sweat from his forehead with a napkin. The sight of Ali in his *thobe* instead of a police uniform made everyone jittery. Adhik waited outside under the impression Ali wanted to interview everyone alone. Manu wanted to give Ali the inside story—but he couldn't, having found none.

"We were waiting for you," Manu gestured at the two chairs. "For few hours. Then the friend came in with a key from the cleaner. We went in to look around."

Ali tapped the entire story into his phone. The fluorescent lights bounced off his gold cufflinks. A fragrance, woody, emanated from him.

"They didn't want to wait for police," Ali noted. "Then?"

"We checked everywhere, found her in the bathroom," Manu swallowed. "I saw the body, and called you again." Manu's voice cracked on the last few words.

Click, click, click, went the words into Ali's phone.

Manu's legs shook. He gripped the edge of the counter.

"Let's start with the guard."

Manu opened the door and beckoned to Adhik, who sat perched above the lower step. His head bowed, gaze focused on the ground. He crouched on his haunches like many South Asians did while waiting for a bus or a train.

"Hey," Manu called.

Adhik jerked his head up, the whites of his eyes showing in alarm. Street-lights cast whitish pools of light throughout the darkened streets of the compound.

Ali remained seated as Adhik came in. "And his relationship with the teacher?" He indicated Manu should translate.

"In what way did you—"

"I speak English." Adhik stuck his hands in his pockets.

"No chances of mistakes." Ali indicated Manu should continue.

"In what way did you know the woman, Lauren?"

Ali's eyes flickered to him at the addition of the deceased's name.

"She is a resident. Been here a few months," Adhik responded in English.

Ali unbuttoned the collar of his *thobe*. He ran his finger around the starched neck.

"The last time you saw her?"

"Yesterday." Adhik looked at his shoes when Ali questioned him but would sneak glances at Manu when he wrote notes in the phone.

"And the nature of your relationship with her?"

Manu repeated his original translation, though the two men ignored him.

"I am not boyfriend."

Ali stood. "No one said you were."

Adhik shrunk against the back wall. "I didn't do anything."

"No one said you did," Manu said.

"We're finished here," Ali said.

Adhik left in a flash, and the door rattled behind him.

"You can't give people assurances in an ongoing investigation," Ali said.

Manu fidgeted, sitting down. "I don't think he did it."

"Why?" Ali scrolled through his notes. "There's no husband, no boyfriend, and a teacher is unlikely to have enemies, so it has to be one of the men here on the compound. Opportunity."

"But motive," Manu protested. "Why would someone want to kill a teacher?"

"She's not a teacher out here. She's a woman on her own." Ali filled a cup with water from the dispenser and then drained it. He drank another one.

"What do we do now?"

"We question the friend," Ali said. "The one who found her."

"She's very upset," Manu warned. "We could barely get her out of the apartment. She collapsed."

Ali sighed.

"And the family?" Ali snapped his fingers. "Call the employer. What school?"

Manu flipped through the binder on the residents. He named one of the international American schools.

Ali groaned. "And the embassy. Might as well call them. They'll call us as soon as the reporters find out about this."

"What about the family?"

"The employer should call."

The cellophane covers on the pages slid across Manu's fingers. So many people. So many lives, and they were as vulnerable as the men he worked with on the construction crew.

"Alright. Let's get the friend in," Ali said.

Manu went to the door and asked Adhik, "Can you get Reem?"

Adhik now leaned on the lip of the window of the clubhouse that faced the entrance to the compound. He veiled himself in a cloud of smoke ;an expensive habit, Manu knew from the men in his village who bought single cigarettes as a treat. A clump of men in shorts stood nearby, talking in hushed tones, grey plumes rising around them.

Adhik flicked his cigarette away, and the tip kept burning on the pavement. He returned with Reem, the tall, headscarf-wearing woman Manu spent an hour trying to calm while they waited for Ali.

She trembled, making her way across the street to where Manu stood on the back stoop of the guard station.

"A few questions," he said.

Reem's red-rimmed eyes took him in without saying a word.

He opened the door.

"*Salaam alaikum.*" Ali indicated that Reem should sit.

She held herself on the edge of the seat, clutching a wad of tissues streaked with her mascara.

Manu missed most of the interview because Ali spoke to her in Arabic. Reem's replies came hesitantly at first, then they grew more pleading.

Ali asked a question, as gentle as if he were talking to a child.

Reem burst into tears. "I don't know, I don't know," she sobbed. She pressed the tissues into each eye socket.

Manu passed her the tissue box. She swatted it away.

"Why would someone kill her?" She gave a ragged laugh. "Why would someone kill her?" she repeated, her voice breaking. "I don't know." Another fresh stream of tears began.

"Call the EMT," Ali said.

Manu left the station and took a big gulp of air as Reem's grief rang in his ears. Adhik still lingered there on the clubhouse ledge. The knot of ex-pat men made their way over to him. A fresh cigarette dangled in Adhik's mouth and they were talking over the top of each other.

"Medic?" Manu called.

Adhik disappeared around the corner to the parked ambulance on the side of the compound pool.

The male residents turned their attention to Manu.

"What can you see there, mate?" one called out, adjusting his waistband so it rode over his belly instead of cradling it underneath.

Manu squinted, focusing on each sound so as to stitch them together to make sense of the man's accent.

"On those screens—who did you see enter?"

Manu shook his head.

"Please tell me you have the training to get to the bottom of this," another man called out. The streetlight shone on his bald head, giving him a halo in the growing gaze.

No, actually I don't, Manu cried silently. *I'm here to find out which one of you is smuggling prostitutes, and instead we have this mess.*

"Stop looking at us with those unblinking eyes," the man sneered. "Show some emotion, damn it. A woman just died."

The door behind Manu opened. Ali glimmered, the whiteness of his *thobe* backlit by the office's overhead strip of fluorescent bulbs.

"Where's the medic?" he muttered to Manu.

At the sight of Ali, a local, the crowd in front of Manu dispersed. They stubbed out their cigarettes and slunk into the clubhouse, where other residents huddled together, trying to piece as much of the story together as possible.

"Thank you," Manu whispered.

Ali squeezed his shoulder. "I know this isn't what you thought you were investigating, but I need you more than ever. The headlines on this are going to blare. We have to solve this as soon as possible."

Adhik emerged from around the corner. A much larger man in the grey uniform of an EMT plodded behind him. They both entered the guard station. Ali held the door open.

"Out." He jerked his head to Adhik. "Closed interview."

Adhik cut his eyes to Manu.

"He stays," Ali said. "With me."

Adhik turned on his heel and left before Manu could say a word.

"Now." Ali pulled the chair underneath him. His legs spread wide, he stretched his arms in either direction. "Time of death?"

Manu translated into Nepali, and the coffee-skinned EMT pleaded, "Hindi?"

Manu translated the question again.

"Around noon," the EMT replied. He kept his eyes trained on Manu while answering Ali's questions.

"Cause of death?"

"Strangulation, but they'll run an autopsy."

"Fingerprints?"

"Gloves, by the look of the impressions on the skin around the throat."

Ali tapped into his phone again. "You have the paperwork for the hospital?"

The EMT nodded, licking his lips. "What about the burial?"

Ali considered Manu.

"He wants to know about the funeral," Manu said in English.

"She's not Muslim, so we have time," Ali said. "Send her to the morgue, and call me once the coroner has a report."

"We need permission to embalm the body," the medic said.

Manu struggled to get this across in English, miming a body in repose. Ali stared blankly, and the medic stared at his hands. Out of frustration, Manu strode to the fridge and stuck his head inside. "Keep body?"

"After the autopsy." Ali mimed cutting his stomach open.

The medic nodded. "Finished?" With Manu's confirmation, the interview ended, and the EMT scuttled out of the office.

Manu slumped into the chair vacated by the EMT. The ambulance Ali ordered arrived within a few minutes. Paramedics shouldered past Manu, Adhik, Reem and her friend, and drew a blanket over Lauren's prone figure. Her bare feet, pointing toward them, peeked out as if to plead she not be forgotten.

Manu gave the room a once over, searching for anything out of place. Lauren's smiling face confronted him at every turn. In one picture he saw her with someone older, with the same features—her mother? On the edge of a boat, the blue sky shimmering in the sun behind them.

There she stood, hands on her hips, in a long, blue-striped dress. Children stood in a line on either side of her, and everyone showed their teeth.

"They wait outside," the EMT said as Reem's wails grew louder.

The friend, his hand in the small of her back, took Reem into the hallway.

In the silence, Manu bounced around the living room, not wanting to sit or touch anything, avoiding the smiling gaze frozen in time. The gurney squeaked into the room. In another picture, Lauren looked the age of Sanjana, give or take a few years.

The boundary walls he thought made her compound so safe, the ones he longed for while tossing and turning for sleep in his worker accommodation, now seemed sinister, like the ones looming on either side of the guard station. What these walls contained could prove as sinister as what they prevented from entering.

The worker camps were stuffed with men, like objects, stacked on top of each other in bunk bed-crowded rooms. *But in the rest of the city,* Manu blinked as sweat rolled into his eye, *the veneer of safety is a pretense.*

"Drink some water," Ali called. His voice sounded far away, as if coming through a metal tunnel.

"I'm okay." Manu's teeth chattered.

Ali passed him a cup.

Manu took it, his shaking hands scattering droplets. His throat convulsed.

"Toilet," Ali ordered.

Manu dashed through the wooden door, fell to his knees, and retched. He crawled to the toilet, missing as the contents of his breakfast projected onto the wall. His stomach heaved and heaved.

Manu reached for the trashcan, tossing aside the swinging lid. The spasms continued until only yellow bile emptied into the plastic liner. He pushed aside the trashcan and leaned his back on the wall.

"This couldn't have happened, couldn't have happened here. Impossible. They did it and brought her here." The compound manager's voice rose with his anxiety.

Ali's voice rumbled in reply to the compound manager's protests.

Manu tapped his head against the cement wall. Once. Twice. What made him think life as an undercover detective suited him? He who spent most of his life in a rural village, sitting cross-legged in a dirt-floor classroom, taking notes on a chalkboard.

"Call the cleaners," Ali said curtly. "We are opening an investigation. And you worry about liability later."

The door creaked open.

"Sorry," Manu stuttered. He tried to sit up.

A man in yellow overalls scuttled in with a mop. His eyes flickered in dismay from Manu to the specks of vomit and back. He left, leaning the mop to one side.

"If you didn't react to a dead body, I'd be concerned." Ali stepped around the lumps of Manu's breakfast and extended him a hand.

Manu's lip trembled. He grasped Ali's palm, surprised by the smoothness and strength of grip. He repeated, "Sorry."

Ali hauled him up to his feet and away from the body fluids. "You keep apologizing, and I'll have to tell everyone."

Manu managed a smile. He welcomed the fresh air after the stench of his stomach acid. "Now what?"

Ali adjusted his *ghutra,* flipping the ends over each other, first to the right and then to the left. To Manu these movements looked like adjusting locks of hair.

"Now we fill out paper, repeat the story millions of times, and do damage control when the international media finds out."

"And the killer?"

Ali raised an eyebrow at him. "Yes, we have to try to find of him, of course."

They contemplated the clutch of grieving, scared women and men through the clubhouse window.

"You should call your sister." Ali squeezed Manu on the shoulder. Outside, he dispersed the people as the medics wheeled the sheet-covered gurney to the ambulance.

Manu's fingers trembled as he dialed the second of two numbers stored in his phone.

"Hello?"

He swallowed, his throat convulsing at the sound of sleep making her voice thick and slow. "Hi," he managed. This would be a short call.

"Manu?" she said several times, her voice getting stronger. "Are you there?"

His mind raced, wondering what he could say. *I found a dead person. A woman. Worse than any of the guys in the camps.* The medics were struggling to hoist the cot into the ambulance without a ramp. Ali bent to help them. The body teetered on the unbalanced mattress. "I dialed by accident," he said. "Call you later." He hung up on his sister's sputtering questions about what he ate and how much he slept.

"One, two, three," Ali counted. They pulled it up, hoisting it waist-high to clear the wheels of the ambulance.

Manu's knees buckled to accommodate the weight of the bed and the woman's inert form. All three of the other men, Muslim, shied away from the body as it rolled onto the bed.

"You didn't strap this down?" Ali said sharply.

"We called for a female medic," the older one said. "The friend put her body up."

Manu switched hands, using his left to catch her head as it bobbed to one side. Her blue eye stared at him from the slit between her eyelids. He gasped.

They'd gone too far in for recriminations. The bed went up, into the metal floor of the ambulance, the wheels rolling it forward, taking Lauren away from them into the interior.

He stepped back, and the contact with the cold flesh sent tremors through his arms.

"Stay here, finish your shift," Ali said into his ear. "I'll get the report started."

Manu rubbed his arms, watching the taillights of his contact disappear.

"Show me the video again!" The manager returned, sweat dotting his bald forehead, the weight of his belly straining the buttons on his shirt.

Manu trudged back to the office. Adhik slunk in behind him. The manager pulled up to the desk as Adhik manipulated the machines, showing the footage from earlier that night of vehicles arriving and departing.

"Impossible, impossible," he muttered to himself. "Do you know what you did?" He swung around in the swivel chair, glaring at Manu and Adhik. "Now they'll all want to move out. They will say that this place is not safe. No, no, no." He covered his face with his hands. "This is your fault."

Manu stood against the wall as Adhik tried to find other footage to distract the man. He couldn't argue. A more experienced cop, an actual officer, would have seen something amiss. Maybe he would suspect they should be worried about a killer, not someone buying sex.

Chapter Six

It is a truth universally acknowledged, that a single man in possession of a good fortune must be in want of a wife. However little known the feelings or views of such a man may be on his first entering a neighbourhood, this truth is so well fixed in the minds of the surrounding families, that he is considered as the rightful property of some one or other of their daughters.

"Oh, God," Maryam said, to no one in particular, alone in her bedroom. From writing exposés to responding to women's fiction – these elective courses peppered the curriculum. The paperback turned over like an ignored baby. *Pride and Prejudice*—what a joke. Or what a joke it would be if stacks and stacks of bridal magazines weren't spread throughout her room.

She perused the University's student-run news blog in frustration. This blog, the stories they wrote about, the tongue in cheek critique of society – this led her to choose journalism as a major, to cut her teeth on the stories of the day. Not to learn the finer points of literary analysis. Beloved Friend of Professor Missing. She clicked the link to see a photo of her English professor arm-in-arm with a dark haired woman, both of them sporting red-lipped smiles. The brief piece said Dr. Erin met the woman, Sandra, during their medical screenings when they first arrived into the country. The brunette worked for the national air carrier. Last seen leaving one of the capital's many five star properties after the nightclub closed for the evening. *The professor and the flight attendant.* Maryam composed the headline in her head. An imaginary list of questions followed, populated with interview subjects and suspects. *Did she know the people she left with? Were they men?* Maryam searched the Internet but found no stories about the missing Sandra in the local English or Arabic newspapers. Typical. They were scared to report anything that wandered outside standard press releases of VIP events and could get them into trouble with the government authorities. Or maybe there were journalists like her, who wanted to tell the truth, but their points of view ended up on the clipping room floor of the censor. Maryam's face contorted in a scowl, full eyebrows gathering like dark clouds. A journalism degree meant very little in this media environment which consisted of newspapers printing event press releases. *Focus,* Maryam chided herself. *This is your life now. At least until the wedding.*

Following the engagement party, the household returned to normal, most of the members of the family ignoring her, everyone else ruled by her father's business and social obligations. University life allowed for some variety, yet even there her father's prohibition against any more criticism restricted her movements like a spotlight.

Maybe students at the sister campus in America laughed at the mores of 19th century British society during their class discussions. For Maryam they were no laughing matter. She seethed at the desert sky visible from the corner window, a ribbon of blue above the partition that screened their property from their neighbors' intrusive eyes. *Keep your women under wraps at all costs, even while at home in their gardens.* Not that she ventured beyond supervision for a moment—her parents were making sure of that. Waiting to announce the date for the wedding. Her parents were eager to make things official, but Ali's mother and sister asked for time to order their dresses. Custom-made—only the best for the wedding of the eldest and only son—in order to showcase Maha at her finest. Maryam's family could hardly say no. During this waiting period in life, her father's restrictions applied. With marriage, she could be restored to her full mobility—with a lenient husband.

Her stomach flip-flopped at the thought of the man who would become her husband. *Husband. Ugh.* She kicked a foot free of the cover, where a brooding Darcy loomed in the background while a demure Elizabeth looked into the distance. Maryam gave the book another kick. With a satisfying *whoosh*, the paperback sailed through the air and brought down one of her mother's teetering monuments to fashion, scattering the magazines in front of the doorway. If only reclaiming her life could be so easily arranged. Her mother's selections of pastel fabrics for tablecloths stood in stark contrast to the bone-white walls Maryam insisted on once she started high school. The years and the layers of paint hid the toy-aisle-pink of the room Maryam grew up in. Fatma created two collages of sweeping bridal trains, composing them from the dozen or so images deemed most likely to impress an expected audience of six hundred women. Give or take a hundred neighbors and friends of friends.

You will not call anyone in class to see what they know about Dr. Erin's friend. The reminder sent her into another spiral of despair. Her computer allowed the only connection to the outside world. No phone.

"Here you are." Nasser's profile emerged in the sliver of the doorway as the wood caught on the edge of a copy of *You and Your Wedding.* "Still hiding?"

"It's not like I can go anywhere besides uni," she retorted.

"You can come out of this cave into the rest of the house." He bent down to pick up the magazines in his path. "Wow, *Ummi* went out of her way— this is from London."

"And Italy, and America, and…" Maryam waved around at what resembled the fallout from an explosion at a bridal fair.

Nasser perched on the edge of the padded brown chaise longue, angled toward the bed. "She needs a project."

Maryam threw herself against the pillows. "Why doesn't she get you married, then?"

"I'm training to be a doctor." Nasser laid the magazines on her bedside table. The novel ended up back on top.

"I'm training to be a rented womb," Maryam muttered.

Nasser snorted. "Come on, Mimi. This is too bleak, even for you."

She gave him her shoulder. "See what my room is filled with? Know what I would find in yours?"

"How are things so bad? You're marrying a good guy. A guy you like. Who likes you."

"Our standards are *so* high," Maryam said, her voice muffled by a pillow.

"Should have thought about that before you went night-riding all over the Industrial area like a superhero." He sat on the edge of her bed.

"That's right. I should be at home waiting for my life to start, like a Disney princess." She popped up from the shroud of sheets.

"I'm not the enemy," Nasser said. "You're getting a good deal, and it's better than the one I'll have."

"You?" She sank back against the wooden headboard. "When you decide you're ready, you'll have aunts and sisters and cousins of brides lined around the corner waiting to get in here to say hi to *Ummi*."

"You were the same, but you found reasons to say no to every one." He found her feet with his hands. "Things aren't so bad. You could be in Saudi. Then we'd never see you."

"Exile or marriage. Great non-choices." Maryam scooted away.

"You're still studying." He flipped up the end of the duvet. "Apologize to them, instead of defending your actions. Things might lighten up."

"I have nothing to apologize for," she said. "I saved a man's life."

"You were out with a man at night, alone." Nasser grabbed her foot under the sheet and began tickling it. "Confess."

"We weren't dating," she protested. "We were working."

"You're a university student," Nasser said.

His nails on the bottom of her foot were unbearable. She shrieked with laughter. "Stop, please! Stop."

"Confess." He gripped her other ankle in his hand.

"Alright, alright! I confess to being a woman with half a brain."

He released her ankle, and she drew her feet beneath her, catching her breath.

"You have to grow up, Maryam." All traces of mirth disappeared from Nasser's eyes. "I'm not going to be around to get you out of these scrapes."

"What does that mean?"

"I'm up for my residency in New York. I'll be gone for twelve weeks."

"When?" The question came out in a whisper. Since Nasser enrolled in the six-year medical program, they knew this moment would come.

"As soon as they set the date for your reception."

"Oh." She grabbed the pillow next to her. "And I thought you might miss all the fireworks." With a shriek, she whacked him on the side of the head.

"You two."

Their father's voice brought them to instant stillness.

"As close as when you were children." A smile hovered on the edge of his lips.

Nasser dropped both of her feet.

"You are not children any more." The possibility of a smile disappeared into the hard line of their father's mouth. "Don't you have studying to do?" He directed this at Nasser.

Nasser moved away from Maryam. "Yes, *Yuba*."

"Though I don't see why you want to service people when you could be managing them."

Nasser said nothing, pinned to the floor by Jaber's glance and the age-old argument between father and son.

"The empire isn't quite what it was," Nasser said.

Maryam held her breath.

"That is thanks to your sister's investigations into our company's business practices."

She shrunk against the headboard, wishing she could disappear under the sheets. Her blog posts about company labor practices caused a stir in the local press as well as in their family.

"Doing good comes at a price," Jaber said.

"We can afford it," Nasser said. "At least a little good."

"You children have no idea what you are squandering." Jaber waved away Nasser's words. "It's your inheritance."

Neither Maryam nor Nasser responded. Their father's eyes burned with the fierceness he turned on their childhood exploits. The last time Jaber glowered at them, they were almost teenagers, pretending to lose their Eid money in order to get more.

"If your mother's plans for this wedding don't ruin us."

Without another glance, Nasser left.

Maryam swung her legs over the side of the bed. Anger shimmered from her father's taut face. Nasser's advice echoed in her ears.

Jaber crossed over a few more magazines and handed her a Nokia mobile. "This is so you can talk to your fiancé."

Maryam took the phone, no bigger than a voice recorder, the first she'd seen in weeks. Without a camera or applications, the device weighed as little as a bar of soap.

"He has the number. You may message and talk as often as you want. But no meetings." His eyelids formed hoods now.

She couldn't read his face. Maryam ran her fingers over the grey letters and numbers.

"Is that clear?"

"Yes, *Yuba*."

He picked up the novel and eyed the blank document on her computer. Maryam's cheeks warmed. "And classes?"

"Going to every one," Maryam said.

"Assignments?" He flipped through the book, satisfied with all the text and put it back on top of the magazines. "Anything with interviews or reports?"

"Taking all electives," she said, eyes downcast. "Mostly argumentative essays."

"Your mother is planning the reception."

Maryam's throat burned with unspoken words. She wanted to lash out at this transformed version of her father; he bore no resemblance to the one who dandled her on his knee. As a teenager he regaled her with time-lapse photos of the skyscrapers their company built downtown.

"University and home," he said. "Until the reception. We'll set the date for three months from now. When your brother can come back in December. When they're having Christmas."

"Okay," she squeaked.

The time that Nasser would be away yawned before her like a sentence in solitary confinement. Her friends' parents were keeping them away as well, because of Maryam's online activity.

"*Yuba,* I wanted to——"The words 'I'm sorry' lodged in her throat.

Maria popped into the room, her eyes wide at the disarray. "Sir, there is a visitor for you. In the *majlis.*"

"I'm coming." Jaber adjusted his *ghutra* in the mirror above the dresser before leaving.

"Oh, so messy," Maria moaned. She wandered through the room in a trance, touching each sample wedding favor with a reverence Maryam imagined Catholics used for lighting their candles. "Why, why, these are beautiful." Maria lined them up on the dresser, her fingers caressing the pink box with a glittery ribbon.

"Take it if you want," Maryam said.

"Ma'am?" Maria jumped. "This for me?"

"Take them all." Maryam swept her mother's first option for a wedding favor; a lace, paper, and glass bauble into the tote bag.

"These ones have chocolate in them," Maria said as if they were gold coins. She cradled a set of flat gold-plate disks.

"Don't eat them all at once," Maryam murmured. She shooed Maria out the door and closed it firmly against any other visitors. They were supposed to read fifty pages of the novel and post two hundred and fifty words by midnight. A hundred or so still to write. A loud buzzing, like the sound of insects, came from the bed. Her family-approved phone. Sweat moistened her palms. She stared at the Nokia for a few moments as it bounced around her bed like a wounded bird. He didn't text her as other people did. He called.

"Hello." Silence from the other end. "Hello?" She scrutinized the number. Without a contact list, the phone displayed only digits, no registered numbers. But only one person knew this number. A thrill shot through her, like that of a spy receiving a secret message.

"*Al salaam alaikum.*"

"*Wa alaikum as salaam.*" Maryam returned the greeting a beat later, recognizing the deep timbre of the caller. She kicked the edge of the bed and winced as a spark of pain shot from her big toe up her hip. Over the phone, Ali sounded much more formal than in person.

"I hope you are well."

"And I you," she said, closing her eyes. Days passed since the engagement, when she last saw and spoke to Ali in person. Months since they drove around town, she in the front of his SUV, united in their mission to find Manu. "My mother has filled my room with wedding samples," she said, her voice shaking.

"That's good." He coughed.

Maryam glanced at the pile of magazines. He wouldn't have an opinion on any of those. Or want to be involved. Would he? As the first of her close friends and cousins to go through this ritual into adulthood, she felt at a loose end. Other girls used wedding receptions as a pretext to flaunt their latest designer dresses, earrings, shoes, or purses. The only parties Maryam attended were under duress, escorted by Fatma in order to show off her unmarried daughter.

"I'm calling about something else, actually."

Her attention snapped back to the person—the man—at the end of the line.

"Your friend, the American one. I need you to call him and make sure he doesn't say anything about how we know Manu."

"Daniel?" Panic turned to confusion. Maryam sat down on the bed with a *plop*. Now a freshman at her university, her high school friend hovered in the margins of day-to-day life. His childhood nanny was also the sister of Ali's secret agent. Their lives were like a web, the government lurking in the corner like a spider, watching over them all.

"Yes, the boy. Make sure he doesn't say anything to anyone. Especially his parents."

"Is Manu in danger?" A short silence lingered. Maryam checked the line to make sure they were still connected. "Ali?"

"He'll be fine."

Maryam's mind whirred through the possibilities. "He's staying undercover?"

Silence again, twice the length of the previous one. "Yes, that type of assignment. But you don't know that, and neither does he. None of us can talk about this. To anyone."

"Alright," Maryam said. "Believe me, I don't need to get in any more trouble."

Ali surprised them both with a chuckle. "Send him a message, and make sure he realizes this is serious."

"But I don't have Daniel's number. They took my phone." *After they caught me helping you.* Men enjoyed all the luck, allowed to make contact with the world willy-nilly.

"Right." Ali read out the numbers.

Maryam scrambled to write them down, settling for a sample eyeliner pencil her mother left on the nightstand. She scribbled on the back of her hand.

"Not a word to anyone," Ali repeated.

"I got it."

"No writing either," he added, his voice gruff.

"Fine." Maryam itched to throw the phone in the direction of the remaining stack of magazines.

He cleared his throat. "I'll message you later. Have to go into the office now."

Maryam made a non-committal sound of acknowledgement.

"For paperwork."

They said *ma'a salama* at the same time. The line went dead.

She stared at the phone in her hand. Unaccustomed to speaking to her fiancé, she forgot the questions about Sandra's disappearance. If anyone could find out, it would be Ali, giving Maryam the scoop of the year.

The phone buzzed.

I'd like to see you.

She frowned, unsure if he meant this or sent it as an afterthought.

Ask your brother if we can arrange something.

She read the words several times. Her father was quite clear that there were to be no meetings prior to the reception. Ali didn't seem to have received the same instructions.

What do you know about a missing flight attendant?

Nothing. And nor should you.

She wrinkled her nose. No sense in arguing. On the reporting front, Ali and her father were on the same page. With Nasser headed to America soon, in a few days Maryam would be on her own. She entered Daniel's number, the keys alien to her touch. Gone were the days of *tap, tap, tap* on her smartphone. No, now she pressed down a number and held it, waiting for it to blink, then kept pressing until she saw the letter she wanted. Typing Daniel's name proved even harder. Her patience snapped when the 'I' key refused to cooperate. Maryam pounded the phone on the coverlet. She never thought she would miss autocorrect.

Don't tell anyone about Manu. Five words. That's all she could manage on this ancient device. Maryam put the phone down to return to her reading. The connection between British literature and a degree in journalism eluded her, but this counted as an elective, and she preferred it to science class, which seemed an even further reach.

... he looked for a moment at Elizabeth, till catching her eye, he withdrew his own and coldly said, "She is tolerable; but not handsome enough to tempt me; and I am in no humour at present to give consequence to young ladies who are slighted by other men. You had better return to your partner and enjoy her smiles, for you are wasting your time with me."

She released the book onto the bed. She'd finished the first fifty pages required for the next class. Maryam pulled the laptop toward her. Two hundred and fifty words on any reactions, no summary, of the assigned reading. She pressed her fingers against her eyelids.

"Mr. Darcy sounds like a local mother," she wrote, knowing what her mother thought of Maryam marrying a policeman. "Thinking he's too good for anyone and yet knowing everyone wants him in their family."

"Faisal," her mother sighed, once and only once after her father accepted Ali's proposal. "His family vacations near us in London." Precisely why Maryam wanted nothing to do with Faisal, her classmate. *No one but family is good enough. The more closely related, the better.* Her fingers flew on the keyboard, the topic resonating with the last few months of her life. She and Ali were related on his grandfather's side. The side slightly less wealthy, the children of the second wife, darker in skin tone. These were the things that mattered.

"Mr. Darcy and the average mother in the Arabian Gulf would rather be alone than marry beneath their station." The buzzing phone startled her from the paragraph.

Yeah, okay. See you at lunch tomorrow?

She avoided Daniel and the open-air courtyard because of all the watchful eyes. If someone said something to her mother about Maryam and her American male friend—well, that could put this delicate truce with her parents in jeopardy.

They dealt with this in high school when her father answered the house phone, wondering why a boy dared call the house to ask for her. Her family prohibited her from attending any class birthday parties, although the school required that everyone in the class be invited or at least classmates of the same gender. Guys didn't invite girls to birthday parties after the age of eight unless they liked them. So Daniel's intentions were clear. Adults from both cultures misunderstood their friendship. The school and her parents: they were at cross-purposes. Now she must factor Ali's attitudes towards mixed friendships. Considering their escapades resulted in marriage, he couldn't be far from her father's point of view.

Yes, she typed back. *Seriously, not a word about Manu.*

After the ease of typing on the computer keyboard she grit her teeth at the blinking phone cursor. So far from the glamorous life of a spy like James Bond with a million gadgets at his disposal.

Got it. Have a piece we need to assign to someone. About the bad health care options for the guys who work in our building. Interested?

She started at the question for a few moments, the letters rearranging themselves into a string of sounds instead of words. She sent back, *No. Can't do anything with workers or rights or anything like that.*

He's in bad shape this guy. Cancer apparently. But okay if you can't. Your dad or the university?

Both, she lied. The University legal team advised her and Professor Paul to keep a lower profile. Paul fought tooth and nail, on the grounds of academic freedom, to keep writing about labor conditions. For Maryam, there would be absolutely no bylines of any kind if she wanted to stay under her father's roof.

Running for student government?

If she knew her stint as student body president in high school would be her heyday, she might have enjoyed it more. That girl may as well have been another person. *Focusing on my GPA,* she wrote.

Come on!

She giggled, despite his seriousness. Daniel knew better.

I'm thinking of running for treasurer. Would be fun to rule the school again.

Yeah. If she continued in this vein, she would be living in the past or a fantasy land where she did whatever she wanted, whenever. Both paths would only lead to a frustrated present. Maryam deleted the messages, including the ones from Ali. She couldn't risk the high price of Daniel's extracurriculars. If her father discovered she messaged anyone beyond her one-person allotment, the small window of freedom would close. She consoled herself because Daniel of all people should know how to read her silence: as a polite no. With life as a wife on the horizon, she couldn't fathom fitting in at school, much less running for an election.

In other news, there's rumors of a missing woman. A flight attendant or something. They want it covered for the journalism blog.

I saw! What do you think happened?

No idea. She fell asleep somewhere and hasn't woken up? There hasn't been a murder here in who knows how long.

That they tell us about, she reminded him. The bleak headlines came out of the other Gulf countries, particularly about housemaids. Every now and then a Kuwaiti or Saudi headline reported a national beating a housemaid within an inch of her life for a minor infraction. The last gruesome report, about a Sri Lankan maid, younger than Maryam, described the girl with nails in her hands and arms, pounded there by her employer. She shuddered at this line of thought.

You interested in doing some research? Phone some sources?

Yes! Yes, this is the kind of stuff I love, she thought.

I can't, she typed. She sounded like a semi-prisoner. *I can't do anything with workers or news.*

Ask a few questions. We won't quote you.

She tossed the phone aside in irritation. Daniel dangled a plum assignment in front of her—the kind of piece she would have put all her energy into. Were there two missing women? Or one, the same one that Manu called about? What did Ali know about either? Maryam chewed on the edge of a strand of hair. How to get her fiancé to share what he knew? Maybe if she fudged the truth, said the university newspaper would release the wrong details, he would give her the right ones. She jumped up from bed, the novel sliding off the coverlet, taking Elizabeth Bennett's troubles with it. They would have to meet face-to-face. She knew from personal experience he found it much harder to resist her in person.

Chapter Seven

Horns sounded, filling the morning air like the buzz of a flock of angry birds. In over ten minutes of waiting, craning his neck to see the source of the problem, and making out the hoods of cars for half a mile, Ali pounded the wheel in frustration. The red numbers of the clock glowed at him from the dashboard. At this rate he would miss the briefing meeting with his boss, Khalifa. A meeting with potential to reverse the downward spiral of his career. His fingers itched to join in the general honking of dismay.

The ringing phone filled the vehicle's interior.

"Not now, Hassan," Ali growled.

"How did it go?" His cousin's drowsy voice surrounded him. "Why don't you return my calls? Then we can go out and celebrate."

"It went," Ali said. "I don't go to those places."

Separated by a few years, Hassan's lifestyle suited that of a much younger man. A twenty-something ex-pat boy, to be precise.

"Listen, you don't have to do anything when we go out. You can look, you know. That's still legal."

Ali palmed the wheel, pulling his car up onto the sidewalk, riding down the pavement, dragging the undercarriage on the pavement stone. "I have work to do," he said.

"Okay, okay. Seriously, we can go out and get juice or whatever is your thing. Celebrate."

Ali hung up on Hassan's full-throttle laughter. The other drivers gave him glances before noticing his police uniform. He kept his gaze on the road, approaching the knot of cars at the roundabout. All of the streetlights were blinking in each of the four stations, causing mayhem on this, the main interchange to get in or out of the high-rise development on the eastern part of the city. He groaned. A signal outage meant traffic would be backed up for hours. *8:30*, the clock taunted. Ali looked left, right, across the roundabout, and then left again. No traffic police in sight. He estimated at least fifty cars in the double column of traffic approaching the roundabout from the north. A glance in his rearview mirror said there were twice as many behind him.

"Yes, what is your emergency?"

Ali twitched at the sound of the English answering his 999 call.

"There's a problem with the signal down by Lagoona," he said.

"Yes sir, thank you. There is a power outage in that side of town."

"Power outage," Ali parroted. "For how long?"

"Sir, we don't know. They are working on it." Irritation laced the man's singsong intonation of the English words.

"Send traffic police," Ali snapped. "The roundabout is a mess."

"Yes sir, but they are responding to other parts of the area as well."

"How long?" Ali asked again.

"Excuse me, sir?"

"How long before someone gets here?"

"Sir, I am sorry, sir, but I cannot give you an approximate time—"

"I am a police officer," Ali gritted his teeth over the subservience of the call center. *8:45*, the clock reminded him. "I can get out and help."

"Oh that would be wonderful, sir—"

"Until they get here. Tell them to hurry. I have other things to do." Ali gave the dispatcher his name and supervisor details. "Can you tell them I'm helping out, I'll be late into the office?" He turned off the engine and slid out of the car. Heat slapped his face in a palpable wave. Ali raised a hand, stepping out into the gridlock of the roundabout as cars inched forward. He put himself in the lip of the southerly entrance, indicating that cars approaching the roundabout should stop. His aim to clear the cars jamming the three lanes of the roundabout and thereby restore some semblance of peace.

Within a few minutes, the lanes behind him flowed with SUVs and Italian sports cars, signature vehicles for this side of town. For this system to work, you needed two men; preferably four, one at each entrance to the roundabout, holding and releasing drivers in timed intervals. A human intervention to what the lights failed to do. The traffic signals blinked yellow, then red, then green, uselessly, as Ali stepped into and out of the roundabout. A simple, labor-intensive system, used by smaller neighborhoods throughout the city.

Sweat dripped on the inside of his collar, causing the uniform to stick to his neck. Instead, he stood in the middle of the roundabout, a baleful desert sun glaring down on the clumps of SUVs to his right, as others passed through on the straightaway, strangers witness to his misery, their flickering gazes evidence of their own.

"Go!" Ali stepped onto the curb of the roundabout, his boots inches from the purple petunias wilting in the rising temperature. He motioned with his right arm like a frenzied flight attendant, releasing the line of cars stopped for five minutes. He lived his worst nightmare; serving as the lowest on the totem pole of police officers. Traffic duty. Drivers honked further up the road. Ali checked his phone. The wait to clear the roundabout averaged twenty minutes. Ali buzzed 999 again, this time with no answer. Residential towers rose behind him, standing tall on either side of the street, structures with luxury boutiques in the bottom level and apartments in the top fifteen stories, extended down towards the bay. The failure of a power station here meant wealthy ex-pats and locals going without for a few hours. Ali gave a grim smile at the idea of the foiled plans for the day. His wouldn't be the only one ruined.

"Finally," he said, thirty minutes later, as the blue lettering on the white SUV of the traffic police vehicle rode into the roundabout.

"*Al salaam alaikum*," the officer said, swaggering up next to Ali.

"*Alaikum a salaam*." Ali returned the greeting of peace, though he couldn't see the shorter man's eyes, obscured as they were by sunglasses.

"Thanks for calling this in. They gave us no warning when the outage happened. Cars were stuck all the way to the university. Looks like we'll be out here all day. No idea when the power plant will be back up."

"That's two kilometers away," Ali said with surprise. His mind skidded to Maryam. If she sat in traffic this morning, she didn't send him any grumbling messages.

"So which station are you in?"

"Hm?" Ali jerked his attention back to the moment at hand. They contemplated the trickle of cars into the roundabout.

"Are you in one near here, that's why you were the first one on site?"

"Oh, I don't do traffic," Ali mumbled.

The other man peered at him over his sunglasses.

Ali now saw the shadow of a beard, close-shaven for maximum effect, a look now popular among the younger men. The man took in Ali's non-descript blue uniform, indicative of the intelligence unit.

"But then why——"

"Have to go. *Ma'a salama*." Ali jogged to his car before the junior officer could ask any more questions.

This late into the morning, drivers entered mostly from the south, as cars sped into the roundabout to come into the development for shopping and coffee, or ladies made their way out for lunch. He climbed into his vehicle, cranking the air-conditioning and pulling on his seatbelt, avoiding eye contact with the officer now joined by another car with two more men. In typical fashion, the traffic police were understaffed at a key moment and now overstaffed with minimal requirement. Ali stepped on the gas, his tires screeching as he took the curve of the roundabout, several hours late for the meeting of his life.

Section for Missing Persons. Ali cringed at the black Arabic lettering on the door as he hurried past to the captain's suite. He arrived, huffing, to have the secretary, murmuring on a cellphone, wave him into an empty waiting area with a lift of his chin. Sweat beaded in Ali's stubble. Was the meeting still on? Canceled? Without anyone to answer these questions, the secretary would be no help at all, nor would Ali give him access to his anxiety. He entered the bathroom of the palatial office suite, dabbing at his sweat-soaked back with tissue from the brass-studded box on the granite sink. If Khalifa sensed the nerves, hope and fear this summons triggered, Ali would lose the upper hand. White fibers dotted the left side of his face. In the mirror, his fingers shook as he pulled them out.

"Focus." He threw drops of water on both sides of his face and dabbed it with a cream towel his mother would have envied. The outer door to the office clicked. He started out of the bathroom.

"*Al salaam alaikum.*" Ali snapped to attention at the sight of his superior seated on the low cream sofa in front of a bank of windows. Desert sunlight refracted around the office, temporarily stunning Ali from the semi-dark of the bathroom.

"*Alaikum a salaam.*" Khalifa held out a basket of chocolates to Ali.

"*Mabrook*," he replied automatically. The chocolates meant congratulations were in order.

"*Allah barak feek*," Khalifa tilted his head, indicating Ali should sit next to him.

Ali complied, careful not to sink back against the inviting leather cushions. He would wrinkle his uniform—and he'd just earned back the right to wear it.

"The chocolates are for you."

"Me?" Ali chose one of the smaller squares, wrapped in thick, glittering paper. "I'm sorry about this morning. On the way in—"

Khalifa raised his hand, his eyes narrowing, all of his attention focused on Ali. "You did the right thing," he said. "They're still trying to sort out that mess. People calling in, complaining all their food is rotting, restaurants losing business because they don't have A/C. The media writing about the luxury development without any power. It's a circus. You actually helped hundreds of people get on with their day."

Ali nodded, swallowing past the lump in his throat. A few words of praise meant so much to him, especially from the man who worked closely with his father before his illness and death. He switched his gaze to the low table in front of him. Photography books of Arabian horses and aerial shots of the country's various landmarks littered the table's surface. Nothing about this office resembled the seamy underbelly of a growing capital, the thousands of hands that toiled to make the very room they were sitting in. Hands of men, the laborers, who, until recently, Ali took little notice of.

"We need more men like you, Ali. Those who stop to help, no matter how low the task."

He felt rather than heard the last phrase, like a punch in his gut. Did Khalifa think low level tasks now suited Ali, an internationally-trained military expert? An expert who spent most of the morning directing traffic. Potholes riddled Ali's road to redemption—much like the well-traveled neighborhood streets in their city-state capital. The path back to good standing would not be not straight, nor smooth.

"You're getting a promotion."

"Promotion?" Ali echoed. "But I haven't found the murderer." He laid the piece of chocolate, still in its wrapper, on the glass-topped coffee table.

"You will." Khalifa's face remained impassive, made craggy during the additional decades that Ali's father, Khalifa's friend, didn't get. "There are only two people it could be. A boyfriend," he raised a finger. "Or an ex-boyfriend. Question all the men she knew and you'll find him." The lines around his eyes and mouth guarded against any sign of emotion. "But you have a bigger mission now. Now you're a two-star sergeant."

Pinpricks of joy burst across Ali's skin, along with the niggling feeling of something amiss. The increase in rank would mean more prestige. More prestige would make him respectable. And more eligibility meant that

Maryam's family—

"I'm adding a secondary set of duties," Khalifa continued.

Ali couldn't bask in this moment. His morning's do-gooding put him on level with the traffic police who stood at roundabouts and signals in the heat of the day, alternately waving through cars and making them stop. They caused bottlenecks rather than solving them. Ali recoiled at the thought of spending any official time on traffic detail and further wasting his Sandhurst education.

"You'll set up a vice squad and choose the men you want to work with you. The Nepali is a must. Good recruit." Khalifa handed over a sheaf of papers.

"Vice squad?"

Maryam's luminous face, those liquid eyes trained on him, faded from Ali's mind's eye. Worse than him standing on the side of the street would be her wanting to write about his work.

"Yes, this is the newly identified priority—tackling those people who are brought here for services. Also counts as trafficking. Missing Persons is your cover, if anyone asks."

Ali leaned one hand on the folder and pulled at his collar with the other. A man who worked in busting prostitutes wouldn't be high on anyone's list, regardless of how many stars he might have.

"Vice—"

"Top secret." Khalifa held up a leathery hand. "No one will know about this. You're a secret department working directly for me."

Secret. Ali could tell people he worked on anything. Even a security detail. "No one else?"

"No," Khalifa said. "There's a leak somewhere. Keep your eyes open."

Ali took the folder, thoughts swirling in his mind like grains of sand. He stood and headed for the door.

"And Ali?"

He turned at the door.

"Keep this under wraps. No media. Especially not that professor your man stayed with. Or any of his students."

"Sir."

"And check in on that last file. There's another woman missing."

Ali raised an eyebrow.

"Unlikely to be serious," Khalifa said. "Safest country in the world, especially for women."

Depends on the woman. Ali thought of Manu's sister, the first time he met her in the police station, trembling in fear at the sight of so many locals.

"She probably went on a trip or a cruise and didn't tell her employer. You know, American. Someone said she skipped work. Young girl, teacher."

"Yes, will do."

"Good luck."

A flush spread up Ali's neck. His boss's neutral tone made it difficult to know whether the words were a criticism or benediction. He swung on his heel and left. Khalifa knew about Paul's journalistic aspirations. Even worse, he knew about Maryam's involvement in exposing the labor violations of the hiring agencies. Ali pulled out his phone to send Maryam a stern message. At the thought of her, he hit the 'call' button instead.

"The number you have dialed cannot be reached at this time," droned the singsong automated voice in Arabic.

Ali crossed the marble foyer, blinking as he stepped into the mid-morning glare of the desert sun. Maryam's family kept close tabs on her until they confirmed their relationship with a wedding reception. He put the papers on the dashboard and let the SUV's cooler air hit him in the face, first to ease the blush Khalifa caused by his deliberately vague mention of Maryam and second to combat the heat trapped inside the car.

Her parents could watch over her for now. Ali needed to launch an investigation. Solving this crime was the next step in rising in Khalifa's esteem and resolving his own problems.

Chapter Eight

Sanjana clutched the plastic envelope stuffed with printed documents. Passport copy, resident permit, no objection letter from her sponsor. The sedan slid along the highway, transporting her to meet destiny.

"People behind you!" her taxi driver shouted. He slammed on his brakes, flashing his lights. Cars screeched to a stop on the bridge. They shuddered to a standstill. Sanjana braced herself on the back of the seat in front of her, her nose inches from the seatback.

Glowing numbers on the dash said she would be late.

"Is it an accident?" She chewed at her lip, clutching the dossier.

He swore again at the SUV that cut over from the right-hand lane, obscuring the view.

What was his name? Her nerves were so taut she couldn't comprehend the familiar landscape and, for a second, she found herself disoriented on the streets she traveled everyday. They passed a men's sandal shop and a row of tailors. Then the Hardee's.

"Make a right cutting," she said.

He met her gaze in the mirror.

"Go, go." She pointed out the window. They swerved off, missing by inches the guardrail on the ramp to the bridge.

"You know where you going?"

"Right." She clung to the door as the car wheeled around the roundabout. "And straight." They bounced over a series of speed bumps, Sanjana's head hit the top of the car. "And left."

This brought them to the straightaway after the bridge where traffic flowed at a normal pace.

"You drive?"

"Madam knows all the shortcuts." She fidgeted with her braid, tossing it back over her shoulder.

"I come to your compound," he said.

"Yes." The tops of trees waved at her from behind the boundary wall of an estate. Signs of green made her miss home. "For sir."

"For... supply." He mimed a drink with his finger tilted to his mouth.

She kept her gaze on the window.

"You know your madam's son—"

"We are here." She gripped the door handle, half hearing him.

The security guard's forehead puckered as he gave her the once over. He stood behind a low white gate that formed a box in front of the large gate shielding the nursery interior from the street.

Sanjana tugged at the bottom of her shirt, the cotton fabric loose at her waist. The waiting taxi's engine hummed in the row of parking spots next to her. She wanted to rush straight in, out of the watchful gaze of the driver.

"You picking up a child?" His dark skin made his teeth gleam, picking up the white of his button-down shirt. Sweat beaded on his forehead. "What's the name?"

There were dozens of men like him scattered across the city in shopping malls and behind reception desks in offices. A few were posted at the entrance to the compound where she lived with Madam Cindy's family.

Sanjana gave them all a wide berth, those guys from India and Sri Lanka, who joked with the madams and were known to harass their maids. Between the guards and the maintenance men, the compound meant living under constant masculine surveillance. Here, at a nursery, a lone security guard appeared at the front gate as an afterthought. She gathered her scattered nerves. No one would run off with a child in this country, where the penalties were so severe you'd never see the outside of a prison again.

A silver pick-up truck whipped through the street behind her in a squeal of tires. The reversing SUV slammed on its breaks.

"Slow down! This is a neighborhood street," the dark-haired father called out the window at the retreating vehicle.

Less security and more traffic police. Manu's boss swam in her vision. Tall, broad-shouldered, thick across the chest, and heavy in gait. Someone to inspire fear or confidence. Nothing like the man who stood before her, clutching a sign-in sheet. Nor like her brother; a boy with persistent questions. *What help could Manu be to the national police?* She brushed the thought aside as the man in front of her clicked his teeth at her. Kenyan, Sanjana guessed. Maybe northern Sudanese.

"I have an interview," she said in her best imitation of Madam Cindy's curt tone, given to inattentive drivers. *I am supposed to be here.*

He appraised her again then opened the iron gate secluding the nursery. She stepped through and the metal clanged shut behind her.

Sanjana entered a courtyard strewn with three-wheeled bikes. At the far end, children played in a sandbox with shovels, scattering grains around as women with dark hair and collared white t-shirts shielded their eyes.

To the left she saw a glass-fronted room filled with colored mats and shapes that younger children toddled around. Her heart squeezed at the sight of dimpled legs and cheeks. She made her way toward the two-story building in the middle. She hoisted her purse, a black leather tote bag - one of Madam Cindy's nicer Christmas presents - over her shoulder.

"Excuse me," she said as a mother wearing tight black pants and a tank top came out clutching a wailing infant, trailed by a boy in a striped uniform. She stood to one side like the maids in the malls, waiting for their mistresses to exit before following along. They passed her by without a word. Sanjana entered a sunlit reception area with a white desk and set of glass double doors.

"Can I help you?" The woman behind the desk peered up over purple-rimmed glasses. Her accent gave Sanjana pause. Her sharp vowels were harder to follow than Madam Cindy's, or Daniel's soft ones. "Picking up someone?"

"Yes, I'm here for an interview," she said. "Sanjana."

"Oh, right." The woman wheeled back in the chair to reveal a rounded belly. "I'll get Betsy."

The woman waddled with the weight of pregnancy from behind the desk and into the next room. Sanjana stood next to a tiny green leather sofa meant for children. A bulletin board facing the desk announced photos of the Tiny Tots.

She studied the faces; children with fair, milky skin and blue eyes, many of them staring back into the camera without blinking. There were darker-headed ones too, with dusky skin and thick lashes. These were blurs of movement, not looking at the camera.

"Yes, hello."

Sanjana swung around. She extended her hand to the blonde woman as she rehearsed with Sir Paul. Sanjana looked her in the eye, which he insisted would give a good impression.

"I'm Betsy, the director of Kids Corner. Why don't you come back here?"

Sanjana followed her through the open set of doors, the top part made of glass, and into an indoor play area.

"Sorry, these are the only chairs we have."

Sanjana perched on the wooden child's chair.

"They're sturdy." Betsy gave a laugh.

Sanjana smiled. "This is application." She handed over the final set of papers, filled in block letters, having discarded others riddled with errors.

Betsy took the documents, rifling through them. "You don't have any experience?"

"I am housemaid for ten years," Sanjana said. "I take care of one boy, most of his life. And I have my own brothers and sisters."

Betsy nodded. Her eyes crinkled at the corners. "Children of your own?"

"No," Sanjana managed. The word knifed through her insides, causing her stomach to tense. Approaching thirty, without children, living far away from her siblings. She clutched her hands in her lap, hoping the woman and her school could give her some meaning again. "My boy," she corrected herself, "the boy in my family, he a teenager now." *Doesn't need me.*

"You might need a new job soon." Betsy rolled the papers into a cone and tapped it on the round yellow-topped table beside them. "We're looking for people with a bit more experience, with more children."

Squeals interrupted them as a stream of children filed through, holding on to a rope, led by two women toward the courtyard. One of the women said, "Come on Omar, stay together."

They were both Filipino.

"Hi, hi, hi." Betsy waved to the children approaching.

A dark-haired girl with wide eyes, her skin the color of brown sugar, stood out like a raisin in a pudding. She marched at the end of a line of children with milky-white skin and yellow tufts of hair.

"I do have one opening," Betsy said in the silence following the mini-parade.

"Yes? I can start soon. I am available during the morning times and when the children are here." She and Madam shared their schedules, making sure someone would be home when Daniel arrived after his sports and club activities.

"Our cleaner went back to Ethiopia for family reasons, so we do need someone," Betsy said. "You'd come in around two o'clock as the day is winding down. Clean all the rooms, the bathrooms, the outdoor play area, and take out the trash."

"A cleaner?" Sanjana's mouth dried up. She wanted to run out of the room after the children who recently left. "I want to be a teacher's assistant."

"We can see how it goes," Betsy said. "You could start, and the next opening we have, you could be considered. Have a think on it and let me know by the end of the week?"

Sanjana fumbled for her bag, following Betsy back to the entryway like a chastened child.

"Thanks for coming in," the pregnant woman trilled as Sanjana left.

She blinked her way through the courtyard, tears blurring her vision of the playground on the right, children swinging in bucket-seat swing sets and clambering over a wooden bridge. These children—she wanted to teach them, yes, but as she brushed past the guard's stare, through the gate and into the street outside, her stomach tied in knots.

She thought being out of the house, doing a job, the newness of it all, would cheer her up. Humid air filled her lungs with the lingering heat of summer.

"Excuse me," she said, stepping into a woman's path.

"Watch where you're going." The woman pushed past, not breaking her stride, into the nursery courtyard.

Sanjana paused at the gate. Something stirred in her memory at the sound of that voice. She scanned the other woman's profile for clues. Indian, judging by the dark hair and printed *kurti* that ended at the woman's hips. Jeans that a younger woman would have worn, with diamanté accents on the back pockets.

"Laxmi Pande," she said to the receptionist as the door to the front office swung closed.

Sanjana froze. The name sent a chill down her spine. Her hands trembled at the proximity of her adversary after all those weeks calling the embassy and searching for signs of her brother. Laxmi. The woman who arranged for Manu's visa then sent him to work in construction after promising him an office job. Sanjana's mind whirled. The woman enrolled her child here. She peered through the double glass-fronted doors. Betsy's eyes were trained on the computer screen at the desk. No sign of Laxmi. Sanjana re-entered the lobby, clearing her throat.

"Did you forget something?" Betsy glanced up, a smile fixing the edges of her lips.

"I, ah, I thought about it, and yes, I would like to clean here. For you," Sanjana stammered.

Betsy folded her hands on the white desktop.

Sweat prickled under Sanjana's arms. *Don't say no now,* she prayed. *Not when I need to stay.*

"Okay." Betsy rummaged in the cabinet behind her, handing over a sheaf of papers. "You get your current sponsor to provide you a letter, bring in all these copies, and we'll get you started."

"Tomorrow?"

Betsy stood, her elbows on the lip of the counter. "Let's see how long it takes you to fill out this paperwork."

"Yes, yes," Sanjana said. She stuffed the papers with their English words, swarming in lines like ants, into her bag. "I will return." She gave a big smile, showing all teeth.

"Goodbye for now." Betsy gave her a small wave.

Sanjana crossed the courtyard of the nursery, passing a glassed-in play area filled with toddlers running on vinyl-covered mats. The brown-sugar-skinned girl must be Laxmi Pande's daughter. Her heart in her mouth, Sanjana ignored the guard who asked her if he would be seeing her next week. She needed to tell Manu. His police officer would surely help catch that awful woman and make her pay. She climbed into the waiting taxi, one arranged for her by Sir Paul. "Home, please," Sanjana managed. She slipped on a pair of sunglasses to hide her trembling chin. A cleaner. She would start all over again, cleaning up after the children of rich ex-pats to whom she would remain invisible.

"Good news?" the driver asked.

"Yes," she sniffed, though not in the way he meant.

In the constant cool breeze of the air-conditioner, her thoughts slowed. Did she do the right thing in saying no? Sanjana seethed at the Filipina teachers with their fair complexions and their singsong English. A small voice inside her said she didn't want to take care of other people's children at all, not even as their teacher. So she knew where Laxmi Pande sent her child. A child who called that woman Mother. Sanjana felt an unfamiliar pang, a twist in her gut: envy. An empty lot, with scattered rocks marking the stations for an improvised cricket field, flashed in her periphery. Laxmi promised Sanjana and Manu the proper papers to work for a company in an office job. Instead he spent months on construction sites, as men were injured or died on the job. If she did it to Manu, maybe there were other men in similar predicaments. The thought sent a chill down Sanjana's spine.

"Hungry?"

"Excuse me?" Sanjana said. The driver's question startled her out of her morose musings. He regarded her in the rearview mirror, his eyes hidden behind black sunglasses.

"You hungry? Nice curry in shopping center. I take you."

"No. No, thank you," she stammered. The guy—what did Sir Paul say his name was? Mohammed? Ahmed?—served as a shadow to the family, taking Sir to the airport for years and driving the couple around after they drank too much.

"This is close to where I stay." He switched to Hindi, pointing across the passenger seat to a set of clustered apartments.

She shrank against the back seat, noting the accent. Maybe Sri Lankan after all. Sir said African, but brown, black, these shades were all the same to white people. She flipped open her phone, pretending to read a message.

"You want to see," he said, swinging the wheel to the left.

"My madam is waiting for me."

"Come and try. The food is hot. You not have to make it."

She snuck a glance at him. Clean-shaven, a glint of a thin gold rope necklace beneath his crisp shirt. No dark bags hung under those eyes like the city taxi drivers with their long shifts and high quotas. No, a glint of honey-colored flecks were scattered in his eyes. "Maybe one dish," she said.

The car swerved into the service lane, eliciting a few honks from those behind him. He gave her a broad grin, a flash of white teeth. They pulled into a complex of one-story shops, many with their metal grates down for the afternoon break while the sales clerks went for lunch. He gestured to one with the picture of chicken on a blue background, the blood-red plumage cresting above the rooster's head. Between the glass face of the eatery and their parking spot stood a red steel box on wheels, with four vertical spits. A man in an oval paper hat wiped it down.

"Nights they roast chicken," he said, smacking his lips.

She climbed out of the car, pulling at her clothing. He strode ahead of her, into the café with four tables. He sat. She took a chair opposite him, trying to look as though she ate lunch with a man every day. The menu hung above the counter with photos and letters—her heart pounded in her ears when she wondered how to make out what to eat.

"Two chicken meals, Pepsi," he said. His arm stretched across the back of the seat in front of him.

The waiter shuffled off. "Sure."

A prick of irritation at his knowing air. "You said there curry."

"That another place. This one closer." He waved a hand around his head, as if swatting at a fly. "You not from Sri Lanka like most of the nannies."

"Nepal," she said. "You?"

"You could pass for Indian," he said. "Kerala."

"Oh." *Mighty India.* The geographic neighbor loomed large in the politics of the subcontinent. And also here in the Gulf where many of the skilled jobs, like cooking or driving, were taken by Indians, leaving tasks like construction to Nepalese, Pakistanis and Bangladeshis.

"You could pass for Indian." He laughed. "Big eyes. Not Chinese."

A waiter, bent over his phone, looked up at the sound.

"Yes," she said, regretting this decision. In her siblings the iteration of features repeated themselves in a wide variety of ways. He wouldn't be so kind about Manu's flat nose, for example. Her thoughts roiled in elation at the idea of being near Laxmi Pande everyday, to mild discomfort at this, her first outing with a man. What would her mother have said, seeing her daughter in a gas station restaurant with a man not her father, brother or husband?

He eyed himself in the mirrored paneling behind her, turning his head left, then right, smoothing out his hair. Fine bone structure, she admitted; a nose like an unbroken mountain peak, giving his profile a regal air. He caught her staring and winked. Sanjana blushed, clutching her hands in her lap. What to do with her hands?

Another couple came in, the wife wearing traditional Indian clothing, printed flowing pants and a matching top with a gauzy shawl. Her husband wore a button-down shirt and slacks, their daughter sporting twin ponytails, in a striped white dress. She bounced on her chair. Sanjana's appetite disappeared. The waiter made his way over with two trays of food.

"You have family here?"

She bit a French fry to distract herself.

"No," she said out of habit. *Yes,* she thought, but she didn't correct herself to Vinay. Her brother's job remained a secret. The policeman explicitly instructed they were not to talk about what he did. She couldn't contact him. His calls were rare. Not that different from when he went missing or lived across the Indian Ocean. If he knew his sister ate lunch with a stranger, what would his reaction be? Manu of the village, careful and playful, may have teased her. Here, hardened by his months of labor, he might think this driver beneath them. "No." She rolled pieces of chicken in the flatbread, stuffing them into her mouth to chase away her family's displeasure. She chewed, savoring the rare treat to have food made by someone else.

"Me neither." His phone rang. "Yes? Yes, yes, Madam. I'm coming now.

Lunch bag? Okay, sure, sure, sure." He hung up. "These kids, they forget everything. Their mothers too busy to go and take it to them." He laughed again, a sound that made the girl next to them jump, and the mother scolded her for spilling her drink.

Sanjana reached for her purse to give him some money for the meal, but he waved aside her attempt to contribute. "How you have so much?" she asked in halting admiration.

"Business is good." They walked back to the car. He put his arm out, so her feet weren't run over by an SUV pealing through the parking lot. "Plus I have lots of side projects."

Sanjana flushed at the protective gesture, confusion over-riding any follow-up questions. She wished to be more like Madam Cindy, whose frosted beauty made men nervous rather than the other way around. She would know how to deal with this proximity of contact, whether to encourage it or move away with a frown. A car pulled up at the fruit and vegetable stall next door, laying on the horn until an employee scurried out to take the order. Sanjana hesitated at the car. Sitting in the back as she did in cabs now seemed formal, borderline rude. Yet sitting in the front would seem forward.

"Yes, come, come." He threw open his door. "Will be nice to have company."

She sat in the front, holding her purse on her lap.

The radio blared to life with the engine and they pulled out into the stream of traffic, like a tadpole searching for a place to nest.

"We do that again," he said.

She cracked the window so the words could fly out into the moist air. Did he mean like a date? If she were a film heroine, like the Hindi ones Manu loved so much, she would offer a toothy grin, maybe lean closer for him to catch a sniff of her perfume. She wasn't. She didn't, not now, her first time, alone in the front seat of a car with a stranger. She leaned away.

He took the hint and said no more. The wind swept her face, yanking tendrils along her forehead. He slammed on his breaks and swore at the car in front of them, honking for stopping suddenly.

The force pressed her back into her seat, and she silently thanked Madam for instilling in her the insistence on wearing a seatbelt, even in the back. The driver behind them returned the favor. A volley of horns ended as traffic surged forward.

No, she would not become some driver's girlfriend.

Sanjana wanted to raise her motherless siblings. She reached for her phone to text Manu. The cursor blinked at her in the TO line. Sanjana had no way of getting in touch with him.

The beige landscape streaked by as she sped back to the only home she'd known for the last decade. She shivered, raised the window, and adjusted the air-conditioning vent so it pointed downward at her feet. She tossed the bills into the front seat, avoiding eye contact, and scooted out of the car.

"Keep it," he said.

She paused, gripping the headrest.

"Next time I come for supply, you tell your boy, and he give me discount."

"Daniel." Awareness dawned on Sanjana. "What kind of discount? What are you doing with him?"

He laughed. "You not worry about me. You worry about what your boy do when you are not at home."

She left the money where it lay and huffed her way to the front door. As if she didn't have big enough problems, now Daniel needed minding to keep him out of Sharif's latest addiction. Maybe she should consider it a blessing to live so far away from her siblings.

"How did it go?" Of course, Madam Cindy, head hanging between her legs, arms stretched on the mat, peered at her from the living room.

"Your car is not here."

"Maintenance," Cindy called over her right shoulder, bent over in a triangle. Her head disappeared behind her leg. "That's why I skipped class and came to workout at home."

"I got a job." Sanjana walked around the hot pink yoga mat.

"That's great news!" Cindy straightened. The black of her tank top blended perfectly with the black of her exercise pants. "Vinay find the place okay?"

Sanjana blanched.

"Lost? Or speeding?" Cindy wiped her face with a towel. "I don't know why Paul insists on using that guy. He's reliable. That's his one virtue."

Dumb, dumb. How could she have thought the man could be a love interest? Someone to have a child with, like the round-cheeked girl she'd seen in the café.

Sanjana's phone rang. She rifled in her purse as the Bollywood tune began again. The caller gave up. The unlisted number meant she couldn't call back. Manu? Or one of the kids, using a calling card in the village shop?

"He is friendly man."

"Sounds like you two hit it off."

"Nothing like that." The words were ridiculous, now that she'd said them out loud.

Cindy followed her through the bottom of the house and out onto the back porch as Sanjana fumbled for her room key. "You okay?"

Tears filled Sanjana's eyes, and the door handle swam in her vision. *I'm not okay. And I have no way to get okay.*

These were not words to say with a roof over her head and her family safe. *Can't I have more?* she wanted to shout. *Is this all I can ever have?*

"Tired," she said. "New people, new place. I will rest." She shut the door without her standard 'You need something madam?' before Cindy could ask more questions. Sanjana flopped on her bed, allowing the tears to take over her, muffling them with her pillow. Resentment pinched her heart like a weed. She let out a pent-up breath when Cindy's shadow moved back into the kitchen. She wasn't a heroine in a love story. She was a housemaid who couldn't read or write English and barely spoke it properly, having spent her twenties in the service of a family with one teenage child. In a twist of fate, taking care of Daniel kept her more sheltered than if she stayed in the village. Then she would have seen men, on the way to and from the river, or at festivals and gatherings like weddings or funerals. Instead, she spent a decade or so tucked away with benevolent ex-pats for whom Sanjana performed adult tasks like child-minding and yet also remained their responsibility. A knock on the door startled her from the downward spiral of her thoughts. Too late to turn out the light. Sanjana held her breath. Maybe if she held still, they would think she fell asleep with the lights on.

"Hey." Daniel poked his head around the door.

"What you need?" She sprang off the bed into action.

"Nothing." He braced his hands across the doorway, green eyes like a tractor beam. "You okay? Mom said you were down."

"Fine," Sanjana sputtered. "I'm fine."

"Yeah, okay. You know, you can talk to me."

She stared at him, slack-jawed. What did that make her, if a teenage boy sensed her listlessness?

"Just saying." He limped back into the house.

"Uh, thanking you," she called after him. "What happen to your leg?"

"Basketball," he said without turning. "Should be fine in a week. No more dribbling for a while. Water sports only."

The door clanged shut, the blinds rattling. Tears stung her eyes. A teenager came to check on her. She should have given that man her phone number.

If only because he was the first one to ask for it. What did it matter that she couldn't remember his name? Her deceased mother would be horrified at the extent of her daughter's desperation. She locked eyes with the photo on the wall above her bed. *I'm an adult orphan. No one cares where I'll end up.* Her eyes filled with tears. Sanjana ground them out with the heel of her hand. Once the hero, being the top earner, then bringing her younger brother to this country, now he surpassed her. While Manu solved crimes in the city, she folded sheets. She took two tablets from the bottle of cold medicine Madam gave her. In addition to curing colds, the blue-green liquid capsules brought the blessing of sleep. *Something must change,* Sanjana vowed.

The medicine would take a few minutes to set in. She plotted her revenge on Laxmi Pande, deported with her family in the middle of the night with hastily packed suitcases. Images of children playing on airport tarmac persisted in Sanjana's dreams.

Chapter Nine

The once-cream villa hunched at the edge of the street like a sleeping crone. One-story houses littered both sides of the street and rusted metal garage doors maintained the privacy of the residents. Cats bickered in the gunmetal-grey dumpster. Their cries pierced the night like the wailing of babies.

Manu shivered in the humidity that wilted his shirt to his spine. The other men on the van, resembling a color palette for the hue 'earth', ambled forward in the aisle and then off the van. The driver called out in Hindi that the next van would return for the morning-shift guys.

"Five hours. Don't be late."

Manu slung on his backpack, one of Daniel's discards, filled with what he needed for his new life as a security guard. They trooped across a dusty entryway. No boundary wall or entry gate to this property. The freedom of it—compared to the previous camp where Manu stayed as a construction worker—disconcerted him.

"Cigarettes?" An older man with white hair and fair skin splotched with darker patches squinted up at Manu from behind a desk.

"No, sorry boss," Manu said in deference to the man's age.

The others trooped past into the kitchen. There were stacks of foil packages, rice and beans, and pieces of cold naan—not the homemade meals he'd enjoyed while in Sanjana's care. With a hunger pang, Manu regretted not further indulging the hospitality of her employers. Now he would eat cold bread in his own company for the foreseeable future.

"Come with me." The elder's husky voice led Manu to the room in the back, where four twin beds were placed, one in each corner. "You have that tonight. Chum is out on duty."

The man shuffled away, returning to his post in the villa's entryway. A guard for the guards. That seemed the way of it in this country, someone to watch those living here on the fringes. Manu swallowed past the rising panic, thankful that the dim interior wouldn't give away his fear. Scuff marks from men's shoes marred the white paint in the corners of the rectangular concrete room. He discarded the company uniform on top of the other supplies they gave them: two shirts with the Group 4 insignia, one black pair of pants, and a thick-soled pair of black boots. His underwear and shirts he rolled into the space on the right side of a drawer under the bed. Another man's socks and undergarments took up the space on the left.

Everyone else stripped down, so Manu did the same. Sleeping in his undershirt. He pushed away thoughts of the airline pajamas waiting at his sister's. *Come quickly, sleep,* Manu pleaded. The morning would bring its own set of troubles: a whole day off with nothing to do.

"Hey, you still awake?"

Manu jumped as Adhik came into the room.

"Yeah, too much water." Manu made his way to the bathroom, one in every room. Still five or so men to a toilet but that was much better than the latrine he used in the labor camp. When he came out, Adhik peered at him from the semi-dark. "You?"

"Snack." Adhik held up a twist of crackers. "Want some?"

"No thanks," Manu said. They would crumble in his mouth like dust as he remembered the home-cooked meals his sister prepared for someone else. "What is everyone doing tomorrow?"

"Oh, your first Friday!" Adhik clapped him on the back as they went up the stairs. "We go to lessons."

"Lessons?" Manu echoed. "On how to take IDs?"

Adhik chortled. "No, of course not. Not working. English lessons. Taught by some special teachers." He wiggled his eyes.

They made their way through the dark room toward their cots.

"Special?" Manu wondered what the teachers' qualifications were.

"*Women,*" Adhik breathed as if saying a prayer. "Get some rest. You'll need all your brain power for these sessions."

True to his word, the next morning Adhik waited in the common area for Manu to finish his breakfast of *roti* and lentils.

"They send a bus for us, and we head to the big camp where they house most of the guys working in malls and such." He rubbed his hands through oil-slicked hair and gave himself a once-over in the window. "And there it is."

They crowded out, some of the other guys with backpacks slung over their shoulders.

"Myself, I'm working on the Reham equation." Adhik threw himself onto the seat next to Manu.

Manu's sister would have called him a blabbermouth. Manu found the stream of thought comforting. With Adhik by his side, he didn't have to think about Sanjana waking up, having a day off, and spending it alone, in her room, watching Hindi movies and eating instant noodles from a packet.

"Reham?"

Adhik gave a low whistle. "You'll see."

The van sliced through the city's empty streets on a Friday morning. There were no cars because people were preparing for prayers at the mosque or sleeping in. Manu took in the cranes that towered over an empty lot to the right of the intersection and shuddered. A few months ago he was one of the guys breaking concrete, putting pieces in place for the new office buildings. He shaded his eyes from the sunlight, blocking the columns of rebar from his line of vision. As they approached the outskirts of the city, sweat broke out across his skin. This street, or the one next to it—they blended together out here, more or less the same. The roads resembled a teenager's pockmarked face, faded clothing dried on lines strung in doorways.

"Poor bastards," Adhik murmured as they rumbled past a group of men in high-waisted jeans. The tires churned up dust and sand on those waiting on the side of the road for someone to have pity and pick them up to take them a few meters closer to the center of the city. "Can you imagine living out here like this? Why didn't they stay home?"

"Maybe they didn't know," Manu blurted. "It's not their fault."

"Huh?" Adhik rested his hand on the seat in front of him and faced Manu. "You know someone who works out here?"

Manu's throat constricted. "I mean, yes. Why would any more come? Maybe they didn't know."

Adhik nodded, tapping out a beat on the edge of the seatback. Music blared from the ear bud in his right ear. His profile niggled at the edge of Manu's memory. The slant of his nose, the rise of his forehead, reminded him of someone. *Adith.* A shudder ran through Manu. Adith seemed liked a friend at the beginning of Manu's days in the labor camp. He turned on Manu, reporting him to the agency goons who tried to shut him up for his organizing others to demand their rights.

Report to me everything. Ali's voice reverberated in Manu's mind. *Trust no one.*

The van shimmied to a stop in front of a chain-link fence. Manu propped an elbow in the window to keep his teeth from chattering. The barracks in this compound sat on three sides behind the guard station, opening into a shared courtyard. Almost identical to the kind of camp Ali rescued him from, though much newer and better-kept.

No trash rolled in the breeze around the courtyard. And the windows to the rooms were closed, suggesting air-conditioning like Manu enjoyed in his new villa. A one-story building stood in the center, and this is where the men disembarked.

"Hello, good morning," a tall, thin woman said from the door. Shuffling noises of those entering competed with her soft-spokenness. She wore black slacks and a cotton *kurti* with long sleeves.

"Morning, Ms. Reham," Adhik said in a singsong.

The girl's eyes flickered in acknowledgment. Her gaze did not linger.

The men trooped into a room set up with dozens of computers. Their footfalls thundered on the thin carpet. Plastic siding, the color of cedar wood, couldn't hide the fact they stood in a temporary facility, built on a platform. Any movement up or down the length of the rectangular room sent vibrations throughout the structure. Rows of fluorescent lights buzzed over their heads. There were no windows but banks of desks, with computer stations.

"Hello, hello, hello."

A yellow-haired woman stood at the back of the room, swinging chairs around and offering seats. "I see we have some new learners today. Hello, I'm Erin." She pressed a hand to her chest. "Erin."

Manu followed the slope of her fingers that pressed the flesh above her breasts. Shame rose in his cheeks. Other men were doing the same.

"Let's begin with your names. I'll take the new people and Reham will continue with the others on their computer skills. There's an exciting new module today on how to use ATM machines."

Adhik winked at Manu. He sat as close to the front as possible, watching Reham's every move. Manu and two other men shuffled toward a square table and four chairs at the back of the room. They sat around a whiteboard, and Lauren uncapped several markers of various colors.

"I'd like you each to write your name please." Her blue eyes crinkled at the corners.

The other two shook their heads.

Manu selected the red marker and made his letters. The marker felt awkward in his hand, like a foreign object. His fingers slipped. "Don't we all know how to do this?" he muttered.

"Pretend you don't," Adhik hissed, his face still forward. "Or you hurt their feelings."

"There are men that can use these lessons," Manu insisted. "The guys on the construction sites. They haven't even been in a room with a computer."

"Shhh," Adhik hissed.

"Good." Erin swung the board around so she could see the letters. "Very good." She passed white sheets of paper to the other two men. "I want you to learn these."

They glanced at the paper and then each other. Manu translated in Hindi.

"We know, brother," the stout one said with a wink. "But the teacher likes to be helpful."

"Here, let's practice." Erin stood between the men, taking up a marker. The stout one nodded, his partner focused intently on the curves moving under her shirt.

Manu shook his head in disgust.

"We can see how many more words you know." Erin gave them each a worksheet with a different paragraph of text on it.

Manu's heart seized at the sight of so many words in English.

"Don't worry." She laid a hand on his wrist. He jerked his eyes to her face. The other two eyed him with envy. "We'll work on this together, and take our time."

Friday might become his favorite day of the week again.

Chapter Ten

Sanjana wiped sweat from above her lip with the edge of her sleeve. The line of people waiting for their chance to present a ticket to the dry-cleaner bunched up outside the door. *Do you not see me standing here?* Sanjana wanted to shout at the woman who waved in the man in a t-shirt and shorts who'd come in behind her.

"Were you next?"

"Yes," Sanjana charged forward. *God bless Americans.* At least someone knew right and wrong beyond color. She presented the ticket to the woman, who used the edge of her scarf to wave air toward her chin.

"604," she called over her shoulder to a man in a hotel uniform. Two rows of hanging garments shrouded in plastic white bags buffeted him. He pawed at the hanging garments and repeated the numbers like baby babble. He stood on a step and reached for them.

"You have three riyals?" the woman asked.

Sanjana shook her head.

The woman's watery eyes took in Sanjana's blouse and jeans as her fingers flicked through the various sizes of notes. Biggest for fifty, the smaller tens, and blue and green fives.

"No change."

"No, sorry." Sanjana tucked the receipt into the back pocket of her jeans.

The man who let her in line in front of him shifted from one foot to another. She gave him a nod, as she left the pick-up counter. She navigated around the teenagers waiting to buy candy in the main part of the mini-market at the front of the compound.

The wand at the security gate went up and down as the guards screened vehicles entering the compound. Sanjana stayed on the sidewalk, conscious of the time. She'd need to get dinner on the table soon. She hoped they liked the homemade pizzas she mimicked from the lesson at the Italian restaurant Madam Cindy sent her to.

"Hello?" a maid called out. The maid's long black ponytail swung in time with the tail of the dog. She approached Sanjana in a peach uniform with white trim.

Sanjana doubled her pace to avoid Madam Amira's newest maid. Sanjana wouldn't bother with the effort to get to know her. The compound's pickiest employer would be rid of her in no time. *That boy the maid was responsible for, Sharif, was the one who needed to be gotten rid of.* Sanjana snapped on the hallway light to halt the dark bend of her thoughts. As long as Sharif stayed away from Daniel, what did it matter to her what Amira's family did? She hung Sir Paul's shirts in the closet in the spare room. During Manu's stay, she took a selection every day to hang on the chair in the other bedroom, to minimize the awkwardness of bumping into each other in the morning. Sanjana hung Cindy's dresses in the wardrobe. Downstairs, she scrubbed the inside of the sink until it gleamed. Manu made thousands of rupees doing who knew what for the police officer.

The front door slammed.

"Daniel?"

"It's me," Sir Paul called, from the front of the house.

"Hello, Sir." Her gaze darted around the kitchen, wishing for a pretext on which she could leave the house again on some errand. He returned from an overnight trip, to Dubai or Jordan—she stopped trying to keep up years ago.

"Vinay wants to say hi." Sir Paul's rumpled suit came into view as he wheeled his carry-on to the foot of the staircase. He ran his hands through his hair – fuller and longer than most men his age - those blue eyes searching her, reading clues she didn't know how to hide. "He's waiting for you." He shooed her toward the front door.

Sanjana blushed and ran a hand over the crown of her head. The humidity did a number on her hair at times like this.

"Hello." Vinay lounged in the driver's seat, a cigarette dangling from his left hand.

"*Chee*," she said, running down the two steps to the street. "Don't smoke."

"You're an old lady," he laughed at the consternation drawing her mouth into a tight line. "Come for a ride with me."

"I can't." She stepped back onto the curb. "Sir is home and I have work to do."

"He won't mind. He's happy. Said two people he liked now liked each other."

Two spots burned on her cheeks. "You say this to him!"

"Relax." Vinay's hooded eyes raked the length of her. "Nice jeans."

"Goodbye," she snapped.

"When will we go eat again?"

"I'm busy."

"Okay, I pick you up for work."

She paused, her hand on the doorknob. He laughed as the realization hit her. She would need a ride every day. Using the national cab service would be unreliable and expensive. Sanjana had no one else. "Okay."

"See you tomorrow." He blew a smoke ring at her, rounding his lips in a kiss.

She retreated inside the house, only to find Sir Paul standing exactly where she left him. A smile played at the corners of his lips and eyes. "So you're friendly."

She walked back into the kitchen, ducking his knowing gaze. "I need a ride to work."

"You got the job."

Her step faltered. "Kind of."

"So they'll try you out on probation. You're so good with kids. I said that in my letter." He gave her a round of applause and a huge grin. "Things are looking up."

"I mean to say I got a job. Not teaching. Cleaning." She clutched the folds of her cotton skirt, willing away the tremor in her voice. "They said no openings for a teacher. Only for a cleaner."

"Well, you are great at cleaning." He rummaged in the fridge.

"I can make you something," Sanjana said between clenched teeth. "You are hungry?"

He pulled out a green apple and took a sizeable bite. She put the breakfast plates away to break the contact of his steely eyes.

"Plan B."

"What is Plan B?" she asked. Much of conversing with Sir Paul, the professor, involved humoring him so he could hold forth on opinions about all and sundry.

"Plan B is what you do when Plan A didn't work."

"I take job," she said, avoiding his gaze. Dishes away, she stood at the counter, her hands hanging by her sides. "I no make Plan B." *Not for me. But for revenge, yes, that plan I have.*

"I know. We'll make one now." He shrugged off the blue coat, slinging it on the island in front of the fridge. A few more bites and the apple disappeared. He slid magnets off a notepad on the fridge. "Let's sit."

She perched on the edge of the bench at the breakfast nook. Sir Paul drew lines on the paper, dividing it up into three columns.

"What you are good at." He labeled the first column accordingly. "What you want to do. And job openings."

Sanjana shook her head. "They don't want me. They want Filipinas."

Sir Paul stopped writing headers for the three columns. "Excuse me?"

She hid her shaking hands under the table. "All the teachers in the school, none of them are from anywhere like me."

He pushed back from the table. "That's racial profiling. There's no reason why nationality should come into this. In the U.S., that would be illegal."

We are not in the U.S. She bit her lip as the unspoken thought ricocheted across the table. "They are thinking maybe my English not so…"

He ran his fingers through his hair again. "It's only one nursery. You can try others."

"Maybe I cannot speak to the ex-pat parents. That is maybe why. I stay at this nursery," she said, heart racing.

He snapped his fingers. "Tutor. We'll get you a tutor, and you can apply again."

"Hey." Daniel halted his slouch into the kitchen. His green eyes flickered at the sight of his father.

Nothing. She jutted out her chin. *I said nothing.*

"Hey, yourself. Come join us." Paul beckoned with his arm along the back of the breakfast nook.

"Can't," Daniel called over his shoulder. "Have to go ice my knee. And homework."

Paul raised an eyebrow.

"He's been like this since the injury," she said. "He hurt his knee during training." She ached at the growing gap between Daniel and his father. She couldn't solve this for either of them.

"Well, he can still get around," Paul said.

Sanjana clicked her tongue. "Not getting any better, and doctor said he should take it easy."

"Teenagers," Paul muttered. He wrote 'English tutor' across the incomplete chart.

"You could ask him to go swimming," Sanjana suggested.

Paul leaned in to hear her.

"Swimming, the doctor say is good for him. No weight. So easy on the knee."

He tapped the pen on the notebook several times. "Says."

"Hm?"

"The doctor *says* swimming is good for him." Paul rose from the table, adjusting his belt. "And good idea. Tell Cindy to find you a tutor. She'll be glad to help."

"I don't have time for tutor," Sanjana protested. Plus, the idea of asking Madam for anything, after the antics of the past year, made her nervous.

"Your job is part-time," Paul shot back. "Take the language lesson as a job. Take it seriously."

"I am too old for learning."

Paul's forehead creased. "That's ridiculous."

"I not go to school," she said with a shrug. *Like my brother. Like my siblings.*

Paul snorted. "So what? Your life is finished? You're not yet thirty and you want to shrivel up in service for another fifty years." He grabbed his phone, pushing away from the table. "I've got to take a call."

Sanjana slumped against the table. The flicker of derision in her didn't compare to the rivers of loathing streaming through her veins.

Chapter Eleven

Everything Ali knew about the case could be summed up on a few notecards. One: Lauren, a do-gooder so everyone went to her for help. Two: her do-gooding tendencies led her to unsafe places, namely the camps for the workers. Three: her American friendliness meant half the men thought she loved them. The other half loved her. All of them with alibis for the night of the murder.

Ali flipped over his buzzing phone and answered it. "Yes," he said to his unseasoned partner. "Feeling better?"

Manu repeated himself several times, Ali still not understanding. "Sir, sir—they say we shift to another compound."

"There's a problem with your villa?"

"No," Manu said. "No, we live same place. But the work, the manager from compound, he change security company. They get new guys. More expensive. Western trained. We get new station."

Ali pinched the bridge of his nose. Khalifa's informant said that someone smuggled women into that compound. Without Manu there, he couldn't verify who came in or out. The sight of new guards might appease the residents, particularly if they sounded like westerners.

"Do you know where they're sending you next?"

"No." Manu's voice sounded tinny, as if he were calling long-distance, not from a few kilometers away.

"Did you complain?"

"No," Manu said.

"Okay, you did the right thing," Ali said. "I'll check with a few people and call you back."

Silence came through from the other end.

"Don't worry," Ali said. "I'm keeping track of you."

"What about the murder?"

Ali rolled his neck and pressed his finger into a knot at the top of his spine. "Don't worry. That's my responsibility now."

"Who would anyone want to kill a teacher?" The persistent question became the refrain of the case.

Ali leaned back in his chair. The man sounded lost, like he'd lost a friend or lover. "Did you know her in some way?"

"What? No," Manu stammered.

An infatuation then, Ali surmised.

"She taught some of the guys English classes," Manu said. "On Fridays."

Ali straightened. "How many people?"

These men were away from their families for so long, no wonder they developed attachments to people they barely knew. She captured the attention of many. Easy to do when so many were far from their families and out of contact with women in their daily lives.

"Twenty, maybe thirty."

Ali's mind whirred. To question that many men, he would need help. He couldn't blow Manu's cover without progress on the prostitution ring. "Where?"

"The company's headquarters."

"Do you think any of them could have done it?"

"Why?" Manu's voice broke. "She helped them."

Ali sighed. They were back to the glaring blank that could not be filled: Motive. Who or what did Lauren irritate before her death? "They need more male volunteers in that program," he said. "Men teaching men has got to be more effective." He got more details about the class from Manu and said he would call back with a new plan.

"No one would come to class."

Ali rubbed his eyes. "Next one."

The new guard, a stranger, cowered at the sound of Ali's voice. He wouldn't be able to work with Manu until the issue of the ring resolved. Ali could use some of the other man's perkiness, his jovial air about life. This guy was taller and stoic, like a silent human wall. He left the clubhouse without replying, returning with the next interview subject, the last unquestioned resident of Lauren's apartment building.

In came a portly white man, the buttons on his shirt straining to constrain his belly.

"Ralph?"

The man nodded, licking his lips.

"Tell me what you know about the deceased."

"Nice to everyone," Ralph said.

Ali pretended to write notes as the man repeated everything he already knew. Lauren, the country's nicest ex-pat. She helped everyone when they needed it, whether moving in, or out, of the compound, bringing back packages of hard-to-find items when they were home.

"Any boyfriends?"

Ralph shrugged.

Interesting. Everyone else he spoke to responded with a definitive and immediate no.

"Boyfriend?"

Ralph rubbed his palms on his knees. "I don't know if that's what you would call him. One night I saw her coming back with a guy. They parked outside the flat for a moment, you know, for a good night..." he trailed off.

Ali took notes to mask his reaction. People kissing in public in their car. The foreigner would find it hard to believe that an engaged man, married in the eyes of his religion, did not kiss his wife goodnight.

"And then?"

"And then she went into the apartment."

"You were where?"

Ralph paused.

"You saw this how?" Ali reformulated the question, unsure if he expressed himself correctly in English.

"I was walking my dog."

"Anyone else see this?"

Ralph shook his head.

"What time?"

"Eleven. Maybe eleven-thirty."

"What kind of car?"

"White sedan."

"What day?"

Ralph chewed one of his fingernails. "A month ago?"

The most common vehicle out there, next to the white SUVs. Ali noted it anyway. The security log should reveal who—if the guys were taking IDs like they were supposed to.

"Thank you."

"That's it?"

Ali put his hands on the table. "Unless you have more to tell me?"

Ralph scratched his head. "No, I just thought—"

Ali stood. "We'll call you if we hear anything."

The man left.

Ali exhaled, sliding the note into the folder. Hours of sitting made his back stiff as a sandal left out in the sun. He stretched, the guardhouse coming into view through the clubhouse window. Now was as good a time as any. He walked across the street, empty in the middle of the day, and into the one-room guard area.

The two men on duty jumped to their feet. One jerked ear buds out of his ears, cutting off the loud sounds of Hindi pop music.

"Vehicle log." Ali mimed the visitor register. They looked around the counter top under the window. There were stacks of blue notebooks.

Ali took one, as the other two opened theirs. He flipped through the pages, filled with notations in blue ink. His finger ran down the column of dates. The dates indicated last year. He tossed it into the corner and looked over the shoulder of the guy who'd been bringing in interview subjects.

"I want to know what happened to my daughter!" The door clanged behind a petite woman, dressed in all black, wearing socks with sandals.

Not now.

"Who's in charge here?"

Ali stood.

The woman, Lauren's mother, eyed the three of them. Out of uniform in slacks and a button-down shirt, he thought plain clothes would set the ex-pats at ease and get them to open up. But in her eyes, the two men in uniform were the figures of authority.

"Ali," he said.

She stuck out her hand.

He put his on his heart to indicate he didn't touch non-related women.

Hers dangled in the air for a moment, like a fish gasping for air, before fluttering to her side, her eyebrows knitting in confusion. "You're a policeman?"

"I am. I am a detective."

She crossed her arms. "Why haven't we been given any information? Why don't we know what's happening?"

"We are trying."

The guards pressed back in their chairs against the wall.

"I want to know what you know."

"And I would also like to know what you know." Ali kept his voice even.

He motioned to the clubhouse. "Please, join me."

She followed him. Their eyes flared in the sunlight and took a minute to adjust to the interior.

"Water?" He offered her a bottle from the cardboard box.

"Yes, thank you." She sat across from him.

"Mrs.?"

"Martha." She took a big gulp of water. "Call me Martha."

Across the table, he saw the purple shadows under her eyes, the whites of which were criss-crossed with red veins.

"This is supposed to be a modern country!" Martha pounded on the table. "What is being done to get my daughter justice? What?"

Ali placed his sizeable palms on the table, focusing on his fingernails rather than the woman's face in front of him, which twisted with a myriad of emotions: anger, sadness, fatigue.

"Women here aren't safe!"

"They don't hurt women in your country?"

The tirade of complaints halted. Martha blinked at him. Ali kept his gaze steady as the lines around her eyes deepened.

"No, of course, women get hurt everywhere. Lauren wouldn't hurt anyone." Martha gazed over his shoulder out the window on the street.

"What do you know about any boyfriends?" He asked a question that would insult any local mother.

"I mean, she saw people." Martha fidgeted with her collar. "I'm not supposed to say that, right? Dating is illegal here."

Ali folded his hands over the notebook. "I don't blame your daughter for dying."

"That's a funny way to put it." She took a shuddering breath, her eyes darting to his. "Considering someone strangled her in her own home."

"Boyfriends?" He repeated.

"Well, she met one or two men on Tinder. But I don't think she used it very often."

"Tinder?"

Martha blinked again this time in a rapid series, like something was caught in her eye. "It's an app. For dating."

He pulled out the evidence bag with Lauren's phone, passing it along with a pair of gloves to the mother. "Please. We can't get in without the code."

She wiggled her fingers into the gloves as Ali also put on a pair before plugging the device in to revive the battery.

Martha frowned in concentration, the tip of her tongue emerging between her teeth. "Probably her birthday?" The phone buzzed, rejecting the code.

"We tried that."

"Hm, maybe my birthday?" Another little shake - *no* - from the device.

"Okay. Okay. Lauren's memory is terrible. She uses—" Martha took a shuddering breath, "she *would* have used something easy to remember..." Martha's fingernails drummed the table. "Last four of her social? ... Yes!" The phone unlocked, going to a home screen showing Lauren sitting on the pavement, a black kitten in her lap. "Oh." Martha's breath came out in a *whoosh*. "Oh." Her hands flew to her chest.

"Tinder," Ali said. He took the phone back, nudging over a box of tissues. He scrolled through the apps, stopping at the one with the flame over the letter 'I'. They certainly didn't believe in subtlety. The app opened to a bare-chested man reclining on the beach, the azure blue of the Arabian Gulf behind him. "What the hell..." Ali said. The shadow of a beard belied the man's Arab roots, that and the shock of hair curling across his pectoral muscles. *Hassan?* Now he knew how his cousin stocked his stable of girlfriends.

"You swipe right if you like him," Martha said, propping her elbows on the table for a closer look.

"Did she swipe right on this guy?" Ali tossed the phone back to the other side of the table as if it were contaminated. "Did they go out?" His stomach twisted at the thought of Hassan dragging him further into this mess.

"No. The app brings up everyone registered in your city," Martha said, tapping the screen. "He's a new user. Besides, she stayed clear of Arab guys." She cleared her throat, eyes flitting away from Ali.

He wrote it down, ignoring her discomfort. "And then what?"

"You wait to see if he swipes back."

Ali scribbled more notes, asking for Lauren's stats on the app. Thirty matches. They would take ages to track down. He tapped the pen against his lip – did Khalifa know that ex-pats were using this app inside the country? Should he include it in his brief? Confusion clouded his focus.

"Wait, I've seen this guy on the compound." Martha turned the phone around to display a picture of another man's face, close up, blue eyes sparkling but a hint of a double chin wobbling in the bottom right.

"Ralph." Ali said. "She passed right for him?"

"Huh?"

Ali mimed the action that said you liked someone on the app.

"Swipe," Martha corrected. "No, this is in her photos."

Ali took the phone back. The photo featured a close-up of Ralph. Peering at the screen, Ali made out the fine mesh of the window. *A second floor apartment.* Ali took out his phone to duplicate the photo.

"You think this is important?"

"We are doing everything we can," Ali said. He stood to escort her to the door.

"Is this the man who killed my daughter?"

"Everyone is a suspect until we clear them."

Martha pulled her elbow out of Ali's grasp. "You find who did this. If he's on that app, he could be after someone else next." She clutched her bag.

A frisson of worry raised the hairs on Ali's arm. "I'll keep that in mind," he said.

Martha dabbed at her eyes. Ali jerked his head, summoning the waiting security guard to escort the woman from the clubhouse. With the door closed, his attention returned to the phone. For the first time since the case opened, he felt the sorrow of the woman's life ending. Not, as the local community said, a mindless woman alone. But a person with a mother. And a man who habitually watched her movements. He mentally assigned more points to the column of an unrequited lover.

He dialed his cousin. No answer. *You delete that profile right now. No more SWIPING,* Ali texted. The prohibition would ensure a call back within twenty minutes of Hassan waking. His cousin's fascination with ex-pat women spelled disaster. All he needed was his relative's name to end up on the suspect list. Khalifa's henchmen would have a field day with that knowledge. Ali turned his attention back to Lauren. Those she knew confided in her. A sign that she led others along as well without ever knowing it.

Chapter Twelve

Maryam snapped the switch in the semi-dark classroom. Fluorescent overhead lights flickered on. "Are we having class?"

Salma shrugged, her face and scarf lit by the eerie glow of her phone. They were two of the four people supposed to be in the windowless classroom. "I'm taking this pass/fail." A senior, Salma managed to work that tidbit into each class.

"Did you hear about Dr. Erin's friend?"

"Yeah, sad huh? They say she knew the guys she went with." Salma didn't take her eyes from the phone.

Maryam sat at the top part of the square created by pressing four desks together. She eyed the whiteboard, scrawled with numbers in various colors, the X and Y axis of the graphs noted with spidery letters she squinted to make out. Econ, macro, from the way the trends were marked. She remembered that semester, working through the formulas as though learning a new language, failing most of the exams, and being told by professor that a D was actually more like a B, given the complicated percentages he used to calculate a curve.

"Homework, homework." Dr. Erin rushed into the room, dropping a red marker and several sheets of paper with the force of her entry. "You know if I'm not here yet, you can pass your homework to the front of the room." For anyone seeing her for the first time, her skeletal frame took a moment to take in. The bag that swung from her shoulder spanned the width of her waist. From her state of permanent distraction and dishevelment, students thought Dr. Erin's classes would be easy. Maryam discovered the hard way that the diametric opposite was true. Dr. Erin believed in standards. Dr. Erin thought Bs were acceptable. New at the university and a tough grader, Dr. Erin's classes were small.

Maryam placed her assignment on the table in front of the professor, who rummaged through her bag, most likely looking for the glasses perched atop her head. She picked up the discarded paper and marker from the floor, scooped up fluttering Post-it notes, and several paperclips, adding them to the pile of belongings emerging from the bag onto the table. The red marker joined the ranks of blue, black, and green, plus one circular cardboard tube, similar in length. Maryam giggled on the way back to her seat as Dr. Erin jerked the tampon back into the bag's side pouch.

"Oh, it's still so hot out there." Dr. Erin sat across from them, at the head of the square, her belongings strewn on either side. Her hands fluttered like birds around the tendrils of strawberry blonde hair stuck to her jaw like a beard. She removed all her jewelry; first her watch, then her rings, of which there were several silver bands. Then a bangle, the width of a finger, landed with a clunk on the desk. She wound her hair into a bun, stabbing it into place with a pencil. In the process she discovered her glasses. "Oh, there they are! I thought I'd left them in the car. Salma?" Her eyes were red-veined; bloodshot, almost. Dr. Erin's reputation as a scatterbrain made her an easy target for students turning in late work. Maryam peered closer at the bluish circles under her eyes.

"Salma?"

The girl shifted in her seat. "I didn't do it. Spent the night rendering my short film," Salma protested.

"I had a late night too," Dr. Erin said. She scanned Maryam's essay. "You know homework is ten percent of the grade."

"This is an elective," Salma said. "I have to focus on classes in my major."

"Not original, but at least you're honest," Erin murmured. She pulled out a copy of *Pride and Prejudice* with dog-eared pages and multi-colored sticky notes.

Amal strode in, sidling up to Maryam's side of the table. Her *abaya* billowed open, revealing black tights and a hot-pink tank top. "Sorry I'm late, Professor. It was out of my hands."

Not like you were kept by a natural disaster. Maryam couldn't account for the transformation in Amal since their high school days, when she'd been part of their trio with Daniel. She who once eschewed the *abaya* for shorts and t-shirts now came to university wearing make-up and diamanté Manolo Blahnik slip-ons.

"Yes, I see congratulations are in order." Dr. Erin waved at the henna patterns decorating Amal's hands and forearms. "Late night?"

Amal flashed a smile that showed her dimples. She pulled at the corners of her *abaya*. "My cousin's wedding."

"None of us are sleeping that much then, but your reason is the most fun," Dr. Erin signed. "Homework?"

Amal handed over several typed pages.

"Staplers, ladies. Staplers." Dr. Erin dug out a full-size stapler from the depths of her tote bag.

Amal apologized, citing the late hours and the excitement of the wedding. "She's like a sister to me, this cousin, but she doesn't have any actual sisters, so we did everything."

Maryam doodled in the corner of her page, sketching a series of connected boxes, equal in shape, each pair sharing two sides. She could do this to infinity.

"Well, this is a great segue into our reading for this unit," Dr. Erin said.

Maryam added a few more boxes.

"Let's hear your thoughts about the novel. For a change, you can read your logs instead of my reading them later at home. Maryam? Would you like to begin?"

Maryam snapped to attention, her eyes narrowing at the paper Dr. Erin handed back with a red check mark. Noted, credit given. "Uh, sure." She focused on the words on the page, conscious of Amal's gaze and Salma's disinterest. *If only you participated,* Maryam seethed. She read her essay, comparing local mothers to the character of Mrs. Bennett, their society with that of 19th century England.

"Very insightful," Dr. Erin chirped. She bent forward and scribbled some notes on a legal pad in front of her. In her excitement, more hair abandoned the bun and fell into her glasses. "What do you think about these comparisons?"

Salma shrugged.

"Amal?"

"That's one perspective." Amal avoided eye contact with Maryam.

"Would you like to share yours?"

Amal sat up straighter, accepting the returned essay. "The world of Jane Austen's novel is in the past. Thank goodness for British women and also for us locals. Our grandmothers were like Mrs. Bennett. Their daughters must marry and marry well. Our mothers suffered like Elizabeth, so they don't do the same things to us."

"Hmm, very, very interesting." Dr. Erin's pencil scratched across the paper. "Opposing viewpoints. Fascinating."

"That's not entirely true," Maryam said. "Not all grandmothers are so accommodating."

"No? Please, elaborate." At the rate she scribbled, Dr. Erin needed a sharpener.

"You can't speak for the majority of locals," Amal said.

"Neither can you," Maryam huffed. The awkwardness of her engagement dinner would make an excellent exhibit one. Her unease about her impending life with Ali's family, growing like a tumor, came as a close second.

"Well, what demographics do you each feel you represent?"

"Ugh, why are we always talking about locals?" Salma muttered.

"If you completed your assignment," Dr. Erin retorted. "You could tell us about your native society. For now, this is all we have."

Salma bent her head, squinting at the pages of the novel. Unlike Maryam's and Amal's dog-eared copies, hers had a pristine spine.

"Those people who force their daughters to marry are largely uneducated," Amal pronounced.

"Also untrue," Maryam snorted. "There are many reasons people get their daughters married young. Protecting their honor is one."

"These are outdated notions about women." Amal gave an exasperated sigh. "Why are you focusing on the negative?"

"So this is about painting a rosy picture?"

"Ladies, we can agree to disagree." Dr. Erin's forehead ridged in concentration. "What do you mean, Maryam?"

"I mean," Maryam said slowly, "we tell different versions of ourselves to different people, depending on the effect we're trying to create. There's no such thing as the truth. Only the truth as you see it. We learned that in first-semester journalism."

Amal sputtered. "We learned many things, like how not to get everyone in the university in trouble." The dig at Maryam's blog post about labor malpractice went unnoticed by Dr. Erin. Maryam glowered at her former friend.

"Okay, this is excellent. Truth is relative and culture can be as well. Let's see where in the text we can find evidence for each of our points of view. Were there any modern notions about women and marriage in Austen's time?" Dr. Erin hopped out of her seat and passed around a worksheet. "Ten quotes, ten interpretations."

"Can we work in groups?"

"There are only three of you, Salma. You can compare your answers at the end."

Maryam worked through the sheet, filling in the blanks to elaborate on passages in the first half of the book with symbols and metaphors. The tintinnabulation of a cell phone broke their focus.

"Ah, whose is it?" Dr. Erin stood before them, her hand outstretched. "I'll take a message. Class policy, as you know."

"Not mine," Amal said.

"My battery died," Salma smirked.

"I don't have a pho—" The Nokia's ring cut her off. Maryam dug out the phone her father gave her. "Oh, this is new. I'll turn it off."

"Rules," Dr. Erin said. She held her hand out.

Maryam shrank from the outstretched palm.

Dr. Erin's eyes flashed, a line appearing between her eyebrows. "Either give me the phone or leave the room," she intoned.

"It won't happen again," Maryam pleaded.

Erin wiggled her fingers, like a hungry mouth.

Maryam handed over the phone, eyes downcast. So much for being treated like an adult anywhere, even on an American university campus.

"Hello, this is Dr. Erin. Maryam is in class right now. May I take a message?"

Maryam clenched her hands in frustration. It could only be one person. And now her secret would be revealed when Dr. Erin asked to explain her relationship to Ali. Amal would never stand for a guy to call her without telling the whole university about Maryam's boyfriend.

"Yes, Daniel. I'll be sure to tell her to meet you for lunch." Erin handed the phone back to Maryam. "He said he's free at one and to meet him downstairs."

Maryam took the phone, a dead weight in her hand.

"Daniel?" Amal whispered.

"Oh, and he apologized for interrupting class."

There are two people who know that number. Maryam's foot vibrated with agitation under the table. Not having a phone for several months erased the habit of constantly checking for updates. Or keeping track of what she missed.

"Can I come in?"

With relief, Maryam turned to the door, away from Amal's bird-like gaze. There stood Reham, president of the student volunteer club, in black leggings and a long white cotton shift that on anyone else would have been a shirt, but hanging from Reham's angular hips and shoulders, became a dress.

"Reham! Yes, of course. Come in, come in." Dr. Erin waved an arm, sending her bracelets skidding into each other.

"I can wait." The girl pulled at her ear.

"No, I said you could have class time. This is the time." Another jangle of bracelets. Reham came forward. "Ladies, Reham would like to tell you about a volunteer opportunity."

Reham cleared her throat. Despite her flawless skin and waist, the girl's gaze bounced around the room, not making eye contact with any of them. "Yes, well, we need people to teach English and computer skills to the workers in their camp. You know the security guards who sit here all day downstairs, checking people coming into the building? So if you can spare some time on the weekend, let me know. And you can start with some training and the sessions are on Fridays. We need more trainers after an accident." She paused for the first time since she began speaking. "And we've lost a few volunteers since then. So we need more people. Also, we're on Facebook, so you can join the private group to see photos, get updates, whatever." Reham slid a stack of fliers on the table.

Everyone in the room exhaled once the torrent of words ended.

"So by accident, you mean—?" Maryam zeroed in on the euphemism. She suspected this accident linked to the disappearance Ali and Manu were investigating. How many women in harm's way could there be in a city with a population of two million? She filed that question away as a possible framing device for an investigative piece.

"The police haven't told us much. Only a woman, found in her apartment."

"Do you think this volunteering job is safe for women?" Amal's shrillness jarred their professor into action.

"So sad that someone trying to help would get hurt." Dr. Erin took one of the fliers. "Nice to see that isn't keeping others from continuing."

"Alright, then." Without answering Amal's question, Reham gave a small wave and left.

Maryam passed a flier on to Amal. *Help those who help us every day,* the caption said. Her mind raced to recall the conversation with Ali. This must be where the murdered woman volunteered. If Maryam went along to a class, she could get a better sense of the players.

"Can we get extra credit if we go?" Salma gathered her laptop and purse.

"This isn't directly related to class." Dr. Erin sighed. "Remember, you can't bump your grade up a level from extra credit. You can only move it from a minus to a plus." She droned on with a lecture about their civic responsibilities, the homework assignment, and the purpose of a university education in their overall lives.

As class concluded, Maryam brainstormed acceptable reasons for her parents to let her leave the house on a Friday morning, the day for prayer and family time. She swept her notebook and other materials into a tote bag.

"Maryam, I need to ask you about something," Dr. Erin called.

"Yes, Professor," Maryam said, from the doorway. "If it's about that reading log, I can write more."

"No, no, this is something else." Dr. Erin came closer, dropping a few paperclips behind her. "You know, one of the maintenance guys, he's very sick."

"Oh," Maryam said. "I didn't really hear anything about it." She fidgeted with the strap of her bag. Not being religious, she hoped the professor wouldn't ask for prayers like Christians did in the movies.

"We're going to get a collection going, to help send him home for treatment."

"Right," Maryam said. She still didn't see how any of this concerned her.

"Could you ask the students if they want to donate? You know we can't send any emails. The University has prohibitions against collecting money for individuals."

"Um," Maryam tried to think of a reason her professor would accept for crying off. If she said that her parents wouldn't want her to be involved, it would sound like they didn't care about laborers. Her father's company was already under fire, thanks in large part to her piece on the double contracts used by the labor agency they contracted.

"You know Arnell. He converted a few months ago. Now he does the *athan* in the breezeway."

"Oh." Maryam did know the cheerful Filipino. Her professor didn't say that the system, low wages, and high agency fees, made people needy. Maryam's piece on labor abuse made her the pariah of the local community but a heroine in the eyes of ex-pats.

"His name is Ahmed now," Amal chimed in. "I can help too, Professor."

"Yes, sure." Erin tucked her hair behind her ears. "Anything would be helpful. You know how little these guys make." She put her jewelry back on, piece by piece. "I mean, lots of people know this guy. And like him. The international students would love to help but they're limited in resources. The locals…" Erin trailed off.

So that's what she needed. Locals could afford to send him home and they should feel obligated to do so because he was now a Muslim. Most of the girls in their university spent on their handbags the price of a ticket to the Philippines. But Maryam wasn't one of those. Not any more. "Amal knows more people than I do. But I'll see what I can do." Maryam gave a small wave. "Oh, any more news about your friend?"

The professor's shoulders slumped. "Not a word. Her parents call me every night. The authorities don't respond to their inquiries."

"That's terrible," Maryam said. If they called Missing Persons they were being routed to Ali. "What department?"

"I shouldn't say more." Erin straightened as if waking from a dream. "About the only thing they are telling us is to stay out of it."

"See you later." Maryam left, the promise of a lead lending a bounce to her step.

"Still in touch with Daniel?" Amal pounced on her outside of the classroom.

"Uh, I bet he wanted help with public law or something." Maryam quickened her pace.

"Hm. Funny you haven't come to lunch."

Maryam slowed. The three of them, inseparable in high school, were more like strangers at university. Maryam struggled to keep up with assignments while Amal sailed through. "He's running for student government."

"Oh," Maryam said. She forgot how to make chitchat since Amal ignored her for most of their first year. Nasser described their shifting association as one of 'frenemies'.

"I'm thinking about running, too. For president." Amal adjusted her headscarf. "Amal for Action," she said with a flash of teeth.

"Good luck," Maryam said. The pressures of organizing games and national day celebrations were well below her reality. She faced bigger problems. Like how she could get out of the house on a Friday morning and into the camps to volunteer with Reham without her parents or fiancé finding out.

"You know who else is running? So random." Amal didn't give Maryam a chance to respond. "Sharif."

"Really?"

Amal gave her a sideways glance. "Yes, I thought that strange also. He's running for secretary, and Daniel for treasurer. That's all freshmen are eligible for." Amal sailed on toward the elevator.

*

Sharif for student government? Maryam, hunched at a corner table next to the window, texted the question in a flash of irritation. She'd been so caught up in her own drama that she'd forgotten about her friend.

I'll catch you up at lunch.

I can't. Her refrain.

Changing your name in my contacts to Can't. We all appreciate what you did for Manu. I appreciate what you did for Manu. Where's my civic superhero?

His words stung. She made her way to the stairs, choosing the ones on the far side of the building, to avoid the open-air atrium at its heart.

"Maryam, how's the semester going?" Professor Paul fell into step with her.

"Fine, Professor, and yours?" She put the phone in her pocket, paranoid he would see her texts to Daniel.

"Much less drama than the last one." He faked a laugh.

The fallout from her blog post about the conditions of the workers were now campus legend. He paused at the bottom of the stairs. They contemplated the posters together. On the bulletin board on the right hung a slew of campaign posters, a series of *Dan-Dan-He's-Your-Man* with Daniel's face in a range of colors.

"Surprised you aren't running," he said.

"I can't," she said, vowing to find another expression.

"Too busy?"

"I'm getting married," she said.

Professor Paul's laser-like attention focused on her. "To your cousin?"

"Sort of."

"Faisal?"

"*No.*" A group of students; freshmen—she recognized none of them— rushed past to push the button for the elevator door.

"Sorry, none of my business."

"I don't think you know him," she lied. From their work freeing Manu from a labor gang, Paul would have heard of Ali. They were embroiled in overlapping connections like one of Shakespeare's tragic-comedies. "Someone I met recently. Not my cousin. Not arranged, exactly."

"Congratulations." His voice sounded unconvincing.

Maryam pulled at her bag. She owed him no explanation, particularly after the fallout from her reporting project for his class. She saved her university career and earned an A, but she'd brought that bane of all local women, attention, to herself in the process, largely as a part of his encouragement to get him a unique story.

"Well once you get settled, maybe you'll want to write for us." Paul beamed, rattling off an update on what he thought would be the answer to the media chokehold in the country. "We have a few stringers, and a great contributor for the daily beat. Would love to give you a column. Will launch soon. You'll have to be there."

That their project, an online news site, continued without her, rubbed salt in the wound. "See you later, Professor." She walked across the green AstroTurf, bumpy over the rocks and dirt underneath. He called after her, but Maryam kept going. She couldn't be furious with Professor Paul. His assignment was instrumental in introducing her to Ali. The man who would determine her future. Fake grass radiated like fingers across the approach to the buildings, reaching out into the parking lot. *A land of make-believe.* That's what one of her high school teachers said, describing the countries of the Arabian Gulf. The bike rack made her smile. Ambitious Americans – they thought they could influence a car-based society into becoming anything else. Babu waited behind the wheel of a white Mercedes, Maria sitting in the backseat. Mundane repetitiveness would suffocate Maryam before marriage could transform her life with its magical properties.

Maria got out and started over to Maryam, her hands reaching for her bag. In the line of waiting cars, other maids hovered next to passenger doors, waiting to do the same thing, as local female students minced their way to the parking lot in high heels.

"I can do it myself," Maryam snapped.

Maria shrank back and slipped her hands into the pockets of her uniform.

The vibrating phone halted Maryam from getting into the car. "*Salaam alaikum,*" she said, greeting Ali.

He dispensed with the pleasantries. "Tell me what you know about Tinder."

Maryam paused, sweat beading on her nose. "This is a trick." The fan in the idling SUV went into overdrive, whirring like a jet engine. If she said she knew about the hookup app then Ali would have grounds to divorce her and call off the reception. Though they were legally married, the period before they lived together was an engagement used to suss out unsavory activities such as these.

"No, I thought you might have heard about this. It's an application."

"I know about Tinder," she said. Babu and Maria sat behind the tinted windows, their still silhouettes waiting for instructions.

"How many 'likes' is a lot?" Ali said gruffly.

"I don't know that much about it."

"I searched for you. You're not on there."

She pinched the bridge of her nose. "No I wouldn't be." She conjured up what should be an appropriate level of outrage.

"I'm trying to understand it. How do people use it for dating—should I set up a profile for myself?"

Maryam laughed. Ali joined in. "It's for hook-ups. They say it's for dating. Some see it that way but most people use it as a hook-up spot. It's sleazy."

"So thirty 'likes'?"

"Matches," she said.

"Matches."

"Average, I think," Maryam said. "Maybe even low. What I've read, there can be hundreds. Depends."

"On how much people like you."

"On whether you choose one sex or both, whatever age and proximity range you choose."

Ali went quiet.

"Hello?"

"Thanks," he said. "You know this how, again?"

Maryam laughed. "Social media and gender class. Wait—Lauren used Tinder?"

"I'll speak to you later." Ali hung up.

Maryam stared at the phone in her hand, a mix of emotions coursing through her.

"We go home?" Babu twisted in his seat to ask.

Anywhere but home. On an impulse, she pushed Reham's flyer to him. "Let's go here."

Babu took it, studied the map on the paper. His eyes met hers in the mirror. "This worker accommodation."

Maryam sighed. She rubbed her forehead. "I want to see where it is. That's all. Find location."

He kept his foot on the brake.

"We are going."

The last time Babu followed her directions into the Industrial Area, he'd ended up with three cracked ribs, courtesy of an angry Ali.

"You settling down, getting married."

"I have a father, thank you," Maryam snapped, her voice rising. "Take me there now." Babu flinched, dropping his gaze. The driver's sudden deference reminded her how much power she held over him. Her stomach lurched as the car shifted into gear.

Chapter Thirteen

Manu stood at the sink, combing gel into his hair. Light from above the mirror spilled onto the floor a few inches from his feet. He welcomed the anonymity of the night in the last few moments before dawn. His thoughts centered on the coming day's lesson with Reham. When the food service dropped off the meals for the day, the rest of the men in the house stirred from their sleep. He itched to leave, but they waited and waited for the bus.

By the time they walked into the computer lab, half an hour remained in the session. But Reham brightened, didn't she, when they—well, he—walked in the door?

"Quickly," she said in a strange way of speaking he associated with people from England. A gnawed pencil stuck out the top of the bun on the top of her head, tendrils of new hair curled on her neck. "Take your seats." Her hands rested on the chair next to him.

Manu's body tingled with their closeness. She smelled like fresh rain, and her hair shone under the harsh overhead light. His fingers trembled on the keys.

"Slide the mouse—the white arrow—over to the photo of the money."

He did as she said. She rewarded him with a smile.

"Good, Manu."

Adhik tapped his screen, as if hoping to direct the white arrow with his finger.

Oh, the sound of his name from those lips. Manu's heart squeezed. Though he continued staring at the screen in front of him, his mind went to a green pasture on the top of a hill, white-capped mountains behind him. Big-budget Bollywood films with European sequences. Alps for him and his Reham. The best.

She in a sequined pink sari, he wearing a white, double-breasted suit, and they would sing.

Adhik's somber face came into view. He'd taken the seat next to Manu.

"Today's the day," he whispered.

Manu leaned closer. Adhik's lips were tight, his skin flushed. "You feeling okay?"

"I'm doing it. I'll tell her today."

"The bus won't return for another thirty minutes," Manu reasoned. "Try the lesson. It's fun." He maneuvered the mouse to show how the arrow bounced across the screen. There were fewer of them today. Some stayed home because they didn't want to associate with the dead woman's project.

Adhik raised his hand.

"Everything okay here?"

The familiar voice caused Manu to start. He swung around, knocking the mouse off the desk. At the sight of Maryam, the local girl who helped him out of the agency's clutches, Manu started.

"Fine," Adhik said. He sat straighter and put his fingers to the keyboard.

"We're working with the mouse today," Maryam enunciated. "Mouse?" She demonstrated on the machine next to him, taking the dark shape into her hands and twisting it around the desk.

"Yes, yes." Adhik did the same, going through the motions, causing his mouse to jump from one end of the screen to the other like Manu's thoughts. "I know how to use a computer," he stuttered. His friend's eyes swiveled in alarm at the proximity of a local girl, one of the ones whose father or brother or uncle could bash your head in for looking at them too closely from the bus or, for the lucky few, the mall.

Maryam, the girl who saved him from prison, arguing with Ali on his behalf, sat next to him. *Did she know about his assignment? Did Ali send her to help him?*

"Now slip on your headphones, and listen to the module." She mimed putting them on.

"I'll be right back." Adhik slid away from the desk, approaching Reham.

Manu reached for his headphones, wanting to call him back. His friend's bow-legged walk gave him a swaggering air as he strode towards the unsuspecting girl.

Maryam used the empty computer on the right, pretending to test the module. On the screen, a blonde man in blue slacks and a white shirt waved. "How are you?" she asked.

"Fine," Manu mumbled.

The upward tilt of her eyeliner gave her a mysterious profile, making her prettier than he remembered. Or Adhik's obsession with women had rubbed off on him.

"No, don't look at me."

He forced his gaze straight. Then again, he reasoned, she wasn't this close to him during their first encounter in the police station. Maybe in his terror he missed the scent of jasmine as well.

"Is the work interesting?"

Sanjana's questions about his job revolved around safety. Interest, he hadn't prepared for. Maryam slipped the headset off one ear, as the conversation between Adhik and Reham grew more animated.

"I'm flattered, really," Reham said, taking a step backward. "But we aren't allowed to be friends with our students. Plus, you know, you send your salary home."

"I have money." Adhik's voice rose, causing others to look away from their modules. "You not have dinner with me because you not like me."

"No, it's not that," Reham protested. She clutched at the desk behind her, fingers hitting the keyboard.

Maryam and Manu shared a glance. "What is going on?" Maryam whispered.

"He's not well," Manu said in a low voice. "Ever since the teacher died."

"Killed," Maryam corrected him.

"Killed," Manu acknowledged.

"I am man," Adhik said, his hands clenching and unclenching in fists. "I man like any other man. Not nice for you?" Other men turned from their monitors at the sound of Adhik's raised voice. "Security man not enough for you?"

"You are nice," Reham stammered.

"I don't know how to stop this," Manu said. His face burned with embarrassment on his friend's behalf. A twinge of irritation accompanied his panic. Now Adhik ruined anyone else's chances of making a go of it. Reason told him to be relieved—he escaped humiliation. The other men were murmuring amongst themselves, casting sidelong glances at the flustered man.

"Okay, so let's start the next tutorial," Maryam said, jumping up and clapping her hands together, as if she were directing children.

Adhik blinked, glancing around the room. Manu gestured to him to come and sit down. Reham drifted away, mouthing 'thank you' towards Maryam.

"Going to the toilet," Adhik muttered. He shuffled off.

Maryam relaxed and slipped into his seat while the others stayed engrossed in the new skills test, on using something called a cash machine. "How much do you know about the woman who died?"

"Nice woman," Manu said. "You help? Her body is stuck here."

Maryam fidgeted with the mouse.

"Her mother, she apply to take the body, but they say no."

"Why?"

Manu shrugged. *Your country,* he wanted to say. *If you don't know, how would I?*

"That's terrible." She swung the mouse around, clicking a few times.

"That's all we have time for, everyone," Reham called out. She asked them to shut down their machines.

He missed precious moments of observing her. The way Reham tucked her hair behind her ears to give her full attention to whoever spoke. The wrinkle that formed between her eyebrows when she concentrated on the screen.

"I don't know how it works with ex-pats," Maryam said quietly. "I'll try to find out."

"Will I see you again?"

"I don't know," Maryam said. She helped Reham power down the machines as Manu watched, a mixture of fear and wonder on his face at the easy way the two girls chatted with each other. He wanted that, one day. To move as easily in their world as they did in his.

So went the morning of this, their one day off. They came back to their accommodation in the van and spent most of the rest of the day indoors, watching DVDs of old movies. Tinfoil rectangular containers of Arab appetizers: *tabouli*, hummus, bread—none of it what their South Asian palates craved—crowded the fridge, untouched. His roommates devoured the white rice topped with caramelized onions, making do with a vegetable gravy locals called *salona*. Everyone loathed spending their earnings on themselves and on something as mundane as food. Manu said nothing about the advance Ali passed him with his uniform. He sent most of it home and kept a thousand riyals with him. Clutching the bills at night while the others' snores filled the room gave him comfort when sleep eluded him.

So nice. Why would anyone want to hurt her? Questions ran in his mind like the wild horses that grazed near his village. Like those proud beasts, they were difficult to pin down. The chicken turned to fibers, dry in his mouth as he chewed, the garlic sauce coating his tongue like a paste. This must be what it felt like to eat sand.

A few of the men were arguing about whether to call a taxi or try to catch a ride to the nearest shopping mall.

"Friday, no way," a thin, boyish guy called Sanjany said. He shook his head from left to right. "They see us coming," he pointed at Adhik and himself, "they turn us away. Family day."

"Yeah, we get a woman to go in with us and then we are a family," Adhik said in a nasal tone.

"Where we going to find one of those?" Sanjany snorted.

"He's got a sister." Adhik jerked his thumb in Manu's direction.

"Your family is here?" Multiple sets of eyes turned to Manu in surprise.

"She's a housemaid," Manu protested, giving the guy a dark look. The less others knew about him, the better. Having a sister working in the same country made for a memorable detail. One that made him stand out and one they were unlikely to forget. "I'm sure she doesn't have a day off like us."

The men contemplated their lunches, their hopes for an outing dashed.

Outside, a horn blared. A blast of a film score tinkled past. Manu's favorite distraction, a Bollywood film, seemed like a pastime enjoyed in another life, one where women were protected, not harmed.

The phone bleated in his pocket.

"Yes?" Manu answered.

"Can you go through all the guys' things?" Ali cut straight to the point of his call, without preamble.

As the only person he spoke to regularly, Manu yearned for more of a conversation. "What?"

"Search the villa. See if you can find something of the deceased. Maybe one of the guards took something of hers."

"Like what?" Manu stammered. There were two other men here—Adhik and a new guy—plus Manu. The three others left for the night shift at their new assignment, a high-rise apartment building in the business district.

"Photos or clothing. Something the killer might have kept as a memento."

"Uh, there are people here." Manu threw away the remaining sandwich.

Papers shuffled on Ali's end. "Yes, I thought so."

Manu leaned back against the wall in relief. No cloak-and-dagger for him. The light from the upstairs stairwell cast a halo into the semi-dark living room and kitchen. He was a spy who hid out in the open.

"I'll got a team together," Ali said. "To come in and search. Yours will be searched as well. They know about you, but don't give yourself away."

"When will you—"

"We're outside the door."

The pounding started before the call ended. Manu froze as the hammer-like sound reverberated through the concrete structure.

Adhik rushed down the stairs, his hair on edge, in an undershirt and shorts. "What is that racket?"

"Someone at the door," Manu said.

Adhik opened it.

"Police," Ali said. He strode in, thrusting Adhik aside with an arm. "Turn on the lights," his voice boomed through the interior.

The sight of Ali's boots spurred Manu into action. He whisked forward and pressed the white switches in the living room and in the kitchen.

Adhik retreated to the kitchen.

"Papers, everyone's papers."

The two thin, wiry policemen behind Ali said nothing. They went quickly to work, overturning the cushions on the couch, shoving aside the sofa to peer behind it. They moved as a unit, like shadows.

"Upstairs," Manu squeaked.

Ali turned his laser-like gaze on him.

"I mean, papers are upstairs."

"Wait here." Ali stomped up as his men pushed past Manu into the kitchen, rattling all the drawers and pans.

"There's a guy sleeping up there," Manu called.

"How could anyone sleep through this?" Adhik whispered.

The newcomer appeared a few minutes later, his feet thrust into plastic sandals, a wide-eyed look of panic on his face. He huddled with Manu and Adhik in the kitchen doorway. "What is going on? Are they deporting us?"

"They're looking for someone or something." Manu told the guy to go to the bathroom and pull himself together. His button-down company-issue shirt splayed open, revealing his ribs. He had forgotten, or had not been given the time, to pull on pants.

"Yeah, what are they looking for?" Adhik drew closer to Manu.

Stop talking so much, Manu berated himself. "I don't know that for sure. I assumed they have some reason to be here."

The policemen left the kitchen and headed upstairs to join Ali. The noises of the search sounded like a stampede as the boots tramped back and forth across the ceiling.

"What's your name again?" Manu asked the new guy, who emerged from the bathroom with slicked-back hair and his shirt buttoned. Lucky for him, the tail of the shirt shielded his essentials.

"Sanjany." His voice shook.

In the garish light of every fixture being turned on in the middle of the night, the dark circles under his eyes dominated his face.

"How old are you?"

A shudder ran through Sanjany's body. "I lied on my passport. I lied to get this job."

Adhik laughed, a sound that echoed in the empty lower level. "They're here for you, then."

Manu put up a hand. Shouting came from upstairs. "They want us up."

A few seconds later, one of the policemen, a guy with a thin mustache and no beard, emerged on the second step. He beckoned to them.

They hurried up the stairs with Manu leading the way and the other men stepping on his heels.

The shared bedroom resembled a disaster zone. Sheets hung from overturned mattresses like his sister's discarded shawls. Backpacks were empty. Papers, earphones and water bottles lay strewn around like a child's playthings.

"Who this?" The thin-mustached officer waved the plastic food box Sanjana sent with Manu. She filled it with his favorite hard candies, various colors in yellow wrappers.

"Mine," he said.

Ali frowned. "Everyone out."

The officers protested.

"All of you," Ali repeated.

Adhik and Sanjany scampered for the door. The officers trailed them, glancing at Ali several times before exiting.

"Why you have a woman's ring?" Ali hissed. His agitation eroded his language skills.

"I don't." Manu drew closer.

Ali held out his palm. In the center, a perfect oval diamond shimmered in the streetlight slanting through the window. The circular band would not fit on either man's pinky.

"Where did you find that?"

Ali nudged the food box with his toe.

"No," Manu said. "Impossible."

Ali searched his face. He closed his palm into a fist. "Are you saying someone planted this on you?"

"Planted..." Manu scratched his head. The English word eluded him but he surmised the gist from the worry in Ali's frown. "I not buy that ring. I never see Lauren before she die." Manu flipped a mattress down from the wall, back onto the box-spring which sat on the floor. He witnessed men dying on construction sites. People threatened him to keep his mouth shut against complaining about labor conditions. But living with a possible murderer was not in the job description.

"Six men live here." Ali paced, as cigarette smoke drifted in from his officers in the hallway.

Manu knew of only one who hankered after the victim. Maybe Adhik hid the ring in the box as a safe space. Maybe he didn't mean any harm. To share his suspicion would implicate the man Ali already found suspect. To hide this knowledge would be to fail his duty. "Let's question them all," he suggested. "And see who knows what."

"We start with you." Ali pointed at him.

Manu sat up. "But I—"

"You are still *undercover*," Ali hissed. "All the more reason now than ever." He pulled Manu up by the front of his undershirt. "I'll question you downstairs. *Now*." He pushed him toward the door, where the other policemen loomed. "Come when I call, you two."

Manu marched down the stairs, the breath of three policemen on his neck.

Fear pulled his thoughts outward, detached, he imagined viewing the tableau from a corner in the ceiling. That poor man, innocent, with no way to prove it. How long would they harangue him? Manu knew little about his boss. Other than Ali's rescue from a life-threatening scrape. He hoped it was enough.

Chapter Fourteen

Sanjana trudged up the village road, dragging a suitcase full of presents for the kids. The wheels bumped along the gravel-and-dirt path. She threw the door to the house open, waiting for squeals of delight. Three profiles emerged in the doorway. She stumbled back. She no longer saw the rounded cheeks of Ram and Raja, the twins, but the faces of men. Meena's once shoulder-length curly hair dangled in a long plait, swinging at her waist. Before Sanjana's eyes, their legs stretched and stretched, and their heads touched the ceiling. They towered over her.

Sanjana brushed the tears out of her eyes and scrambled to pull out the packages. Huge feet stepped on her gifts of a board game, paperback novels to practice their English, and boxes of hard candies. They squashed her much-deliberated purchases and exited the house, giants wandering off in the night.

She fell out of her twin bed onto the concrete floor. Sanjana awoke, the scream of anguish dying in her throat. The clock blinked *11.00* at her, causing a fresh stir of panic until her eyes ricocheted to the wall calendar. Friday.

She scooted back until her back touched the wardrobe, the skirt of her nightgown riding up over her knees. She gulped air and shook her head to clear the image of the children as adults with unseeing, unfeeling eyes. Fridays were a day full of fun, at least for the last several weeks, when Manu stayed with them. They made breakfast and relaxed in the house while Madam went out with Sir and Daniel spent the night at his friends'.

Together, as a male and female pair, they could go into the malls, because in the presence of a woman, security no longer considered him a bachelor. She had showed him around Carrefour and taken him to the ethnic food aisle with pride, a display of all the spices and condiments they used at home. He'd shown more interest in the electronics: the phones and tablets and video game machines.

She pushed herself up, her bones creaking, and went through the motions of wiping away sleep and getting ready for the day. She changed into leggings and one of Sir Paul's old t-shirts. No sense in wasting a good outfit on a day she would see no one.

Being alone on a Friday is nothing new. She spent years and years of Fridays in this room or, when Analyn lived here, going to the *souq*. She left her room and entered the main house through the kitchen.

"Wake up, man. Wake up."

Sanjana followed the pleas to the living room.

"Oh, hey, Sanjana." Daniel stopped shaking Sharif, who lay on the sofa. "Wake up, Sharif. Your mom said to be back by lunch or you'd be grounded again."

Sharif made moaning sounds.

"You slept here?"

Daniel hooked his arms around Sharif's torso, but gravity kept sliding them both onto the couch.

Sanjana came to help him, but her foot skidded an empty bottle across the marble. Sanjana bent to pick it up and saw another peeking out from under the sofa. "Daniel—"

He dropped his hands from Sharif and raised them toward her. "I know, I know. Mom and Dad were out, and a few friends came over. Things got out of hand."

Sanjana fished the second bottle out from under the sofa and spotted a third on the bookshelf. "What did they say when they found out?"

"They're out for the weekend," Daniel said. "Help me clean this up, and I promise it'll never happen again."

She put the first two bottles in the crook of her elbow and picked up the third, half-empty of a brownish liquid. She made a face and set it back down, looking for the lid. "Impossible. If you drank all this, your father will find out."

"He won't," Sharif groaned. He sat up, clutching his head. "This is our stuff."

"Yours?" Her wide eyes took them both in.

"I'm going to hurl."

"No, no, no." Daniel hauled his friend up, slinging one arm over his shoulder. "Not here."

They stumbled to the bathroom in the hallway.

Sanjana found the lid to the half-empty bottle on the coffee table, among an array of crushed beer cans and scattered ash. She made quick work of the room, throwing bottles and cans into the blue trashcan by the kitchen door, wiping down the table, gagging while emptying the brownish liquid down the sink.

"Hey, that one was half-full," Sharif protested. He propped himself up in the doorway for a breath.

"Half-empty," she retorted and retched again. "Now gone."

"She never drank alcohol?" Sharif chortled. "You should try that. Probably cost as much as a few weeks of your salary."

"Sharif," Daniel said. "Time to go."

Water clung to Sharif's hair where he'd slicked it over the side of his forehead. "Yeah, okay."

While Daniel saw Sharif out, Sanjana wiped down the counter, checking the living room for other signs of the night's festivities.

When he came back in, Daniel pleaded, "Don't tell them, please? I promise it won't happen again."

"I won't keep secret," Sanjana snapped. "You not remembering what happened last time because of that boy?"

The doorbell's chime interrupted the tirade at the tip of her tongue. "Maybe it's this boy's mother. She remembered she has a son."

Daniel's green eyes clouded. He raced to answer ahead of her. Sanjana couldn't see who waited on the other side. The angle of Daniel's shoulders filled the doorway.

"Oh, hi, Vinay. Dad's not here." Daniel turned to Sanjana. Her feet stuck to the ground.

"Uh, no. I don't think she's around." Daniel drew the door behind him. "It's her day off."

She released her pent-up breath when the lock clicked. A groan from the kitchen obscured the discussion on the other side.

"You." She regarded Sharif's pale face, his body leaning against the wall. "How dare you come back here?" In a country where ex-pats spent an average of three years, no such luck with Sharif, despite his parents' messy divorce.

He moaned in answer and made for the sofa, collapsing on it as if his bones were weary of holding him up.

"Vinay says he would like to see you again." Daniel's grin broadened, his eyes knowing.

Sanjana gritted her teeth. She waved a hand, swatting at his words as if they were flies. "That's not important."

"Something going on between you two?" Daniel gave her a wink.

"*No*."

Sharif groaned again, both hands to his head.

"*Chee*," Sanjana spat. "As if you can speak to me about these things——"

"Okay, okay." Daniel raised his hands. "He seemed like he really wanted to talk to you."

"He did?"

Sharif flipped over, burrowing his face in the sofa.

Daniel drew closer. "Yeah. Is he your first boyfriend?"

Sanjana stiffened at his fingers on her elbow. In the past few years, while she dusted or folded laundry, he gained several inches on her. Their heads close together, the timbre to his voice announced the end of childhood. Daniel becoming a man, knowing things about adult matters – she could deal with Sharif's childishness but not this budding equality. "My business," she said as he so often did to his parents.

"He wanted to see you again." His hair flopped into his eyes.

"And?" She gripped his hand and peeled it off of her arm.

"I told him you were probably sleeping."

A string of sounds like that of a truck backfiring issued from the sofa.

"Ugh," Daniel cried. "Sharif!"

"Focus on this, your big problem. This boy is no good." Sanjana moved away, breaking contact, emboldened by the familiar argument.

Daniel's frown deepened, his emerald eyes glittering. "He's not. Blame me for the hashish."

She didn't argue. Daniel's covering for his friend put them all in jeopardy and nearly cost Manu his freedom.

"But this time we're not hiding anything." He spread his arms out with a shrug, "Just not sharing all the details."

"*We?*" Sanjana snorted.

His pleading began anew.

"Your mistake is being friends with that boy," Sanjana said. "Nothing but trouble."

"His dad is leaving the country," Daniel said.

"He's taking him?"

Sharif convulsed and groaned. "No. I'd be a damper on his lifestyle."

"They make divorce for long time now," Sanjana huffed in a whisper. "Why he go now? And why not take his child?"

"Yes, but his brother is staying. No new school, etc." Daniel tugged at her hands. "Please. I promise."

She turned her face away, but he dominated her vision, standing first to her left and then to her right.

The door opened. Vinay stuck his head around the corner.

"Ah, sorry. I wanted to give this note." He waved a folded piece of paper. His hair slicked back in waves behind his ears, emphasized his wide forehead.

"Not now," Daniel said. His tattered gym shorts and t-shirt made for a drab contrast to Vinay's salmon-colored shirt, tight on his biceps, his jeans hugging his waist.

Vinay locked eyes with Sanjana. She clenched her hands into fists to try to cover the mundaneness of her own outfit.

Sharif began to convulse.

"He okay?"

"He's fine. Leave the note on the table," Daniel said.

Vinay put the note on the dark wood entryway console. "Doctor?"

"Bye." Daniel walked Vinay back to the door. On his way back into the living room, he picked up the note and waved it at her. "You've got this under control?"

"That's mine." Sanjana reached for the note, but Daniel held it above her head. She fisted her hands again in frustration. She leveled him with a stare that once reduced the toddler version of this not-quite-man to tears. "Daniel, give it here."

"I need your help." He stretched out his pinky to her, in the child's gesture they used to agree on keeping secret one of Sanjana's housekeeping mistakes. A broken plate or a ruined dress. She would come clean to Madam Cindy later, slipping in the news during a big task like setting the table for Thanksgiving or three days of packing for the summer holiday. She linked her small finger with his. Daniel passed her the paper with his other hand. They released fingers. She stared at the English script, shame burning her cheeks.

Daniel hoisted a groaning Sharif up. The boys listed to one side, and Daniel grunted as Sharif clutched his stomach.

"Steady." Sanjana crumpled the note into her pocket, rushing to prop Sharif up from the other side. They helped him to his feet. "Bathroom."

Daniel didn't argue. They made their way, at an ant-like pace, between the sofas and across the carpet to the spare room. They kept going, into

Paul's study, the room that in other units on the compound served as a guest bedroom. They maneuvered Sharif onto the closed toilet lid.

She held him in place by the shoulder. "Shower."

"You sure?"

"Fine, make it warm," she added at the doubt on Daniel's face.

The hiss of the water perked Sharif up.

"I'll do it." Daniel came over, pulling Sharif's shirt off.

"I'm outside," Sanjana said. She ducked out of the bathroom into the study. They might have the maturity of boys, but the hair she saw curling up Sharif's neck said their bodies were in the throes of transitioning to manhood. Daniel as an adult sent her thoughts skittering back to Vinay. *He knows where I live. He can come any time.* The realization annoyed and thrilled her. Is this how it felt to have a boyfriend? She wished for a friend to ask, her confusion yet another reminder of her inexperience.

From inside the bathroom came a series of clashes and clangs as Sharif swore. Daniel called, "I need a towel."

A piece of paper fell into a corner. *I'll get that later.* She rushed upstairs to the linen cabinet. When she returned, her arms full of purple towels, Vinay stood in the bathroom with Daniel, the two of them with their arms around Sharif. "What are you doing here?"

"We need his help," Daniel grunted.

Sanjana dropped the towels, averting her eyes from the spread of hair on the boy's chest. Was it possible to be so young and manly at once? She blushed, first in shame and then in embarrassment at her lack of knowledge about men.

She left home with Manu still young, younger than Daniel. The years helped her mother with the children did not prepare her for the muscles she saw straining in Vinay's back and neck or the ropes evident in Daniel's forearms. Her gaze skidded into the hallway, over the photographs in silver frames on the bookcase. The baby, the eyes turning from blue like his father's to green like shards of jade.

"Your shirt," Vinay said. They dressed Sharif in Daniel's clothes, leaving him in his undershorts.

Sanjana kept her eyes on the mantel.

"I take him home," Vinay said.

"Thank you." The gratitude in Daniel's voice flowed like warm syrup.

"No problem, no problem," Vinay said, his eyes trained on Sanjana.

Daniel gave a final wave in the lengthening pause, and closed the door.

She retreated, as quick as a mouse, though Daniel's footsteps echoed behind her, up the stairs. "Your not-boyfriend is really nice."

Nice, is nice enough? She rushed towards middle age with no prospects in sight. Maybe Vinay wasn't so bad. Sanjana pushed aside the hooded glance Vinay gave her. It wasn't a look of adoration. No, it reminded her of the Maoist soldiers who came to their village looking for wives. *Married is married.* Wasn't it?

Chapter Fifteen

Ali marched down the stairs, the breath of the two other policemen on his neck. Now seemed a bad time to question how well he knew his secret partner. He flipped the main switch, turning on the lights in the living room. Ali jerked his chin left, indicating that Manu should stand while he and the other officers sat on the low sofa.

"What you know about this ring?" He began the line of questioning afresh.

Like an errant child, the diamond sparkled atop the glass of the coffee table.

"Nothing." Manu clutched his hands.

"Nothing?"

The other two officers held a rapid exchange. You didn't need to speak Arabic to understand they found Manu less than credible.

"Why was it in your box?" Ali interrupted. If he could keep control of the interrogation maybe they would learn something useful from the other men staying here.

"Someone put it there."

"Someone?" Ali repeated.

Before they could say another word, Sanjany burst into the room from the stairs.

"This ring is worth more than all your salaries combined. So yes, it could use a safer place than that," Ali intoned.

"Sorry, sorry, sorry." He ran across the width of the living room and threw himself at Ali's feet.

"This is an interview." Ali pulled the prostrate man up by the elbow. "Enough!"

Ali bent over, in an effort to distinguish words amongst the sobs.

"I lie on my passport," Sanjany whispered.

"Fake documents?"

"No. Me. I am the fake." He extended his passport.

Ali took it and scrutinized the photo with the image of the man in front of him. "You are not twenty."

"Seventeen." Sanjany's teeth chattered.

Adhik crept down the stairs, his eyes darting across the faces. The two officers stood, protesting the intrusion.

"Is every man in here a teenage girl with something to confess?" Ali asked, slapping the passport against his thigh. "This is a formal investigation."

Manu rose, and caught Adhik by the arm before he reached the table.

"Don't take it, please," Adhik cried. "It is all I have of her."

Ali pushed his hands onto his knees and rose. "Who?"

"Lauren." Adhik's chin quivered. He burst into tears.

Manu caught the slighter man as he stumbled. Adhik clung to him, sobs wracking his body.

Ali raised an eyebrow. He read the slant of the other man's head and shoulders. Manu's look said he knew nothing about this ring or a relationship with Lauren. The burst of emotion ebbed. Adhik wiped his eyes on the sleeve of a shirt he'd put on upstairs.

"You purchased this ring for the deceased? To propose?"

"No." Adhik's gaze rested on the table. He said with a dark laugh, "I bought it for me."

"Don't play games with me," Ali said sharply.

"He's telling the truth," Manu said.

Ali put up a warning hand. Relieved of his burden, Sanjany curled up on the sofa, eyes fluttering to a close.

"I bought it, but I wasn't going to give it to her," Adhik said with a hiccup.

"Excuse me?"

"It is fake. The ring, it is a child's toy. I bought it at one of those shops in the *souq*. I couldn't have given it to her. Other men could give her the real thing. With me, only pretend."

Ali held the ring up to the light. Up close, the stone looked clouded and thick, like plastic. He tossed it to Adhik, who crushed it to his chest.

"A fake ring for a fake girlfriend." Ali nodded.

Adhik crumpled around the ring, a sob rising in his chest.

Another smattering of Arabic as Ali translated the gist of the conversation for the other officers. As they conferred with each other, a growing sense of unease alerted him to the fact that of all those in the room, his fellow country policemen were the ones he trusted the least.

"What other men?" Ali switched to English, hoping to keep one step ahead of them. "Were there many people in love with her?" How many people could one woman keep on a leash? Ali blanched, Maryam's face floating before him. He ignored such things, though the rumor mills were rife with stories of local girls growing bolder, breaking off engagements and walking away from marriages.

"Check the visitor log," Adhik answered. "They should be listed."

The minions; that's how Ali labeled them in his mind, shuffled upstairs, to do another sweep. He remained with the men from South Asia, sitting in a now companionable silence, downstairs. Sanjany fell asleep. Adhik stared into the distance, not far behind. Manu remained alert, back straight as a shepherd's switch, scanning Ali for clues. He gave a slight shake of his head to say no, he couldn't make sense of these tiny bits of information either. A dull ache formed at the base of his neck. The minions trudged downstairs, shrugging their way to the door.

"Nothing else upstairs," Ali said.

Manu and Adhik regarded him in the garish living-room light.

"Let's go to bed," Manu said. "While we still can."

Ali made no move to stop them. Adhik lumbered up, casting about for a few minutes like a new sailor. Manu elbowed Sanjany awake, sending him up the stairs next.

"Adhik didn't tell you about the ring?" Ali hissed, flashing it in front of the other man's face.

"No," Manu protested, palms up. "Who hide it on me?"

Ali discarded the ring onto the table with a clunk. The dozens of ungloved fingers touching it erased any value to the investigation. To hide the ring in Manu's box, however; that smacked of desperation. "Go," he said quietly. "Or they'll suspect something."

Ali went over it again and again in his mind as the men continued searching upstairs, resetting the overturned mattress and other personal items jostled in the search. Was Adhik motivated by sadness from unrequited love? Or did fear cause his left leg to shake like a young goat? Questions swirled in Ali's mind as sand circled in his headlights on the way home. A dust storm approached, tingeing his windscreen orange. One thing was clear: Manu couldn't stay there if one of the other men wanted to frame him.

"You're going back to your sister," he said when he answered the line with a whispered hello. "I'll arrange it. We'll get you a new detail. The school. There's got to be someone there who knows something." He hoped so. Otherwise this case was as dead as the woman at the center of it.

Chapter Sixteen

Sunlight streamed into the room, same as each of the three other days Manu spent in his sister's employer's house. He rolled over, burrowing his head under the pillow. The pillow, the sheets, the weight of the comforter—he couldn't get used to any of it because this wasn't his real life. This was a holding zone before he went back into the city, out into the underbelly, looking for those like him who needed help.

A knock on the door called him out of his thoughts.

"Have some breakfast," his sister said through the crack.

Ali reinserting Manu into the household dispelled the pretense of a guest in this house, on holiday, like any other ex-pat, to exclaim over the differences from home, but his list differed from the things he'd heard people talking about in the malls. His list included things like the cement streets and concrete paths devoid of trees and grass, but with splashes of color at the roundabouts. He wouldn't tell his siblings about the men crouched in the growing grass in these strange places, cutting it with large shears people at home would use to trim their bushes. He dressed in the shirts and shorts his sister bought him.

A wider face stared back at him in the mirror, the cheeks fuller than when he stayed at the house that first time, drawn, malnourished, and beaten by the agency thugs trying to shut him up. He put aside the idea that their managers were still out there, in the tangle of a city that he still knew very little about. The goons couldn't reach him, safe behind these walls. Manu slid into the breakfast nook behind a plate piled high with pancakes, which were topped with three raspberries. He dug into the food, the feeling of the knife and fork in his hands more familiar after the months of staying in the home of these strangers.

Sanjana sat across from him, her chin in her palm, watching him eat. It reminded him of how their mother used to do it—lining up the children against the wall, doling out seconds, cleaning up spills.

They said little, the air heavy with the topics they couldn't discuss. His last assignment. His next assignment. When they would see each other next.

"Delicious." He made quick work of the stack, dispatching them without delay. More meals like these and his t-shirt would get tight along his belly.

Sanjana scooted his plate and utensils into the sink. "Are you scared?" She stood with her back to him, her words muffled by the water.

"No," he lied. "This is safer than the other thing."

Well, that was partly true. He wouldn't be in physical danger of being crushed while working on a building.

"Those people, the agency—they don't know where you are."

"That's right." He stood next to her at the sink. "I'll be fine." He put out a finger and caught the tear before it fell off her chin. "I have you to come rescue me, if I get in trouble."

She gave a shaky laugh, swatted at his shoulder, and wiped underneath her eyes. "I won't know where you find you."

"Mr. Ali will," he said soberly. He turned around, his hips leaning on the edge of the counter so he could study his sister's face more closely.

She took a shuddering breath.

"Maybe you should go home." He forced the words out, and panic at the idea of being left alone in this country closed up his throat. "Get some rest."

"No way." She dried, the towel working across the white surface in concentric circles. "I'm not leaving you here."

"Someone asked about you," he teased, to lighten the mood.

"No," She put the plate in the drainer.

"At home," he pretended to think. In truth, most people thought Sanjana too old to become a wife. Men her age wanted someone younger. And those men willing to consider an almost-thirty-year-old woman wanted her to help with children from other women. Her life as a wife would consist of tasks very similar to those of her ten years as a servant. Only wifehood meant no one would pay her for washing, cooking, cleaning or babysitting. Life in the village would be harder. Much, much harder without the American appliances.

"You're saying that to make me feel better." She put the silverware away. "Laxmi. I saw Laxmi when I went to interview for a job. Laxmi Pande. The one who sold your contract to the construction company."

Manu's attention snapped back to his agitated sister. "Don't worry about that now."

"What do you mean? I call the police. We call that officer who you work for." Her speech wove between English and Nepali. "We send her to the jail."

"No." Manu sliced his hand through the air. "That's not important now. Leave it alone," he said. "Leave Laxmi alone."

"Morning." Daniel wandered into the kitchen, his hair standing on end. He shuffled to the fridge, his torso disappearing as he bent to look inside. "You still here, Manu?"

"Yes." Manu straightened.

He re-emerged, munching a red apple.

"You want something to eat?"

Manu seethed at the conciliatory tone in his sister's voice. A few minutes ago she'd been using it on him.

"No. Remember Mom's rule? No work on Fridays." Daniel tossed the apple core toward the trashcan in a move from around his waist. The remainder of the fruit went through the swinging top. "For the game!" He put his arms up and gave a little jog.

A good rule. The grooves under his sister's eyes diminished since Manu's arrival. They were now dark discolorations instead of variegated bags.

"I make you pancakes, no problem." Sanjana went to the stove. "See? Mix is here." She turned on the gas, the pilot caught with a click, the blue flame hissed to life.

Daniel shrugged. "If you insist." He sat in the breakfast nook recently vacated by Manu.

"No working on Friday." Cindy, his sister's madam, clicked into the kitchen. "Come on, Daniel. We're going to be late for church."

"Not work," Sanjana insisted. She scooped out batter for one pancake. "Making them anyway."

Cindy's hands sat on her hips. The black dress accentuated the contrast between her waist and bust, her jawline magnified by an upward twist of hair. She brightened. "Good morning, Manu."

One person in the house would be happier with him gone. Manu took a seat next to Daniel. Their legs touched before the teenager shifted to make room.

"I suppose we could go to the second service at eleven." Cindy brought out four circular red placements. "Daniel, will you let Sharif and Amira know we're going later?"

"Ahunh." He bent over his phone, hair hanging in his eyes.

Sanjana's head-shake at Manu said not to mention he'd already eaten.

"I'm sorry we didn't plan something more formal. Paul is away, you know."

"No problem," Manu murmured.

"Glad everything worked out." Cindy placed a stack of plates on the table. "You got a great job and you're helping the country."

"Hmmm," Manu murmured. *And not here with you. That's what you care about.* For her part, his sister stood humming at the stove.

Maybe it would be good to get away from here. The unknown couldn't be worse than being sandwiched between the boy who framed him with hidden drugs and the boy's mother, who sucked up ten years of his sister's life.

"Speaking of Sharif, how do you think he likes med school?" Cindy asked.

Daniel gave Manu a sidewise glance as if to say, *Can't your turn last a little bit longer?*

Manu bit into a pancake. He suffered his share of prying questions— before his mother died.

"Sharif says his mom is going to Zumba in the clubhouse, so yeah, later service works," Daniel mumbled.

"Zumba." Cindy glanced at her watch.

Zumba? Manu's gaze cut to his sister. She waited at the stove, spatula in hand, eyes trained on a bubbling pancake.

"I'm going to zip in there, too." Cindy pushed away her plate. "I'll meet you back here in an hour."

Daniel grunted as the first pancake landed on his plate, ushered there with a glass of milk. Manu rose, hoping to escape back upstairs, but the next pancake plopped onto the plate in front of him. Sanjana mimed the fork going into his mouth. He chewed, thinking of the rice and pita bread he ate in the camps, his stomach recoiling. Cindy gave them a small wave as she jogged out the side door.

"What is Zumba?" Manu asked as the door shut behind her.

Daniel laughed, milk snorting out of his nose.

Manu's cheeks burned. "Finished," he said, pushing up from the table.

"Exercise," Sanjana said, passing the boy a napkin.

"I'm not laughing at you," Daniel said, wiping his face. "If you saw them, you'd know it's not about exercise."

His words washed over Manu like a tide of sound. Sanjana's phone rang before she could intervene again.

"Yes, Madam," she said, her eyes landing on Manu. "Yes, I'll send him."

She hung up, slipping the phone back into her pocket. "They ran out of water in the dispenser there. She wants you to take one down."

He raised an eyebrow. One of them worked for the American family and it wasn't Manu.

Sanjana gestured at the multi-liter water cylinder under the counter. She couldn't have carried it.

"I'll help," Daniel said around a final mouthful of pancake. The paisley shapes on his underwear peaked out over his waistband as he bent to roll out the container. They rolled it between them, through the kitchen. "Front door is closer to the clubhouse."

Manu steered past the cream couches, avoiding the sharp corners of the glass-topped coffee table. They left Sanjana on the doorstep, rolling down the two short stairs and down the pavement.

"Hey," Sharif called out the window.

Daniel paused, straightening, and pushing his hair out the way.

"Come up and help me with this campaign slogan?"

"You got this?" Sweat peppered Daniel's forehead.

Manu swung the container onto his shoulder by the plastic handle.

"Okay, then." Daniel's eyes widened.

Manu stepped away, toward the clubhouse at the end of the street. The boy sauntered in the opposite direction, crossing the street and disappearing behind Sharif's door, with the same metallic lattice and glass on every door in the neighborhood. As soon as the door closed, Manu slipped the container back onto the pavement, rotating his shoulder. He arched his back, getting out the kink. In case the boys glanced out the window, and thought him tired, Manu pushed the barrel down the street and over the sidewalk, up the stairs of the clubhouse. The water sloshed inside, bumping up the tier. Manu rested again at the plateau at the top, like summiting one of the many mountains around his village. Sliding glass doors swished open, dousing him with a blast of cool air. His eyes adjusted to the clubhouse's dim interior. Leather sofas waited for ex-pat residents to lounge in their expansive arms.

Music pulsed from behind a door to his left. Flickers of light from underneath said this was his destination. Manu hesitated, remembering the stories from the camps about not looking too directly at women.

"There you are!" Cindy burst into the foyer. "It's hot in there."

Manu's gaze fell to the floor at the sight of his sister's boss in a top that bared her flat stomach.

"I'll give you a hand." Cindy came over to him, standing the drum on its wide base.

Manu kept his gaze on her shoes. Even the street workers in the capital wore more than this when trying to attract clients.

"I got it," he said, using Daniel's slang. He hoisted the barrel onto his shoulder, keeping it in place with his left hand.

Cindy stepped back.

He basked in the admiration in her eyes, allowing himself a glance at her orange shorts, parting to reveal the rise of a plum-shaped rear end. *She's someone's mother,* Manu chastised himself. The door to the exercise room opened, deafening him for a moment. He needn't have worried about offending Cindy. Once inside, female flesh surrounded him in the bare legs and arms of the women dancing to the beat of a drum-heavy solo.

"Shake!" A tall woman, cinnamon-skinned, stood with her legs braced, bottom shaking in a circle from the front to the back.

His step faltered, confronted by the reflected images of the six women bouncing to the beat. Manu scurried to the water dispenser, putting down his burden next to the plastic tower.

The song changed—someone let out a cheer. Manu worked at the plastic seal on the drum, keeping his back to the women gyrating in the back of the room.

"Make it count, ladies, it's beach season." Her aqua-blue tank top matched her sneakers.

He hoisted the drum, clenching his teeth, and turned it over, the nozzle pointing down into the interior of the dispenser.

"Thank you!" Cindy called after him, taking three steps to the left, pivoting before taking three steps to the right.

Manu made it to the exit without meeting her eye. He closed the door behind him, leaning on it as if it were Pandora's box, his heart racing. Somewhere in here danced the other boy's mother. Western women weren't that crazy, he consoled himself. At least they were inside, not out in the open like he heard happened in nightclubs.

"Aw."

Manu started at the four men in blue overalls standing to the right of the column in the foyer. Their sightline gave them an unrestricted view of the exercise room.

"Brother, can't you wait a few minutes?" A swarthy man chuckled. His paunch jiggled as he gyrated his hips, imitating the exercise leader.

"I'm memorizing the blonde," said another, the lines in his face and white hair making him the senior of the group.

"That's my sister's employer," Manu said.

They regarded him more closely.

"You in villa 2?" The swarthy one pushed away from the pillar, squinting.

"Visiting," Manu stammered. He left the clubhouse before they could regale him with other questions or discussion of the women. Yes, exercising behind closed doors was the safest thing for those women. Manu hoped his mind would delete everything. In order to do that, he probably needed something or someone to replace the images.

Chapter Seventeen

An inky night sky blanketed the neighborhood. In these hours before the dawn call to prayer, even the most rambunctious teenagers slept, their 4X4 vehicles waiting for daylight and the chance to terrorize the neighborhood streets. Maryam yawned, spreading out on the bench in the foyer. She could have stayed in bed; he would have come to find her. But she wanted to be awake for these last few moments.

Nasser came through the sliding glass door in a matching blue-and-white tracksuit, trailed by their mother. He kissed the top of their mother's head. Fatma turned away, wiping the corners of her eyes. Maryam blinked rapidly to prevent tears from building in her own.

Nasser came closer. She swallowed past the lump in her throat.

"I'll see you on Skype." His eyes were shadowed by a baseball hat with the New York Yankees' insignia.

"Yeah, sure. Don't forget me while you're in the big city." Her voice broke on the joke.

"I'm going to be trapped in the hospital for most of the day and half the night," he said. "Not glamour. Keep up with those grades."

"I'm not a kid," she muttered.

"No, you'll be a wife soon," he whispered in her ear as they embraced. "Don't mess this up." They drew apart. He chucked her under the chin. "I'll be back in no time."

"*Enshallah*," Maryam and her mother said at the same time.

He left. Two black suitcases filled the rear mirror. All he needed for his future as a doctor. She pulled aside the curtain in the front room, watching as he climbed into the cab, beside the driver.

Her mother's hand weighed heavily on her shoulder. "We'll be so busy with the reception, we won't notice he's gone." Her mother swayed back and forth.

Maryam wasn't convinced. "*Ubooy* isn't going with him to the airport?" She made an argument to go but her mother forbade it. The hugs and tears that would ensue were not fit for public consumption. She didn't trust herself not to break down completely so didn't push further.

Fatma sighed. "Your father—these are hard days for him."

Maryam belted her robe without answering the accusation that hung in the air. She and Nasser were constant sources of frustration for their father. She wondered what he thought would happen, with their international education and foreign teachers.

"Your cousin, Mohammed. He is going into the business."

"That's great for him," Maryam said without rancor.

Fatma gave her a searching look, grasping her hands. "Don't worry about your brother. You're starting your own journey. You won't miss him one bit once you get settled."

The taillights disappeared through the front gates. There went Nasser, off to pursue his future. Leaving Maryam to make what she could of her fate. She kissed her mother's forehead, in a sign of respect and affection, and her mother wrapped her in an embrace.

"I'll see about breakfast." Her mother released her grip first. Maryam suspected Fatma left the room to hide her tears. She headed back to her room. Her parents' door hung ajar. Her father stood at the window, in sweatpants and a t-shirt. He stood motionless as the gates swung closed. His shoulders were stooped; he lacked the electrical energy that crackled from him during the day.

She played her a part in her father's disappointment, but Nasser broke his heart.

"*Yuba*, I'm sorry," she said in a whisper that he showed no sign of having heard. She slipped away, around the corner, and into her room, a sob rising in her throat. She blinked away tears, looking for something, anything, to distract her. She picked up the novel. Why did people think white women were so much more independent than Arabs? From what Maryam could see, they were under as much pressure to get married as anyone. Arrogant Darcy could not end up with Elizabeth Bennett. Her eyelids drooped—the endless descriptions of houses and countryside were unnecessary.

Are you awake?

The bleat of a text jerked her awake. *Yes.* Maryam flopped onto the bed. So Ali woke for *fajer*, the pre-dawn prayer. A question at the top of her mother's list for previous grooms.

Can I see you?

The phone fell from her grip, smacking her in the face. *Now?*

Whenever your parents will let you out.

Maryam rubbed her forehead, squinting with one eye at the screen. Did he want a relationship? Hope unfurled like a small flower in her chest. With Nasser gone, movement became even more restricted and life much more mundane. She couldn't do anything outside of her routine, unless she wanted to alert her mother to the burgeoning relationship. The idea of becoming friends with Ali, in addition to his sleuth, and wife, was so new, she couldn't share it with anyone. Especially not her mother, who would take it as a good sign of things to come.

Maryam knew about the divorce rate. She remembered the look on Ali's sister's face when she first entered the room during the engagement.

Maybe in a few days, she texted. *I have an exam.* His refusal to answer any questions about the case irked her, not least because she suspected this would be his approach after marriage. Also, Daniel kept expecting her to update him. There was nothing to share. The unfinished book lay spine-up in her room. *Reading exam,* Erin called it, to make sure they were keeping up. From what Maryam could tell, life in England in the 19th century involved mostly sitting around and waiting. The four walls around her didn't feel that different. She popped open her laptop, scrolling through Twitter for amusement, wishing sleep would claim her from the drudgery of college life. #Notsafeforwomen appeared as a hashtag trending nationally. Maryam clicked, fatigue falling from her eyes. She scrolled through the feed, an aggregate of the Gulf Cooperation Countries, grouping them as one region since individually they were too small to quantify for a mega data-miner like Twitter.

@expatwoman *First the dead teacher and now body parts in the desert. All the single ladies better get out of the emirate.*

Maryam read the entire page, her horror mounting at the news about the flight attendant. Another woman now dead. The remains of a Sandra Booth were discovered by a hawker and his bird a day ago. Her frustrated parents released the news to the media because the government failed to respond.

"I told you there was a flight attendant," Maryam said hoarsely, talking over Ali's mumbled hello. "And now she's dead." Tears sprang to Maryam's eyes. While the rest of the girls her age swanned around shopping malls, she confronted the grittiest parts of society.

"What are you on about?" Ali said gruffly, as though speaking through a can.

"It's on Twitter," Maryam said. "Twenty-something flight attendant, remains found burned and buried in the dunes."

A scratch and then a scramble. Ali exhaled in a *whoosh*, the sound much closer. "Wait." There were a few clicks, she imagined him finding the app on his phone to read the hashtag stream. "I've got no messages," he said. "Nothing official on this."

Maryam closed her eyes, her mind swirling. "Two women? Here? What if it's a serial killer?"

"Slow down," Ali said, his voice regaining some of the firmness she was used to hearing. "There aren't serial anythings here. This isn't television. I'll find out what I can. Say nothing," he added.

Her mouth opened and closed like a drowning fish.

"No tweeting, no confirming or denying. Stay out of this."

"Fine," Maryam managed. Thus far there were no photos. They could thank state-controlled media for that small blessing.

"I'll be in touch."

The line went dead. Maryam fell back on her bed, the phone falling out of her outstretched hand. One account, *#justiceforsandra*, featured a series of photos of the woman, maybe only a few years older than Maryam, smiling in her daily life in the emirate. Sandra on a *dhow* in the middle of the corniche, glass-fronted high-rises reaching for the sky in a crescent behind her and a circle of smiling friends. Maryam squinted at the pixelated photo. In the middle of the gaggle of women, arms wrapped around each other, bikini strings tied around their necks and poking out the neck of their tank tops, shone a familiar face. Dr. Erin looked very different on the weekend.

We raised 30,000 riyals for Arnell came the next text from a number not registered in her phone.

Who is this?

Me Amal silly.

Maryam squinted at the screen. Amal texted around Maryam—rather than *to* her—in university-related group chats about specific classes. *Sorry new phone.* A well-known excuse, used to cover deleting someone from your contacts list. In point of fact, this was the truth since her father deleted everyone from Maryam's phone.

Dr. Erin will be so happy. They're going to let me write the piece about it.

Maryam closed her eyes in disgust. Of course Amal would write if it meant she could gloat. If the flood gates were open for communication, maybe she could use them to her advantage.

What do you know about Sandra?

Nothing. Haram. Amal wrote back, calling upon pity for the dead woman. Maryam grit her teeth in frustration.

But there's video of them leaving the hotel, Amal continued.

Whose video?

You know, Sharif. They were at the hotel that night. He saw them. System says this user cannot receive multimedia?

She smacked her forehead in frustration. Her Nokia in no way resembled a smartphone. She scrambled for her tote bag from the foot of the bed and grabbed her computer. *The good phone is broken,* Maryam lied. *Can you send me a link?* She held her breath. Maryam racked her mind to think of an excuse if Amal asked what happened to her 'real' phone. All she needed was for her former friend to know about her complicated engagement to Ali. When the link came, she sighed in relief, twisting her hair into a bun. On the third try, she got the address loaded. Her nose a centimeter from the screen, she followed the female figures in tank dresses and sequined shoes exiting a hotel lobby. A revolving glass door bisected the view. "That's Erin, as in Professor Erin," a male voice whispered off camera. The video shook as it followed the women through a side door, standing a few meters away as they climbed into the backseat of a Land Cruiser. "Guess she's got friends in high places." Sharif's face filled the screen for a second before the camera swung back on the three-digit license plate.

"Me first, then Sandra," Dr. Erin's voice said, clear as a bell. A white arm hung out the window, silver bangles reflecting the chrome of the revolving door. The driver revved the engine before pealing out of the hotel's semi-circle driveway.

In the second the video finished, Maryam hit 'play' again.

Chapter Eighteen

Manu sat at the desk, doodling. With no Adhik to entertain him, the hours crept by like ants trying to get a picnic. His new assignment was beyond boring. None of the glamour of the compound entry office. He sat at the desk in front of the school as parents paraded in, flashing their security badges.

"You have to sign in," he said.

"Huh?"

Manu pushed the sign-in sheet toward the mother who hurried through the metal detector.

"I've never done this."

"For drop-off, it's required," he said.

"Really? But—"

"Yes, you do," said another mother. She hoisted her baby higher on her hip.

"Really?" The woman brushed her hair back.

The mother nodded, her daughter gripping her ear.

She signed, her name a scrawl instead of letters.

"Thank you," Manu said to the second mother.

The mother smiled at him. "No problem. Happy to help." Pity laced her words. She wrote her name on the sheet and went in.

Two people tried to use the narrow entrance at once.

A short woman in pastel-blue uniform scurried in while a man in national dress strode through on the phone. She bounced into his girth and shied away.

"Look where you're going," he bellowed at the housemaid. She stepped to one side, hands at her sides, rushing through after the man exited to the parking lot.

Manu tracked her retreat through the open window. She paused at the stop sign for the guards to beckon her across the walkway. She made her way across the dirt parking lot, disappearing into a black SUV with tinted windows.

He thought of his sister, thankful she never wore uniforms. Her jeans and skirts gave her more dignity; she could be like any of the other women coming in and out, like the dozens of mothers dropping off their children at this international school.

He missed the cadence of compound life. People leaving like a tide in the morning, an afternoon of stillness, the maintenance guys coming in from the heat for a chance to rest, to tell stories of home, escape the confines of the electrical closet where they languished in the heat since the management failed to make good on their promises following Lauren's death.

"Nice watch," he said.

The cleaning lady, the one whose smile reminded him of a much younger version of his sister, smiled back. "Thank you."

He thought of Adhik's smartphone and gelled hair. Did the cleaning lady make more than him? Maybe she didn't have as many people to support.

"How much?"

Her eyes widened.

"I mean, I'd like to get one for my sister," he stammered.

"Oh, my friend bought it for me." She hastened back into the courtyard, dustpan and brush in tow.

"Some friend," Manu called after her. Sumitha's watch, Adhik's gadgets — did no one send money home any more? Manu chewed at his lip. His money disappeared into a pipeline to feed the future of his siblings. His increased pay added to Sanjana's earnings. Maybe he could spare a little for himself. What would he buy? Reham flashed in his mind's eye. Would she like a watch like Sumitha's? Manu pressed the heels of his hand into his eyes. *Down this path lies madness,* he warned himself. The manic gleam in his friend's eye, the dullness of a fake engagement ring, a dead woman's body, waiting to be sent home to grieving parents. He trained his attention on the grainy image of the street in front of the school, made dreary by the overcast weather. A car screeched into the dirt parking lot opposite the booth, a figure jerked in the time-delayed video towards the entrance.

A teenage boy came through the door, the wind sweeping in a gust of dust and sand. His wide forehead and flared nostrils were familiar. Manu trained his gaze above the boy's shoulder in case he recognized him. "High school should use gate eleven," Manu said.

The boy stepped through the metal detector, setting it off. "I'm an alumnus," he mumbled. "Not a student."

Manu stood, not understanding the word.

"I graduated from here. Call Ms. Carson. She asked me to come and talk to the kindergarten students about medicine."

"You're a doctor?" Manu dialed, sizing the boy's wan complexion and stained t-shirt.

"Med student."

"Mrs. Carson, there is a—"

The boy handed over his ID card.

"Sharif," Manu read, "he say he's here to talk to your class." Recognition flashed through him—that boy his sister cared for, this same boy was his friend.

"Yes, send him on through," Mrs. Carson said. "He's late."

Manu gave the boy back his ID. Sharif gave him a smirk, exiting into the lower elementary playground. Each time that door swung open, the orange equipment twisting into the open air, Manu imagined his siblings hanging from the black mesh, like a spider, in place of the white-skinned, blonde-haired children. An alien spaceship would be more normal than such a playground in the hills of his village. His stomach grumbled. He left without eating that morning, avoiding the other men in the kitchen, yet another set of introductions, feigning interest in them. His pretense of sleep on the bus ride to the school melded into reality. He jerked awake when someone tapped him on the shoulder. Separated from Sanjany and Adhik, Manu went through the motions, his day filled with impersonal chatter.

"Would you like some?" A mother came in, carrying a white box rimmed by blue. His eyes skirted over her black spandex pants and hot-pink tank top.

"Uh, what it is?"

She pulled back the cover, revealing a three-tier chocolate cake. "My son's birthday and his class couldn't finish it," she said, pushing the box across to Manu. "We're having another one at home at dinner." A rectangular diamond flashed in the sunlight streaming through the window. "Share it with the other guys, and the cleaners," she suggested.

"Thank you," Manu stammered.

She gave a wave, from behind wide-rimmed sunglasses, disappearing through the door back onto the street.

Manu pulled the box closer. What a place. People with so much food, they gave away birthday cake. Half the cake sat in the middle of a metallic silver circle, like a deflated balloon. Vanilla, interspersed with chocolate. His stomach clenched at the sight of the three layers. He searched the drawers of the desks in the security booth. One plastic knife and several napkins. Manu cut a piece, picking it up with his fingers, biting it in half. Icing dissolved on his tongue.

"I'm emptying the trash can."

Manu started, swallowing the piece, and then choking as bits went down the wrong way.

"Take it easy," Sumitha giggled. She covered her mouth, mirth shaking her shoulders. "The door is open, but you not hear me."

Manu wiped at the counter with the unused napkin. "Want some cake?"

"Who gave you this?"

Manu cut her a generous slice. "I have a friend too," he said with a wink, though he couldn't picture the exercise mom giving him anything as personal as a watch.

Sumitha accepted the piece, enfolded by a napkin. "Good you ate because once others know, there won't be any left."

They munched together.

"Where you from?" Manu asked.

"India," she said. "You?"

"Nepal," he replied.

"Ah, then we speak Hindi," she exclaimed, her dark eyes flashing. Vanilla cake crumbs dotted her full lips.

"Sure," Manu said. A bell pealed from the school's interior.

"*Ai,*" Sumitha darted up, the remaining cake falling to the floor. "I have to mop the cafeteria after snack time." She darted out the side door without a backward glance.

Manu watched her scurry across the courtyard for the second time that morning. The women traveled through the school with ease while he remained trapped in the security box like one of the insects his siblings collected in spare boxes and jars. *What was the inside like?* he wondered. Nothing like the one-room schoolhouse he went to, sitting on the dirt floor and cleaning slates with water by the river. He and his younger siblings were lucky, Sanjana's income kept them sitting on the floor, learning, while others their age were tending flocks of sheep or goats, plowing rows for vegetables, and scrabbling for the food on their tables. *Lucky,* he repeated to himself. Lucky to be here, sitting behind a desk, eating free cake.

The door facing the street banged open.

Manu leaned forward with a smile, waiting for the person to extend her badge to be screened. This woman also wore sunglasses, her shoulders stooped, a black t-shirt stained with white spots. She leaned on a taller woman, who bent towards her, a yellow headscarf blending with her yellow hair.

"Your ID, Ma'am," Manu said.

She stopped at the metal detector, as if waking from a dream. "I don't have one." She clutched the arm of the woman in the scarf as if Manu shouted the request.

"She has a passport," the taller one said.

"Yes, fine." Manu took the passport, embossed with the gold American eagle. He noted the name, Martha, and her passport number onto the visitor sheet as the other woman fished for her ID. Something vaguely familiar about the slope of her nose. Manu gripped the pencil tighter. Yes, he worked for several months in hard labor, away from his one family member, and most women. But he didn't need to get crazy about each one. 'Reem', he read on her ID card.

"She used this entrance every morning?" the woman asked.

"Yes," Reem said in a low tone. "We used to come in together."

"Why, why didn't I come to visit before?" Martha, who Manu realized with sadness, was Lauren's mother, gazed out the window into the courtyard of his morning contemplation.

He kept his gaze averted, in the off chance Reem recognized him as well. Her attention, thankfully, remained on Lauren's mom, who rocked back and forth, clutching her elbows.

"Are you sure you're ready for this?"

"Yes," Martha said. She opened and closed her fists, taking Reem's arm, as she led her forward. "No," she said shaking her head when they stood in front of the other door. "She always helped. Fostering cats. Teaching English, Helping people. She loved people." Martha rambled to herself. "Why would anyone hurt Lauren? She helped so many women. Letting them stay with her."

Like who? Manu wondered. No sign of anyone else in the apartment. No roommate. A pristine guestroom with a full array of toiletries in the shower.

"She could always be relied on," Reem agreed. They exited the guard station.

Manu craned his neck, straining to hear the rest of the conversation. "Will we get to meet any of those girls she helped? I don't know how people here can live with themselves, making money off the backs of other people." He ignored the age-old questions about human rights. *What girls?*

"You know, she told me a few stories. About the cleaner in her classroom. They make like two hundred a month. So these men take them out to dinner, buy them, gifts… you know. She won't get in trouble for that, will she?" Martha's voice faded as the sliding glass doors enfolded the women into the school.

No more than she already has, Manu thought. His fingers itched to place a phone call to Ali. But he needed more information, facts to answer the questions Ali would ask. Why were these cleaners important? Because one of their male benefactors may have resented Lauren's interference enough to kill her, Manu reasoned. With a deep breath, he dialed Ali's number.

"There's something strange about some of the cleaners at this school," Manu said without preamble.

"Hm. I'm still interviewing people from the compound."

Manu stared at the empty courtyard, wondering how long it would take them to interview all the cleaners. There was no way he could talk to that many people without arousing suspicion.

"They make less than me. I mean, less than I made in construction."

"Right."

"But some of them have very nice things."

The *ding* of a text message interrupted Manu.

"I have to go," Ali said.

"What should I do?"

"Get a book or something," Ali said. "I'll look into this. Could be considered trafficking, if it's true and we can get people to talk to us. Two big ifs." The line went dead.

Alone in the guardroom, sitting in the air-conditioning, Manu felt the uselessness that haunted him since the construction site.

Chapter Nineteen

A li dropped the forensics report on his desk. A file so thin, none of the other papers moved. Lauren Miller was in her mid-twenties. She came to teach at the school as an adventure. Her parents lived in Texas. She died in a desert country thousands of miles away. He stared at the passport photo provided by the administration. A thin nose, doe eyes, a wide smile with a slight overbite, dark roots in need of the bleach applied to the ends of her hair. Average—not beautiful, not ugly. A face one would pass in the street without turning for a second glance. The details of her case filled his head so he couldn't think about this other woman, Sandra. He couldn't entertain the notion that the two deaths were connected. To do so meant that crime was on the rise in his country of under two million people. The city's population exploded in the last ten years. And with growing numbers came anonymity. With anonymity, crime. With crime, violence. He shook his head. This was an unproductive cycle for the city and also for cracking the case.

"What happened to you, Lauren?" he said to the photo as if she could answer. "How did someone get so angry that they put their hands around your neck?"

He drummed his fingers on the table. A clean living room; nothing knocked over, nothing taken. The entire apartment looked as if she were sleeping. Her computer and phone sat quietly, waiting for their owner to turn them on. Her shoes were lined up, ready to be put to use.

She lived alone. In a strange country. This was the argument people used to keep their sisters and daughters close to them. While heads wagged in sympathy, tongues clucked at the recklessness of foreign women. On her own, unmarried, living near men. What did she expect? The ringing phone offered no answers, only callers with more questions.

He flipped the file closed, to avoid her persistent gaze. Try as he could, he couldn't find fault with her. A dedicated kindergarten teacher. Class photos decorated her fridge, children as high as her waist, smiling into the camera, their teeth as white as the standard photographer's backdrop.

Girls crowded her knees, boys jostled in the corner. None of them wanted their beloved teacher dead. Maybe an irate parent? He sighed. The children were five- and six-years-old. If this were a question of misconduct, the kind that would make the parent of a kindergartener upset, the school would have records.

He was getting nowhere. Without a partner to talk ideas over with, he grasped at straws. The inert desktop screen stared at him like an unblinking eye. Everything in the office remained still, except for the desk phone. That rang like a banshee. He turned the ringer off, and the red light at the top of the receiver pulsed with each successive call. He tried to field the first few, but the rapid English and flow of questions proved more than he could deal with. On top of that, he tried to piece together the events of the evening and what he should do next. His head throbbed with the cacophony of voices calling about the dead woman. The American embassy wanted to know how the body was being handled. The employer wanted to know what to tell the rest of the employees, many of whom lived in the same compound where the murder took place. Above all these irritants – Khalifa's silence.

Ali threw himself into the swivel desk chair, letting the wheels skid behind the lip of the desk. He could have ridden the chair around the circumference of the office, along the curved bell of the outer wall that served as a bank of windows. On the street below, cars waited at the traffic light. Their passengers were caught up in the trivial details of their lives, unaware that a woman's ended and now Ali's future hung in the balance.

A mess. The whole thing was a mess, and here he was, at the center of it, when he was supposed to be on his way back up into the department's good graces. He needed some answers. He wanted guidance. Ali checked his uniform in the elevator mirror, his stomach churning. Going back to see Captain Khalifa this early in the investigation didn't inspire confidence.

"Is he in?" he asked Fahad, the secretary.

"In a meeting." Fahad's eyes didn't move from the iPad on his desk.

Ali sat. Two other officers sat there waiting, neither of whom Ali recognized. He sat straighter, pulling at his belt. The grey in their beards spoke of years of service.

Both men fiddled with their phones, one messaging away, the WhatsApp alerts pinging with each update. The other watched a video of a police protest in America. Fahad remained unfazed by all this volume. Ali took out his phone.

I have a lead on the flight attendant. Sandra. A message from Maryam.

He cradled his hand around the screen. Irritation and hope mingled together, giving him a sour taste in his mouth. *Tell me,* he wrote.

He thought of Maryam's involvement in his previous investigation as a singular event, precipitated by her connections to Daniel's family. Her continual involvement on new cases was not an option. Not if he wanted to see this marriage through in her father's good graces. Not to mention that his mother would have choice words for him if she knew the kind of information he shared with his fiancée.

The glass door to Khalifa's office swung open. The two men in the waiting area stood, exited with the third man who strode out of the office.

"Your turn," Fahad called to Ali.

"Hold everyone else," Khalifa summoned. "I'm leaving soon."

I have video.

He exhaled. *Meeting. Update me.*

Only if you do the same?

Doubt it, he wrote then deleted the letters. His university days were like a mirage of mirth, shimmering on the horizon of his memory. Maryam deserved the same, not to be drawn into the country's underbelly.

"Are you coming?"

"No, er, yes." Ali put the phone away, message unsent.

Fahad beckoned to him.

"Ali here to see you, Sir."

Khalifa waved him to the chair in front of the desk. He continued to talk into the receiver of the desk phone.

Ali waited, his thoughts churning.

"Tea, coffee, sir?" a man called from a few steps away. He looked to be about Manu's size and age without any of the energy. No spark in his eye, no gel in his hair. He didn't raise his eyes from Ali's shoes.

"No," Ali said. "Thank you."

The man returned with a bottle of water, placed a doily on the desk, and then set the water on top. Despite modern air-conditioning, desert hospitality survived. He scurried away as Khalifa ended his call.

"Okay, so what have you got? Signs of unusual activity?"

Ali started. "You didn't get my folder? Murder."

Khalifa shuffled through the pile on his desk. Ali tapped the brown dossier that held all the reports from the previous evening. Khalifa skimmed them, bowing his head and peering through his glasses at the handwriting. "She was found in the compound?"

"In her apartment. Sir, the embassy is calling. Parents, the company—I thought you replied."

Khalifa peered at him, the bags under his eyes magnified by the bifocal line in the lens. "Those aren't calls about this case," he said, wiping his nose. "Those are for the flight attendant. Gruesome. Naturally, they want those details."

"So who's dealing with that? Should I be looking at files—are they connected?" Ali stopped short. His string of questions made him sound like he second-guessed his boss.

"All of the other woman's details are coming straight to me. So far I see no parallels. Left a hotel late at night with guys. Don't think she was going to drink tea at one o'clock in the morning." Khalifa took off his glasses and rubbed his eyes with a sigh.

"Did we question the guys?"

Khalifa leveled Ali with a gaze. "Have a look at this CCTV footage and tell me if you recognize anyone." He gestured for Ali to approach a monitor on the corner of the desk.

Ali went over, pressing a button in the center of the display. He squinted at the grainy black-and-white images. The movement of the figures on-screen made them shadows. One form darted through a revolving glass door and into the back seat of a white Land Cruiser. "She left with locals? Did anyone make out the plate? Do we have footage of her going in? Alone or with others?"

"I'm tired."

"Sir?" Ali turned from the gray scale of the monitor to his supervisor's ashen face.

Khalifa folded his hands on the desk. "Those guys who were in here, they were checking up on me because I have cancer."

Ali recoiled. That word catapulted him into the heart of his father's illness. The smell of the hospital room. His teenage years spent coming and going from chemo treatment after treatment. Escorting his father with his uncles to London for the best of care—the word 'cancer' brought with it his aborted childhood.

"How long?" he managed.

Khalifa laughed, a hollow sound that sounded part-howl. "You know these doctors. One says months, the other weeks. Months," he said. "Like Yusuf, *allah yerhamo.*"

His father's childhood friend and the most faithful of all the visitors, including the extended family, Khalifa was a bulwark against time. Of everyone, he knew what lay ahead, having witnessed it firsthand. "Stage two, already. It's in my lungs. Too much smoking. All those years on duty."

Ali twisted the cap off the bottle of water, his hands shaking. He drank half of it.

"So they have someone handling the parents and company for the flight attendant." Khalifa tapped Ali's file. "That family is going to the media."

Ali groaned. "That's how it made it to Twitter." Police work was so much easier before the days of citizen journalism.

"You have to act before the teacher's family does the same. Give them something to go on," Khalifa said. "A suspect. Any idea who might have done it?"

"Someone close to her," Ali said. "Strangulation is a classic sign of an angry intimate."

"There's another team working with the guys who found the flight attendant." Khalifa grunted. "You focus on yours. Any sign of a boyfriend?"

"Not yet. She wasn't seeing anyone. But—" The forlorn sound of Manu's voice rang in his ear, "—maybe someone she rejected?"

Khalifa steepled his fingers.

"She ran these English courses for security guards on the weekend. I'm going to interview them on Friday."

"They let women into those camps?"

Ali grunted his concurrent dismay.

"These foreigners, intending good and causing harm at the same time."

She thought she helped. Ali didn't say it; he'd wandered out of line several times already. He thought of Maryam and her interest in the case, her help in finding Manu. Khalifa would no doubt disapprove of a local girl getting involved with migrants, based on his reaction to the ex-pat being there.

"I'll assign some guys to you. Help you get the details."

"Thank you," Ali said. This was the first formal offer of help he'd received since his demotion.

"Don't bring them in on the other project."

Ali's mind swam with the details of the grisly murder of the flight attendant. By comparison, Lauren's strangulation seemed mundane. He leaned closer, embarrassed by his distraction. "I'll need another guy to station at the first location."

"I cleared that compound. The teacher was a coincidence."

How would you know that? We haven't been there long enough to gather information for the first report.

"There is more than one team. They were sent ahead of you, to confirm," Khalifa said in a soothing tone.

Ali clenched his hands. His supervisor read his distrust like a map in the frown lines around his mouth. "Then the team may have seen something related to the murder. Or some connection with this one. Could be a sign of escalation."

Khalifa waved his hand as if brushing away a cloud of smoke, one of the many that contributed to his illness. "They didn't stay long. They cleared the compound and went to another in the area."

If he gives me this mission and assigns others to the same place, then he can't have that much trust in me. The realizations fired like the first push on a set of dominos. *If he doesn't think I can do it alone or wants insurance to make sure I don't miss anything then the reinstatement can't be a sure thing.*

His left eye twitched. No reinstatement, more off-the-books work, or worse—returning to traffic police.

Jaber may have turned a blind eye to his future son-in-law's occupation, but the rest of the family wouldn't be so kind. Especially if they saw Ali, a foreign-trained Sandhurst graduate, standing in the middle of a roundabout directing traffic.

"Find the guy, and let's get back to our real job," Khalifa said. Wrinkles made deep grooves around his mouth and eyes.

"We're trying," Ali said.

"Find him."

"Yes, Sir."

After a few more instructions from Khalifa, Ali left, his hopes of restoration deflated. A deformity was no longer his only limitation. He needed to be better than someone else. Someone he whose strengths and weaknesses he didn't know. Someone who would make a murderer out of a fitting suspect rather than find one.

Footage from hotel security quality is terrible, he confided in Maryam out of frustration and hope that she would let it go. Her reply brought him up short. A series of letters and numbers that opened up a link. A link that showed Sandra still alive, getting into the same car from the hotel footage.

Only this time he could see the three-digit plate that sent a tingle of alarm down his spine. Ali knew that plate like he knew his own vehicle. His cousin Hassan's car.

"This number cannot be reached at this time," said the automated voice.

Chapter Twenty

Submerged animals floated in the soapsuds. Sanjana pushed the plastic ape back under the water. Whitish grime coated his arms, having spent time in the post-lunch grip of one of the younger children.

"Goodbye," called Sarah to a redheaded girl and her mother. Slim-hipped and British, most of the ex-pat parents sought out her classroom, wanting their children to be in one with a native English speaker.

Sanjana drained the sink, running water over the remaining suds. The toys would dry overnight on the long blue towel before they returned to their respective bins, to be mauled again tomorrow.

"Ah, let's send Sajita to the holding room," Sarah called to her assistant. The plump Filipina woman bustled about, gathering the child's bag and water bottle. "Come, Sajita. Your mommy is late." The girl's ponytail bobbed as she followed along, through the common area between the nursery classrooms, a hot-pink ribbon matching her dress and shoes.

This was the moment Sanjana waited for since her first encounter with Laxmi Pande. Today she would confront the woman and threaten to go to the police. Laxmi wouldn't recognize an empty threat and would be too scared to call her bluff. She hummed on her way to sweep the reception area.

"I'm sorry but that's our policy," Betsy said.

Sanjana stopped in the doorway, letting her have her moment with the parent at the counter.

"But we have paid monthly since my daughter started going here."

Sanjana disappeared behind the corner. There was the object of her scrutiny, Laxmi, face screwed up in confusion, painted lips twisted in a frown.

"Yes, new management I'm afraid." Betsy put away office supplies in the drawer: her stapler, receipt book, a ball made of rubber bands. "Everyone has to pay termly."

"That's three thousand dollars," Laxmi said.

"It is a business in the end."

"My daughter loves going here."

"Good afternoon!" Betsy called out to the water deliveryman, startling him on the ramp. "Yes, bring that one in this way."

Laxmi shuffled past Sanjana, mumbling an 'excuse me' on her way to the room where her daughter waited. The girl squealed at the sight of her mother, who knelt and opened her arms to her. "One more week, my girl," she said into her hair, gathering her into a tight embrace.

Sanjana crept across the blue mats in the soft play area, stealing across the open area before they came out. *A week, a week.* The words were a drumbeat in her mind, quickening in pace. She needed more time.

She said little in the car on the way home. Vinay prattled on about how his booming business, so many trips to and from the airport on business. What did her sir do again? Sanjana kept her answers perfunctory, popping out the car when he slowed in front of the house. The still interior of the home quieted her racing mind. Without Manu or Ali to back her up, any of her actions lacked teeth. The doorbell interrupted the downward turn of her thoughts.

She opened the door a crack. "Hello?"

"Hello. Reham." The girl stuck out her hand. She wore her backpack slung over the other shoulder.

Sanjana took the girl's hand, surprised by her grip. "Yes?"

"I'm the tutor," Reham said slowly, enunciating each word.

"Oh, yes. I forgot." Sanjana clapped her hands over her mouth. "Today? Do we have to start today?"

"Daniel said you were interested in learning to read but couldn't come to the classes we offer on Fridays."

"Yes, yes." Sanjana stepped aside. She accepted the offer of help, since the family forced it on her. She led the girl through the living room, over the wool Turkish rugs, to the dining table. "Would you like some water?"

"I brought my own." Reham tapped a plastic bottle with a purple-topped lid. "Have a seat."

Sanjana did as she was told. Her new tutor couldn't be much older than Manu. She wished her brother were in the room with them. The oval table could comfortably seat sixteen.

"Alright, let's begin with this test." Reham placed a blue booklet with a pencil in front of Sanjana.

"Test?" Sanjana squeaked.

"Oh, no." Reham pressed two fingers to her forehead. "That's not what I meant." She folded her hands on the table with a big smile. "Let's begin with an exercise."

Sanjana grimaced. She opened the booklet; the trick would not work on her. There were four rows of words. She could read none of them.

"Okay, what letters do you recognize?" Reham asked, her eyes tracking every facial twitch.

"I—I—"

Reham put her hand on Sanjana's palm. "We'll take it as slow as you need."

Sharif tore into kitchen from the side door with Daniel hot on his heels. "Has your mom got anything to eat?"

"I don't know. We can ask Sanjana to make us something."

The boys stopped short at Reham explaining the difference between vowels and consonants.

"Sorry." Daniel ducked into the fridge, emerging with soda.

"Don't I know you?" Sharif strolled closer.

"I think I've seen you around," Reham said.

Sanjana detected a new stiffness in her tone. The teenagers eyed each other.

"Yeah, I'm at the medical program. So I come over for lunch sometimes," Sharif said.

That boy is going to be a doctor? Sanjana reconsidered whether she'd been too hard on him. Or what the standards were for medicine in this country.

"We're just getting started." Reham waved at the papers in front of them.

"Right." Daniel tugged at his friend's shirt, pulling him up the stairs.

"She's tutoring your nanny? What's the point? Tell her I'll tutor her in a thing or two."

Daniel shushed him.

Sanjana's momentary re-evaluation of Sharif crumbled. "They friends for long time."

"He's got quite the reputation on campus," Reham muttered.

"Oh, for what?"

Her eyes flickered. "Ah, you know, freshmen. They think they're in high school part two." She laughed as though this were a joke they shared. "Let's get back to it, shall we?"

Sanjana wrote the first ten letters. Then she wrote them again, big and small. Then she wrote them again in combinations of words. The fourth time Reham showed her how to write letters, she said she would be right back after a trip to the bathroom. She slipped into the one in the dining area, looking out the window for a few moments, without those sounds buzzing in her ear. Betsy's polite façade mocked her. She knew Sanjana couldn't master these skills. She flushed the toilet and pretended to run water over her hands, letting the gushing faucet flow for a few minutes. Ten minutes left, and then no lesson until next week. She came back to her chair.

"You're doing so well," Reham said.

Sanjana picked up the pencil again.

Reham scrolled through her phone as Sanjana struggled to complete the activity. She focused, vowing to call Meena that night and double check all the kids attended school. She wouldn't let her sister or her brothers end up with this same fate.

She pressed on the pencil, breaking the tip, at the thought that the kids, Ram and Raja, were probably working on activities exactly like this.

"Okay, let's take another break, maybe." Reham took a sip of water.

"I'm sorry." Sanjana put the pencil down with shaking hands.

"Don't be," Reham said. "You're doing better than half the men we teach on the weekends."

"Thanks." Sanjana flushed.

"I mean it."

"Hm," Sanjana said.

"Hey, Reham," a male voice said.

Reham bounced up from her chair. "Professor Paul."

Sanjana straightened as Sir Paul came through the side door. She glanced from Reham to Sir Paul and back. No mistaking the sheen of devotion in Reham's face, upturned like a flower, drawing in the rays of her sun. Sanjana recognized it because she wore it herself. Sir drew women into his orbit, with his urbane manner and broad shoulders.

"How's it going?" He slung his messenger bag against the wall.

"She's great," Reham gushed as if Sanjana weren't there. "Such a quick learner. I told her she's better than most of the students in our learning program."

Professor Paul rolled his neck a few times. "Good, good. Thanks for coming over."

"Of course!"

"I'll see you on campus." He left the room, oblivious of the way Reham trailed his movements.

Reham sank back into her chair. When she saw Sanjana gazing at her, she jumped forward, elbows on the table. "So, back to the letters."

"Yes." Sanjana sharpened the pencil, emboldened by her insight into the real reason the girl sat next to her. She could have told her that Sir Paul's main efforts went towards work, and there was no one who could budge him. His family got the leftovers. But if this girl went to the camps, worked with migrants, and sat here at the table with the likes of Sanjana, maybe she knew this already.

The boys trooped back through the dining room, a duffel bag over each of their shoulders, clinking noises resounding with every step, like the sound of glass. Daniel slouched his way to the door.

"Where you going with that?"

"None of your business," Sharif called over his shoulder. "You're not his mom."

Sanjana grit her teeth.

"Returning some stuff I borrowed to Sharif," Daniel said.

"Your father is home," Sanjana retorted. Nothing could open the closed door to Sir Paul's study, save a bomb blast.

Sharif picked up his pace, leaving the house.

Daniel gave a furtive look over his shoulder towards Sanjana and a silent Reham, then at the closed door. "I'll be back later."

"Someone needs to keep a closer eye on them," Reham said quietly.

Sanjana scratched out more letters. She wanted to tell her to mind her own business, but she knew Reham was right. Sanjana spent hours scrubbing the drunken stench out of the sofa, shuttling the cushions back and forth to the dry-cleaner.

"And he's running for student government," Reham said under her breath.

"What is this government?"

"It's like a group that decides things for other students. And they organize events, you know."

Sanjana didn't.

"They get elected. It's like a mini-democratic process, but we aren't in a democracy. Like they are in America. So it's ironic, being in a constitutional monarchy and having these student elections to teach us about a system that's not our own." Reham giggled.

None of this made any sense to Sanjana. Sounded more like children playing at being grown-ups. The girl next to her knew so much more about the world than Sanjana did. "Do you have boyfriend?"

Reham started. "Excuse me?"

"I mean…" Sanjana took a deep breath. "Are you having boyfriend?"

"I understood the question." The girl drew closer, her brown eyes earnest. "Why?"

"How are you knowing if someone, you know, if you are liking someone?"

"Oh." Reham pushed away the books.

"Or if he is liking you," Sanjana said in a smaller voice.

"Well…" Reham leaned on her elbows. "How many times have you been out?"

"Once," Sanjana said. "To Hot Chicken."

"Right." Reham tapped the table. "And since then? Has he called? Or texted?"

She shook her head. "He no have number." Her difficulty in talking about Vinay hindered her English.

"Did he ask for it?"

The crumpled paper she'd destroyed. "Yes. In a way."

"Did you give it to him?"

She shook her head.

"He's probably confused." Reham tapped her chin. "If he asked and you didn't give it to him, he probably thinks you're not interested. Are you?"

Sanjana cleared her throat. She squeaked, "I don't know."

"Is he a nice guy?"

"Hi girls." Madam breezed in, her heels clicking across the floor. "Oh, you have a friend over."

"This my tutor," Sanjana said, standing.

Reham extended her hand, her eyes taking in every inch of Cindy, from her blow-dry to her neutral manicure.

Sanjana watched it all. *That is your competition. Good luck.* Reham's youth seemed childish to Madam's cultivated beauty, her even skin tone, smoothed by powder, and dresses with darts in all the right places.

"Hi." Madam's eyes flickered between them. "We appreciate you coming in and helping Sanjana like this."

"Yes, sure." This second the affirmation was calmer, less enthusiastic.

"Going well?"

"Yes." Sanjana smiled, perhaps too widely, as Madam gave her a second look.

"Great. I'll let you get back to it." Cindy took the stairs two at a time.

"Sir is in the study," Sanjana called after her.

"Working, probably." Madam's voice drifted down to them.

Reham sank back into her chair. She sniffed. "She's gorgeous."

Sanjana squinted at the handwriting exercises.

"Even the air around her smells good."

Sanjana kept writing.

"Is that a real Hermes bag?" Reham's eyes were unfocused, in the direction of the stairwell.

Sanjana put down her pencil. "Madam Cindy and Sir Paul been married for twenty-five years," she said, leveling a gaze at the girl.

"Of course," Reham stuttered, starting as if from a trance. "I hope you found this lesson helpful." Reham reviewed Sanjana's work, flicking through the pages.

"Yes," Sanjana said, glancing at the clock. Somehow their hour sped by. She jumped up. "I must cook." Sanjana cleared the papers, stacking them in a pile and pulling the pencils together with her other hand.

"Huh, okay. See you next week?"

"Yes, yes," Sanjana shepherded the girl to the door. She should have prepped the ingredients for the lasagna Madam asked her to make. Measuring everything would slow her down by at least fifteen minutes.

"My phone!" Reham turned at the door, rifling through the front and back pockets of her jeans.

They looked around the table and china hutch, searching under Sanjana's homework papers and the chair cushions.

"Can you call it?" Reham read out the numbers. The buzz came from the bookshelf. Sanjana put her hand on the second shelf, the blue-white flash of the screen flickering on the dark wood surface.

As she pulled it out, she recognized a face in the screensaver. "Oh," she exclaimed, fumbling as Manu's grin flashed up at her with each buzz.

"Thanks!" Reham caught the phone with her left hand.

"You know those men?" Sanjana asked, biting her lip against the tirade of questions she wanted to unleash on the girl. Why were there so many of them? Where were they? She hardly recognized her brother as the grinning man in the photo standing close to this girl and a few other white women.

"These are the guys we tutor," Reham said, tucking the phone into the back pocket of her jeans.

"Tutor?"

"Yeah, like you. On the weekends. Only we show them how to use computers. Why?"

Ali's dire warning loomed in front of her. "No, nothing doing, just curious." Sanjana took Reham by the elbow, escorting her to the door once more. So this is what her brother did on the weekends in the weeks since he moved back out on assignment. Why he was too busy to answer her calls or come home for some food.

"See you next week," Sanjana said, injecting a false note of cheer in her voice.

"Yes, see you."

Reham waved as Sanjana shut the door in her face. She leaned her forehead against it, hoping her life would end. Taking English lessons from someone young enough to be her sister while her brother learned computer skills from the same person. Madam Cindy complained about the smallness of this city. A population of fewer than two million people suffocated her. Even in this fishpond Sanjana, and other domestics like her, were invisible to the sea of ex-pats and locals. Yet maybe not for long. She would find Vinay's number, from that slip of paper. Didn't she deserve to have some fun like everyone else? She didn't have to be the good older sister any more.

The kitchen door slammed, a rush of pounding feet announced Daniel and Sharif's return. So much for her own life. She ventured upstairs, to check out what brought Daniel and that good-for-nothing boy back so soon this late in the day. It couldn't be anything good. Sanjana pushed open the door, hoping to find them bent over their homework. Instead, Sharif sobbed on the floor next to the bed, the two boys sitting shoulder to shoulder.

"It's not your fault your father is a loser," Daniel said. "Nobody blames you."

"He cheated on my mom," Sharif sniffed. "With more than one person. One of them a maid." The derision in his voice drove Sanjana back into the hallway. Everyone discussed this in hushed tones; the very public breakup of John, Sharif's father, and Amira after the death of an unmarried Filipina maid on the compound. His mother threw his clothes out of the second story window, disgracing the pilot and eventually getting him fired by the national airline which thought of adultery as employee misconduct. "Now everyone is saying he could be tied to this thing with that flight attendant. You know, a habit, fooling around with women, cheating."

"I didn't know your dad was in the country," Daniel said softly.

"There is no proof," Sharif said, sniffing. "He wasn't here and so it's the rumor mill. And there's no proof he did anything with that maid. You know people on the compound think my dad fathered that baby? Imagine. Me with a half-brother from a maid."

"Maids are people too," Daniel muttered.

Sanjana flushed.

"Now I have to split up everything, alternate this and that. Christmas, then spring break, and summer is coming up. They'll make me choose."

"Okay, so who do you want to be with?"

"You don't understand anything! You have both your parents."

"Hey listen, my dad is always gone and—"

"Your dad is going to win the Pulitzer Prize one day. My dad probably gave someone herpes."

Daniel sighed. His footsteps came towards the door.

Sanjana glanced around for something, anything, to pretend to clean and succeeded in knocking over a few picture frames on the hallway bookcase.

"Is he—"

"Leave him alone," Daniel snorted. "This is what he's like when he's not on alcohol."

"I make you something to eat?"

"Yes," Daniel said, relief flooding his face. "How about steak? Do we have steak?"

"I check," Sanjana said, scuttling down the stairs into the safety of the kitchen. She opened the freezer, standing before the blast of cool air, wishing it could blow away the shame in her heart. Here she hated Sharif, thought of him as a useless child, and all the while, he grieved for his parents. She pulled out the *filet mignon* Madam bought for the rare occasions Sir was home. The boys needed a treat. And after all, she finished her first lesson. She deserved a treat too.

Sanjana bustled about the kitchen, the familiar rhythm of food preparation soothing her into a thoughtless state. Daniel still needed her. These men-in-the-making were more fragile than they appeared. For a moment, she would let Laxmi Pande and the cares of the world rest while she took care of a few members of her family.

Chapter Twenty One

A li paced in the box that was his office. If he could puff on a cigarette, that would give him something to do with his hands. Jaber could use any excuse to call off the marriage before the wedding reception. Smoking separated the men from young kids. He spent most of the night trying to find his cousin, with no success. Short of going into the house and alarming the entire household, he waited for Hassan to make contact. Meanwhile, a host of other problems haunted Ali. At the knock on the door, he started out of his morose circle of thoughts. "Yes," he called.

Ralph entered, flanked by two silent police officers. "What am I doing here?" His eyes scanned the room. When he saw Ali, he flinched.

"Hello, Ralph."

"Do you have a Miranda warning in this country? I want a lawyer."

Ali indicated that the officers could go. "This isn't the movies," he said. He offered Ralph a seat. "But no, you are not under arrest." *Not yet, anyway.*

"Then why am I here? My employer will send you a bill for lost time at work."

"Water?" Ali slid a bottle across.

"Yes, thank you." Ralph's manners kicked in, and he took down half the bottle in one gulp.

"Please tell me what you know about this photo." Ali displayed the photo of Ralph in Lauren's window.

Ralph sputtered water down his chin. "Where did you get that?"

"Who took it?" Ali countered.

"I helped clean her windows," Ralph protested. He clawed at the box of tissue on the desk, dabbing at his chin and leaving behind white tufts of tissue.

"At Lauren's request?"

"Of course! I'm not some kind of peeping Tom."

"Your compound doesn't have people to do this kind of thing?" Ali dropped the phone on his desk, leveling a stare at the fidgeting man.

"Okay, I went up to get a kitten. A cat delivered her litter on the window sill and I helped get them down."

Ali leaned back in his chair. Khalifa was right. This was going to be easy. "Which is it? Dirty windows? Or a pregnant cat."

"Both." Ralph stuttered. "I did both. What's the date on that photo?"

Ali frowned. He read the date back, weeks before her death. Ralph produced another image from his own phone, arms filled with kittens the size of his palm. Plus his utter panic belied the truth. "You frequently helped Lauren," Ali paraphrased, taking a different tack.

"Someone needed to," Ralph said. He took a shuddering breath. "She did so much for everyone else. The neighborhood cats, the maintenance guys, whoever. She would run out of gas on the weekend, carpooling with others to work. And who would she call? Me." His voice broke.

Ali said nothing, allowing Ralph a moment to catch his breath.

"I never would have hurt her," Ralph whispered.

Ali closed his eyes, wishing he could stop up his ears against the next phrase.

"I loved her."

You and every lonely heart in the neighborhood, Ali thought, the memory of the fake engagement ring taunting him. "I only have your word that you were outside her window to help," he said woodenly, out of habit.

Ralph showed him a photo from his phone, tears sliding down his face. In his arms were three black kittens, each small enough to fit in a palm. "September 15," he said. "Two months before she died."

"She swiped left on you," Ali said. He flung the plastic bag with Lauren's phone between them in a last-ditch effort to get to the truth.

"I was her best friend," Ralph countered, eyes lowered. "She told me everything."

"Hm," Ali said. Dead end. But he couldn't let the man go, not when he was his most viable suspect.

"She told me why she let all those girls stay with her. The cleaners from the school. Lauren thought it horrible how little they were paid, how they made up for it with their friends," Ralph paused to give air quotes. "She called it Friendo, a weird type of escort service. So she would let the girls stay with her on the weekend. Taught them how to make American food, watched movies." He hiccupped. Tears streamed down his face.

*

For the first time all day, the line connected. They got the perfunctory pleasantries out of the way.

"I need permission to question everyone at the school," Ali said.

Khalifa wheezed on the other end of the phone. "Most of them are women."

"I'll ask someone from their side to be present," he said. "Are you okay?"

Khalifa wheezed some more. The answer wasn't definitive in either case. "They're coming to unhook the machines. Check with Haytham."

"Yes, sir. About the victim's family—"

"You want to be back on traffic patrol?"

"Excuse me?"

"Do you want to be back in the traffic department? Standing at the roundabout, telling people when to stop and when to go, using your body like a shield instead of a signal?"

"No. No, sir."

"Get on with this and back to the assignment I gave you." The line went dead.

Ali stared at the phone, the swirl of emotions battling inside him. He couldn't look beyond Lauren's death, not now that he'd met the mother and her friends. Lauren was unlike anything he expected about ex-pat women. She didn't sleep around, she wasn't an alcoholic, she helped other women, and she worked hard. She was a teacher.

And she died in his country.

Ali wasn't one to personalize his work, but this case kept nagging at him from all angles. Haytham was his competition. Older, more established. Someone Khalifa fast-tracked after routine physicals revealed Ali's deformity. He drove over to the school. He thought best on his feet. Maybe he would talk to some of the other teachers first, the administration. He strode through the guard station, wondering how much he should share with the principal. She would likely be upset her calls were unanswered.

"Can I help you, sir?" Manu shot to his feet.

He stopped short of the entrance, the familiar voice turning his head. He blinked a few times. There, dwarfed by the guard desk in front of the school, stood Manu. "You're here?"

Manu held on to his hand for a few seconds after the handshake. "Yes, yes."

Ali scratched his head. If Khalifa transferred Manu here, was it because he knew about the connection to the woman's death? They lived in a small country. But that small?

"Good. You can help me," Ali said.

"Someone has to take my place."

"We'll get someone," Ali said. "I'll be back."

He walked the perimeter of the school, shading his eyes against the mid-day light. A massive boundary wall surrounded the school on all sides. As an embassy affiliate, striped bomb barricades could be raised at any moment between the street and the entryway. The entrance to the classrooms sat several hundred yards from the street, a safe distance from a car bomb or would-be assailant. Boys and girls tumbled out into the playground of yellow-and-red play structures. Ali stood still as they milled around him, oblivious to his uniform. He placed them at around second-graders.

"May I help you?" A woman with short brown hair in tight, kinky curls squinted up at him. She kept her eyes on his face. He registered the moment she recognized his uniform.

"Nothing serious," he said. "I'm looking around."

"Do you have children at this school?"

"I'm not—" He couldn't use a term they would understand. According to the law, he was married. According to his culture, he was engaged. "Did you know Lauren Brown?"

The woman blinked. "Yes, yes. She taught in my grade."

He leaned closer. "I'm investigating her death."

Her eyes rounded. "Do you have any leads?"

He pointed a finger between them. "We have to keep this very quiet."

"All guests have to sign in."

"Ms. Craft? Ms. Craft?" a childish voice called to her.

"Don't worry. I won't bother anyone." Ali stepped into the cool, dark interior of the hallway. The noise of the playground drifted away as he wandered the hallways in the kindergarten area. Bulletin boards filled with photos, drawings and paintings lined both sides.

'Book reviews' one said. 'Paintings by Georgia O'Keefe' proclaimed another. He knew that the ex-pats recreated pieces of home—the compounds were one example. The embassy was another. This classroom, however, transported you into another country. Laminated and named cubbies lined the perimeter of the classroom, pastel-colored chairs and desks, and smiling, smiling, smiling children beamed from bulletin boards around the room. He couldn't remember much from his school days; nor could he come up with the name of Aisha's school

He eyed the open supply room, stacked shelf-to-ceiling with papers, pens, markers and glue sticks. He passed a room where he recognized the strains of *The Sound of Music*. He and Maha attended government schools, gender-segregated, taught in Arabic.

Through a window of an empty class, he saw yet another playground. What a place. A land where children learned their multiplication tables while hanging upside down from monkey bars? He felt more alien here than in the Industrial Area or when traveling abroad.

His days at Sandhurst were in recognition of his late father's service to the country. Part of the reason Ali kept to himself in the barracks was because life with his family of mostly women did not equip him to interact with foreigners, and mostly men at that. He knew someone who went to a school like this. Maybe this very one.

"*Salaam alaikum*," he said when Maryam answered in the middle of the first ring.

"*Wa alaikum a salaam*," she replied.

"Did you go to this international school?" He said the name, stopping in front of a row of computers—Apple desktop screens bigger than the one on his desk in the office.

"Yes." Her reply came as part sigh and part laugh. "Why? Where did you go?"

He named a government school for boys, in a low growl, hoping she wouldn't ask him to repeat it.

"Oh, the scientific one."

Did she sound impressed?

"Any idea where the cleaners would be during the day?"

"The cleaners?" Maryam repeated as if this were the most natural conversation to be having with one's fiancé. "Check the break rooms."

"Break room?"

"You know, where they go to rest between their shifts."

Ali didn't know. How would he locate the signs of such a room?

"They're scattered throughout the buildings. Look near the toilets. They're usually closets that they sit in near there."

"Thanks." He scanned the numbers next to each of the rooms. Pre-K, the hallway full of toys, and other objects.

"Still about that teacher?"

"Hmm," he said.

"You should ask the cleaner who works in her room," Maryam said.

"Oh?" He found the male restroom.

"Yes. Some of them are there for years, the teachers and the cleaners. While the assistant teachers come in and out. So they are very close."

"Okay." He stopped in front of the female sign for the bathroom.

Two women sat in the room next to it on plastic chairs, mops and bottles of cleaning supplies at their feet.

"I'll come get you tonight," he said.

"Tonight?"

"If you want," he amended.

"Yes, anything away from here."

The women in the closet were looking at him now.

"Is it that bad?"

She sighed. "Since Nasser left, the house has been like a tomb."

He smiled and tried to offer a friendly grin. The women stiffened.

"Tonight, I'll text you. Let's go for tea."

"Tea?" she repeated.

The wider of the two woman edged towards the door, eyeing the space between Ali and the doorframe like a trapped hare.

"Have to go for now," he said. "I'll think of something more manly."

That sound, he could soon hear it whenever he wanted. If he could keep making her laugh. Ali's smile faded as the called ended, under the watchful gaze of a few women in blue uniforms. He stood straighter, a foot or so taller than the women.

"Hello." He approached them with his hands out, like he would a stray cat. They looked at each other and then at him. Ali's shoulders filled the narrow doorway. If they wanted to leave, they'd have to pass directly by him. "Did you know the teacher?"

They looked at each other instead of at the photo he dangled in front of them. Lauren's last staff portrait, her teeth as white as the startling background, the pink of her turtleneck at odds with the desert temperature.

"No," the chubbier one said. She jumped up, getting together a spray bottle and turning on the industrial sink to fill the mop bucket.

"You?"

The other woman shook her head. She avoided looking at the photo and bit her lip. "Not here."

Ali bent forward to hear.

"Her cleaner not here. Next wing."

"You show me," he said.

The woman didn't move.

He repeated the request, raising his voice above the sound of the rushing water, when she hopped up and dashed past him. He followed her, impressed by how quickly someone half his size could walk.

"There." She pointed a finger toward the left of the building where the hallway split in two. "She's there."

"Name?"

"Sumitha," came floating back to him.

His footsteps echoed in the hall as he walked past closed doors and students sealed inside bubbles of knowledge. He strode through the less colorful older hallways, past rows of lockers, looking for the restrooms and custodians' closets.

"Can I help you?" A bald Indian man, several inches taller than Ali, stepped into his path.

"Yes. I'm looking for the cleaner on this floor?"

"And you are?"

"Ali." He said nothing else, waited for the man to move aside.

"Do you have permission to be here?"

"I am investigating Lauren Brown's death."

"Her murder."

"Her murder," Ali conceded.

The man's jaw worked. "This way." He went around the corner and into an alcove before the elevator. He rapped on the door three times. 'Sumitta' is what the name sounded like in his flat American vowels.

A grown woman about Aisha's size poked her head around the side of the door. "Sir?"

"This man would like to speak to you."

Her eyes rounded at the sight of Ali.

"Here," he opened the door to an empty classroom. "They're in P.E. You can talk in here."

The woman walked behind them, head down. Ali saw her chin trembling. "I'll wait outside," he said.

Ali took a seat behind the teacher's desk. Sumitha sat in one of the student chairs.

"You knew Lauren Brown?"

"Yes."

He leaned toward her in order to hear the breathed words. "How did you know her?"

"I cleaned in her room."

Ali scribbled this down, though he wouldn't likely forget the sorrow that dragged at the folds of her face like gravity, aging her twenty-something features into those of a much older woman.

"Did you know anyone who would want to hurt her?"

Sumitha shook her head.

"Did you hear her arguing with anyone?"

Sumitha shook her head again.

"What do you think happened?"

She shrugged.

Ali tapped his pen on the blank half of the page. No answer. Not good. "I need your help."

She glanced at him, her gaze ricocheting to the whiteboard behind him when he didn't blink or look away.

"Did you ever stay with Lauren?"

The same boomerang of a glance.

"At her house." Ali edged his chair closer. "Did Lauren ever offer for you to stay with her?"

Sumitha rubbed her hands together. "Me, no. Not me. But other girls."

Ali squirmed with impatience. "What other girls?"

A bell sounded.

"I have to go," Sumitha said. "Cleaning time while children are at lunch."

Short of physically restraining her, Ali could do nothing to keep her from leaving.

The man at the door leaned in the frame. "Get anything useful?"

"He said there were girls who stayed with Lauren." Ali pushed up from the chair. "Any idea who they might be?"

The man stepped to the side, bent on escorting Ali out of the high school. "You'd have to ask them."

"How many cleaners work here?"

"One hundred. Maybe two hundred?" He shrugged.

Ali saw himself out to the side entrance and returned to the guard station. Manu's eyes lit up when he saw him. "Did you find her? What did she say?"

Ali flung himself into the chair in the corner. "Nothing. Girls stayed at Lauren's. That, we already knew."

Chapter Twenty Two

Maryam adjusted the long flaps of her *shayla* so they hung evenly on either side of her head. She drew the black fabric tight under her chin, then over the crown of her head, repeating the action in the other direction.

"Get all your hair in there," her mother said. "Not like when you go to university. Not that *abaya* please."

Maryam pulled at the edges, wrapping them around her body. The latest in *abaya* style disregarded the snap buttons that gathered the edges together. The new style, worn like a robe, required the wearer to hold closed the two edges under her arm. As she walked, the wrap loosened, often allowing glimpses of legs, clothing, and shoes. "I'm not going to hide who I am."

Her mother *ts*ked. "No need for such dramatics. You're a month or so away from the reception."

The chimes from the intercom on the front gate stopped the burgeoning lecture.

"Have fun." Fatma pressed her lips to Maryam's cheek.

"I never thought I'd hear those words," Maryam said.

"Not too much fun." Fatma pinched Maryam's arm, above the elbow.

"Ouch." Maryam swept out the side door, thankful to escape her father's scrutiny. Fatma hovered in the window. Her mother's gaze trailed her out until the gate shut. Maryam marched to the passenger side door, pulling herself into the SUV.

"*Salaam alaikum.*"

"*Alaikum a salaam.*" Ali palmed the steering wheel, guiding the vehicle through the neighborhood streets.

"Bad day?"

He gave her a glance. "Does it show?"

She laughed at his forced smile and the deep grooves around his mouth.

"Your right eye is twitching."

Ali glanced in the rear-view mirror. "Where do you want to go?"

"Somewhere private," she said.

"No locals?"

"Without locals," she agreed.

He drove on for a few minutes, twisting through the side streets of adobe-colored houses with boundary walls, until the houses shrank smaller and the walls lower. They'd entered the older part of the city now, away from the steel and glass and glitz of the downtown business district.

Shops occupied both sides of the two-lane road: a Vodafone outlet, a rug showroom, a noodle house and a kebab place. Ali reversed into a spot in front of a flashing sign that said 'Thai Snack'. He stopped the car.

"This okay?" His words came out as a low growl, a challenge.

"Fine by me." She swung herself out of the car and onto the pavement, thankful for her flats.

The Thai waiter sat them straight away at a table in the back, his eyes going from Ali to Maryam and back. He handed them menus and reappeared with a set of glasses and bottle of water.

"What's good here?" Maryam eyed the multi-page pictorial menu.

Ali burst into laughter. "I've never eaten here before."

She closed the menu. "Then what are we doing here?"

His mirth wound down to chuckles. "Testing each other."

"Did I pass?"

"I think I failed," he said.

"Case closed." She pushed against the table to stand.

"No," he put his palm on top of hers.

Maryam turned, the force of both their attention on where their bodies touched. The first time, the first of many that would be his right as her husband. In a country where marital rape did not exist as a legal category, she would be entirely his.

He let go. "I mean, let's stay. If I haven't failed."

She sat. "No one would come here with me. Nasser would have the food delivered."

"You like that I take you strange places?" He took a deep breath and opened the menu. "There's no one to worry about. No one to see us."

She picked up the menu and ordered spring rolls when the waiter returned.

"Hot and sour soup," Ali said.

The waiter scurried away, an electronic stylus tapping away at the screen of a handheld device.

"I like that you take me to a city I've lived in my whole life and never seen," she replied. "No breaks in the case?" That he could surprise her ranked second favorite thing on the growing list of admirable attributes of her husband. His life was interesting. His work was important.

"Not one," Ali said. "The cleaners seemed like a possibility, but turned out to be a dead end."

"There's something we're overlooking," she said because it sounded smart and she wanted to prolong his eyes on her, the focus of all that attention. He listened to her. Not dismissing her like Nasser or waiting for the hidden meaning like her father.

No, he took in every word she said. Her fiancé, Maryam realized, needed a friend as much as she did.

"The mother said Lauren would let women stay with her."

"Yes." Ali accepted his soup as the waiter placed it before him on the plastic table.

"And the cleaner said not all the girls went to Lauren for help, only some."

"Right again." Ali lifted the lid, and steam rose from the broth.

"Why some cleaners and not others?"

"Two hundred people couldn't fit into her apartment."

Maryam bit into her spring roll. Her mother would have a seizure if she knew Maryam chomped down on actual messy, greasy food during this first private meeting with her spouse. Most girls sipped at coffee or juice, demurring any substantive food. They did not use both their hands to grasp fried Asian delicacies.

"Something that caused these women to come to her. Why some, not others? Because they needed something. Something only Lauren could give them. Referrals."

Ali raised an eyebrow.

She flushed under his concentration. And noted that he didn't slurp his soup. "They needed some kind of help."

He put his spoon down. "A type of help that got Lauren in trouble."

They regarded each other across the table.

Maryam's gaze returned repeatedly to his lips. On his sisters, they were wide and plump. On him they looked as sensuous as a model's.

Easy, she remonstrated. *He's still more or less a stranger.* For all her education in mixed gender schools, she became tongue-tied when not talking about crimes with her fiancé.

"They assigned me to the vice squad."

Maryam choked on a piece of shredded carrot. "I thought they were promoting you."

He gulped half of a soda. "This is part of the promotion."

"Vice. I didn't know we had one. You mean like sex crimes?"

He winced at the word.

"They show *Law and Order* on MSNBC," she said. "Or you can download the *Special Victims Unit*."

"That's what you do with your free time, watch television?"

"Should I run for student government?" Maryam retorted. "So I can change the world?"

"You have changed the world," he said. "For Manu. You changed his life."

"One. One in thousands. Hundreds of thousands." Maryam said nothing about her father's anger at her interference in the family business, his irritation at her concern for the workers. "Oh, and I'm raising money to send a guy home whose cancer is killing him."

"Hm. Seems nice of you."

If their food was unusual, their conversation would have given her mother seizures. "A guy who works at the university."

"I hope he gets better."

"I've got to be able to drive."

Ali opened the top button of his *thobe*. "We can get another driver. There will be four women in the house."

"I won't spend my life waiting for a driver to go from one place to another. You don't know what that feels like."

"You're right." He saw the women standing inside the entryways to shopping malls, doctors' offices and schools, waiting to be picked up. The rows of cars in front of hotels for weddings or schools at pick-up time were the bane of the city's traffic flow.

The tension went out of her shoulders. "Really?"

"Yes, you can drive. If you need to."

She kept her gaze on the dishes on the table. "*Wallah?*"

Her noodles arrived.

"I swear," he said. "If you want."

"You're going to teach me?" Maryam took a set of chopsticks from the aluminum holder on the table. She dug them into the noodles, her appetite returning for the first time in several days.

"Let's take one thing at a time." Ali attempted the same task, but the stainless steel chopsticks slipped through his fingers. "There are schools for that, right, teaching people to drive?" His teeth caught the tip of his tongue in concentration as he tried to scoop rice into his mouth with the chopsticks.

A chunk of ice shifted inside her at his earnestness. Most local men preferred knives and forks for meat. Pasta counted as an exotic meal. If they were going to make this work, she owed him some honesty. "I went to the lessons."

"At the driving school." He put the chopsticks down. "So your mind is made up about driving."

"The English tutoring ones. With the workers," she corrected. "I went to volunteer. A group from my university also helps out."

"If your father knew——"

"He won't." Maryam waved her hand. "I saw your guy there. Manu."

Ali folded his hands. "He didn't say."

"I asked him not to."

"He works *for me*." He emphasized the last two words.

"And I will too?" She bit her lip the next instant. She exhaled, placing her chopsticks on the rim of the plate.

"I didn't say any such thing." Ali rubbed his hands over his face. "You finished?" He signaled to the waiter to bring the bill.

"I'm not my father's responsibility any more." Maryam pulled out a pack of wipes and wiped her hands. She handed the package to Ali. "Speaking of whom, he wouldn't be pleased to know about your vice assignment."

Ali pulled out the tissue-like wipe, his eyes never leaving her face. "Are you blackmailing me?"

"I won't be shut up in a house all day, waiting for people to come home, buying plane tickets for the destitute and the dying."

The people at the table next to them looked over. Maryam put her hands down. "I won't. Not his. Not yours." She leaned forward to hiss the last.

"We both want to live our own lives," Ali said.

"In this society, you're the one who gets all the life."

Ali threw his head back and laughed. "You are something else."

She looked away as he rubbed the towelette over both his hands. "My concerns are a joke to you?"

"Can we talk about something else?"

"The body," she said.

He pinched the bridge of his nose.

"Why haven't they released the body to the family?"

Ali closed his eyes. "How is it that we're not married, yet you're already meddling in my affairs?"

Maryam giggled. The memory of Manu's worried face cut short her mirth. "Manu says they won't let the mother take the body home."

Ali's hands rested on the table. "You are not to see Manu again." The levity burned away under the seriousness in his gaze. "Or to go back to those lessons."

"I—" She cursed her hastiness.

"Let's go." He stood and, without waiting for her, left the restaurant.

Maryam followed, reviewing her cover stories, discarding them as she went. *I was gathering information for you.* That sounded like she blamed him. By the set of Ali's shoulders, he wouldn't have anything to do with involving her this time.

I needed extra credit for class. Not likely to win her any points either. She climbed into the car, gathering the folds of her *abaya*, defenseless.

"That woman got herself killed because she hung around men. Maybe even one of them in that room," Ali ground out. His SUV pealed under a yellow traffic light. "Is that what you want? To die? For Manu to call me after finding *your* body like a cat on the side of the road?"

"Way to blame the victim." She gripped the door handle and sat on the edge of her seat. His words sent a chill through her. "No one can get to me at home."

He eased off the gas, glancing at her several times. They coasted to a stop at the roundabout.

"Yes," he said. "You're right."

She adjusted her scarf as the electricity in the air went from anger to attraction in a flash.

"I am?" Maryam crossed her arms in shock. "You're like a split-personality. Which Ali is this? The reasonable one? Please say he's here to stay."

He chuckled. "I can admit when I'm wrong, you know. I live with three women."

He pulled into a neighborhood street, where the houses loomed taller than they were wide. They wheeled past men, legs up, chatting, on wooden benches. Blue lights flickered from a brown-and-white striped tent. Boys played video games in the *majlis*. In the older part of the city, the houses were closer together, less room between the boundary walls of one family's residence and their neighbors.

"Where are we going?" Maryam's heart thudded in her chest, her eyes searched him for a hint.

"Now you want to be cautious?" He grumbled as the SUV slipped between narrow gates, the sensors on each side beeping an alarm. Ali pulled around the side of a two-story house, bordered on one side by a narrow alley, leading straight to a square room which abutted the main house. "You should see where you'll have to live."

Maryam's mind whirled. They were going to his house. The same one with the aforementioned sisters and mother. Curiosity pricked at her. She did want to see where she would live the first few years as a wife. What would his family make of her showing up in the middle of the evening, unescorted? Should she protest, pretend to be concerned about propriety? If she didn't and he were testing her, she would fail if she followed him into the house. She heard stories like this, of men who enticed their brides before the reception, pleaded for consummation and then discarded them, divorced, a few days later, never citing a real reason, while the bride's family scratched their heads. As she ruminated, he dismounted from the truck and strode inside the side chamber of the house as fast as his *thobe* would allow.

Come on, her phone flashed. *Unless you want my sisters to see you. Or the driver.* She scurried up the alley, her heart pounding in her ears. When she reached the wooden door, she held her breath as she stepped through, her mother's warnings ringing like alarm bells in her ears. Even Jane Austen would disapprove of such boldness. Her eyes adjusted to the dim interior of the room. A full bed, half the size of hers at home, sat against the far wall. A dresser, a wardrobe and a prayer mat stood along the other. A low green brocade sofa sat next to the door and Ali sat on it, his *ghutra* and *'agal* pushed to one side, his sandals kicked off beneath him.

Maryam hovered in the doorway.

"Restraint is not like you," he said, his head propped on the back of the sofa, eyes closed. "Though I am pleased to see you have some."

"If that's a dare—" She stepped in, walked around him, paused, then sat one cushion away. "I'm here."

"Predictable." He opened one eye.

She sat at a right angle to his reclining position. Red veins in his eyes pulsed. "This case has upset you."

He rolled his neck to get a better angle at her. "You ever have a boyfriend?" His voice rumbled low, in earnest, not meant to insult to her as it would have from another man.

"No," she said, her voice a low murmur. "You have a girlfriend?"

He shook his head. "Maryam."

Her breath caught at the sound of her name.

"There's something I should tell you."

"You're married?" The accusation burst out of her, raising the volume, and bringing his head up in surprise. She sank onto the sofa in defeat.

"Huh? No." His arm sat along the back of the sofa, fingers close to her shoulder. "No, I have a different sort of secret."

"Oh, God." She looked away from the tips of his fingers. "A child?"

"No." He laughed. "My life has not been that interesting. Not until recently. Can you listen for a second?"

"Okay." She stared straight ahead at the bottle of cologne, a black comb, a pair of cufflinks on their sides.

"I should have told you this before the engagement. That's the rule, right?" He gave a shaky laugh.

"You're scaring me," Maryam said. The bride did have a right to know about anything negative about the groom. "Is it AIDS?" She held her breath.

His blank look led them both into a burst of laughter. "No. It's nothing like that. When I was a child, this illness— it damaged me. I mean I'm fine but— it's hard to talk about this before we're actually married. I should have told your brother and he could explain it to you." Ali turned away.

She put a hand on his shoulder and brought him back around. "Whatever it is, as long as there's no other women or diseases, we can manage."

His mouth opened and closed, eyes roaming her face. Their noses were inches apart. "Maybe I should call Nasser—"

"I knew you were here! I told Maha I heard your truck." Aisha burst into the room. "Have a look at my math homework." She stopped in her tracks, her eyes going from Maryam to Ali and back in wonder. She clutched a red clear folder to her chest.

"Aisha!" Ali jumped up as if to shield Maryam. "Can't you knock?"

Maryam yanked her *abaya* over her leggings and adjusted her *shayla*.

I'm fully clothed. We were doing nothing wrong, she told herself. *We are engaged. We are married in the eyes of the law. We are doing nothing wrong.*

Aisha giggled. "Sorry, sorry. You're busy. I'll come back."

"You dropped this." Maryam handed over a Polaroid photo, the white border framing a woman in a pink uniform who looked straight at the camera. "Who's this?"

"Oh, that's for Art," Aisha said.

"Good composition," Maryam said. The brown-skinned woman occupied the left third of the photo, her mouth a narrow strip across the image. "She doesn't look happy."

"She's the cleaner in my classroom. She didn't want her photo taken. Said she was ugly." Aisha took the photo, clasping it against her other books.

"You shouldn't take photos of people without their permission," Maryam chided. The first rule of journalism, not to mention life in a society of veiled women, whose familial reputation depended on their anonymity.

"She let me." Aisha stuck her lower lip out. "I paid her." Aisha backed out of the room.

"Don't tell anyone you saw Maryam," Ali broke in. "Aisha. Come back here," Ali hissed after the retreating girl.

Maryam clutched his arm. Ali went still, turning to her in surprise. She could make out his individual eyelashes. "Did you hear what she said?"

Ali stepped away, breaking the contact between them.

"She said she paid the cleaner to take her photograph." Her words hung in the air for a few seconds, then Ali smacked himself in the forehead.

"Of course." He took out his phone, tapping in a series of numbers. "They don't make much money. They need more money. They have all these expensive things Manu kept telling me—"

"We'd better go before she comes back and brings the whole house with her," Maryam warned.

Ali made a sound of protest and alarm. "About the other thing."

"You don't have a disease?"

He shook his head.

"No disease, no wife, no child." She ticked off the objections on her fingers. "Whatever it is, it can wait."

They stood toe-to-toe, his eyes searching her. Ali reached out, taking her by the shoulders. "Are you sure? This is the kind of thing you can't take back."

"I'm sure," she said.

"We're a month away," he said. "Your father is spending a fortune on this wedding. Or so my mother tells me every time she lays eyes on me."

"I'm sure," she repeated.

Ali took her by the hand, Maryam keeping his pace as they hurried to the truck. He didn't let go in the ride across town. Maryam kept her eyes on the palm trees speeding by, a smile dancing in the corner of her lips. Okay, so they were holding hands, very Jane Austen. *But he took me to his house.* She married a rule breaker. Things might not be so bad.

With the engine idling outside the gate to her house, she pressed a kiss to his cheek, the stubble sending pricks across her mouth. "Thank you."

He sat still as a hooded falcon in characteristic somberness. She hummed to herself, sweeping out of the car and into the courtyard, pulling her *abaya* tight. As she made her way through the house, Maria jumped into view.

"*Bismillah*," Maryam said, drawing back, resorting to the name of God to ward off evil. "Maria, you gave me a heart attack."

"Someone is here to see you."

"Me? At this hour?"

"Your friend."

Maryam followed the housemaid into the women's sitting area, her mind reeling. There was no way Daniel would have been let inside the house—if he lost his senses and tried to visit.

"Amal," Maryam said. She stood at the edge of the carpet, taking in the sight of her former friend, *abaya* hanging open to reveal black leggings and a hot-pink t-shirt.

"You have to help me." Amal rushed over to her.

"There's nothing due for class," Maryam said. She shed her headscarf and robe on the back of a chair, shaking loose her bun.

"No, it's not that." Amal waved a hand as if at a pesky insect. "Ahmed. I mean Arnell. Apparently he made up the whole thing – a lie. He's not sick at all."

Maryam sank into a gilded armchair as the details came pouring out.

"We collected over sixty thousand riyals for him. And he left. He took it all and he left and he isn't even sick."

"Now that's a story," Maryam said.

"We can't tell anyone," Amal said, her eyes rounding. "Imagine? They'll never donate again. We weren't supposed to collect money to begin with."

Maryam rubbed her temples. "Okay, start again at the beginning. Who else knows?"

When Maryam's mother found them twenty minutes later, whispering with their heads together, she hummed to herself.

Chapter Twenty Three

Rain pounded on the roof of the guard station. Manu shivered inside his company-issued sweater. Water leaked under the door. The droplets streaked past the window like missiles. Rain made their morning journey to the school in the company van precarious as water seeped in from the street and over the bottom step. He sloshed in to the office, his wet socks clinging to his ankles. "This is the desert," he said. The scene outside resembled a monsoon, and the dirt parking lot looked as if an angry child overturned his water pail in a sandpit.

"Every fall," drawled Mrs. Craft, the teacher sent to help shepherd in waterlogged students. She clutched her elbows, two arms merging into a tube of black sweater. "Every winter this rain comes, and we're swimming for a few days." She handed out umbrellas to the parents streaming in, holding their waterlogged children with one hand and shoes in the other.

A *drip, drip, drip* in the corner reached Manu's ear. He scanned the room, noticing at the same time as the teacher the trail of water as it snaked down a corner wall.

"We'll need a bucket for that." The teacher made no move to leave the office. "Call for a cleaner, please."

Manu buzzed the cleaning supervisor. "We need a bucket," he parroted under her blue gaze. "Ceiling is dripping."

"Where's your location?"

"Gate 5," Manu said. "Security room."

"Okay. I send a girl." The line crackled as the man shouted "Sumitha! Go to gate 5. There's a leak."

The phone went dead, the dial tone beeping in rhythm with the rain pelting the roof. Manu placed the receiver back in the cradle. He chewed on his lower lip as one of the female cleaners, Sumitha, appeared a few seconds later, holding the pail over her head, her blue uniform darkening.

Her pants were rolled up to her knees and water sloshed over the tops of her feet.

"You poor dear." Mrs. Craft threw open the door. The wind slapped it on the opposite wall, water rushing into the cabin.

Manu jumped back, grabbing the bucket from the girl, as the hole in the ceiling opened further.

Sumitha wrung the water from the bottom of her uniform.

"Stay here, and wait out the rain." Mrs. Craft waved the girl over to a metal folding chair.

Sumitha huddled on it. Drops of water were scattered through her hair.

"Why haven't you canceled school?" A tall woman came in, shaking water from her umbrella.

The phone rang. Mrs. Craft answered it. "You have your wish."

The tall woman turned from the second door. "Excuse me?"

"School is closed. There's water leaking from the tiles in the elementary section."

The woman sputtered. "Do you know what we did to get here today?"

Mrs. Craft smiled and bent down to be eye-level with the tall woman's little boy. "You get to go home and back into your pajamas."

"I swear, this country." The tall woman pushed up her sleeves.

"I *am* in my pajamas." The little boy pushed out his chest, showing a picture of a grinning pirate. Imprints of ships were scattered on the front and backs of his legs.

"Drive carefully," Mrs. Craft called after them. She turned to Manu. "You have this under control? Tell everyone that school is cancelled for today. I've got to go and help with the buses." She didn't wait for an answer.

Manu went to close the door after her. A stream of parents herded their children back out the security booth. A girl with red hair dropped her mother's hand to twirl in the rain and jump in a dark-colored puddle.

"Alice!" Her mother shouted.

Other children followed suit, wading into shallow ones and covering themselves in mud.

"I would do the same," Manu reflected. "My brothers would, for sure."

"You're with that police officer, right?" Sumitha asked.

Manu couldn't see her expression through the tide of bodies streaming through.

"What's going on?" Mothers greeted each other in the doorway. They commiserated on the lateness of the notification, twenty minutes after the gates opened, an hour after most people left their homes to go to schools and offices.

"You knew the teacher?" Manu couldn't bring himself to say Lauren's name, not in this mass of humanity. The image of her prone figure receded but not the horror of those bruises on her neck.

"She helped me," Sumitha said.

"With what?"

They were alone now, momentarily. He approached her, one step at a time, not wanting to startle her, like a goat he hoped to milk.

Sumitha's eyes were as full as the potholes in the road outside. "Everything. I—I needed money. This salary is so low."

He rested on the edge of the desk.

"She gave you gifts?"

Sumitha's eyes flashed. "She gave me jobs. She let me clean her house, wash her car. She not have children, but if she did, she let me babysit." She let out a big hiccup. "She didn't have. Now she will never have."

Manu passed her a tissue.

"Other girls, they take these offers. Miss Lauren help anybody who not want to take these offers. She take me out for my birthday." Sumitha jumbled English and Hindi, her emotions carrying her along on a wave of memories.

Manu handed over the box.

"She not like these offers girls are taking. She say there a better way. She take me out for my birthday, let me order. I not have to take gifts."

"From whom?" Manu asked.

Sumitha fisted a wad of tissues and hiccupped again. He coughed to cover the urge to tuck a stray strand of hair behind her ear.

"From men," she said.

He leaned forward to make sure he caught the words as she repeated them. The word sent his heart racing.

"Men? The fathers?" His stomach roiled at the idea that the occasional father who trooped through the guard gate, child's hand clutched in his grasp, paid for tricks from the custodians.

"The inspectors. The guys in the neighborhood who see us waiting for the bus to pick up. Anyone." She shrugged. "Anyone who says he will take you for a meal, for your birthday, buy you a present, treat your friend. Many of the girls have no problem. Me—I not like this."

"Wait." He made for the door, blocking her exit, stopping short of touching her.

She shot him a sideways glance. "I told you, I not take the offers. Miss Lauren try to help me. I only bring trouble for her."

She darted out of the office, back into the waterlogged picnic-table area. The downpour abated. Without the sun, the sky remained a stainless steel gray, like a pot left in the sink.

Manu pulled out his cellphone and dialed Ali. "Sir?" Manu rushed. "We interview all the cleaners. It is a must."

"Right," Ali said. "Wanted to call you last night, but—anyway, I'll be at the school later."

Manu hung up the phone, hoping this would not affect Sumitha. He lost Reham to the heights of a college education. He didn't want to lose another potential girlfriend, to prison.

Chapter Twenty Four

Sanjana stretched her arms over her head, pressing against the ceiling of the car, working out the ache in her arms. Working in the nursery was harder than taking care of a family. So many children, so many chances for spills, tears, and messes.

"You have time for lunch?" Vinay glanced at her as she stifled a yawn.

The number of cars in the neighborhood street announced rush hour.

"I have to start dinner," she said. "Maybe tomorrow."

Vinay slammed on the brakes to avoid hitting a black SUV that pulled out in front of them, the driver ignoring a yield sign. "Okay."

"Sorry," she said, her jaw working. "That mother who picks up on Wednesdays is always late."

The woman hurried in, hair flying, heels clicking on the courtyard pavement stones. Sanjana smiled, insisting she didn't mind spending a few minutes with Aiden. The woman was too distracted to notice that the actual teachers' assistants left in their scheduled taxis. Aiden thought of helping Sanjana clean up as a fun game. He brought toys over to her, waddling on his chubby legs.

"You busy woman now," Vinay said. He gave her a sidewise glance. "I'm proud of you." His knuckles grazed her knee.

Sanjana trained her gaze out the window, past the Jerusalem stone office building, and the beauty parlor in a villa with purple trim. A riot of emotions rolled through her at his touch. Embarrassment at first; no way either of her sisters would be allowed to ride in a car alone with a strange man. Pleasure at the look of admiration he gave her. And not for the first time, a sense of pride in the fact a man found her attractive. Still, she swiveled her legs out of reach. "See you tomorrow," she said as the car idled in front of Madam Cindy's house.

"See you." Without warning, he swooped over, pressing a kiss to her cheek.

His lips left a moist spot, their touch like a burning sensation. Sanjana clutched her bag, looking up the street and then behind her.

"No one saw," he chuckled, sunglasses hiding his eyes. "I'll see you tomorrow." He touched her chin gently.

"Bye," Sanjana squeaked. She stumbled up the steps of the house, escaping into the cool interior. She closed the door and slipped off her shoes, out of habit. No pile of sandals here like at home, but she carried them in her hand through to her room. Sanjana changed out of her uniform of black pants and white polo shirt. She unwound her hair, letting it fall to its full length at her waist. She regarded herself in the bathroom mirror. Her cheekbones were still high, giving contour to her face; her waist trim, despite years of good eating from Madam's kitchen. A photo of her with Manu, after being reunited, winked from the corner of the mirror. Sanjana's smile faltered. Now she went to work, not minding the menial labor or the money, accepting her role in the micro-community of the nursery, and losing sight of the entire purpose for being there. Revenge. Laxmi Pande's daughter was sickly and out of nursery more days a week than in. Without the constant reminder, Sanjana's whole reason for being at the school faded away. She embraced the lively environment, the chance to get out of the house, the rides with Vinay.

A knock on the glass part of her door startled her back into the present.

"Hi," Sir said, standing on the back doorstep.

"Yes, I'll go get the dry-cleaning now." She gulped, reaching for the tote bag Madam preferred her to use in place of the plastic ones.

"We need to talk." Paul pulled out a crumpled piece of paper.

"I have the change from the last trip." Sanjana turned in a circle, wondering where she put her purse.

"This is not about dry-cleaning." He tapped the door again. "Join me in the kitchen."

Sanjana whipped her hair back into a bun and did as instructed.

Sir Paul sat in the breakfast nook, smoothing out the note on the table.

She sank back onto the peach cushion.

"Want to tell me about this?"

"No," she said.

Paul leaned forward.

Her head pounded. Without knowing what the note said, she couldn't come up with a reasonable response. What would Vinay have written a few days ago? Try as she might, she couldn't find it when vacuuming the living room. Daniel's antics occupied most of her attention, diminishing her housekeeping skills.

"You can't read it because it's in English." Paul's blue eyes locked on her, pinning her in place. "I'll read it for you." The grave tone in his voice he used for the videos filmed for classroom lectures.

"One bottle vodka, one bottle rum, and any gin. And give me your number. I pay extra."

She bit her lip. *That snake Vinay.* He bought alcohol from the boys, from Sharif. She spent the better part of that Friday cleaning the living room after Daniel took his friend home but never found the note.

"Who gave this to you?" His words came precise, slow. "Vinay writes notes to you. The driver."

"He's a man, isn't he? He has to make money like anyone else." She covered her mouth.

"He is not a suitable person for you."

There is no one else, she wanted to scream. "I'm not your child," came out instead, in a level voice. She clapped her hands over her mouth. Too late, the insult escaped

Sir Paul pushed back from the table and leaned his head on the back of the cushions. "You aren't." He rubbed at his eyes. "You could have been." He leaned forward now, his wiry forearms on the table. "I'm old enough to be your father."

"I cause so much trouble already," Sanjana blurted. Tears filled her eyes again. She was a like a water fountain, she streamed with consistency. "Please don't tell Madam. She will be very angry with me."

"Are you selling our alcohol on the side?"

"Me? No!" She slapped the table.

"Okay, okay." He held up his hands. ""Daniel?"

"No." She rubbed at the surface, feeling the grains of wood under her fingers. Sharif's wan face floated into her mind's eye. A pang of guilt twisted her insides. She knew firsthand about the boy's torment. And yet, wrapped up in her own worries, she neglected to ask after him.

Paul's phone skated across the table like a dancing bug. He slipped on his glasses and held his finger down across a series of numbers. He scanned the waiting messages and mumbled, "An hour flight and you get ten messages."

She exhaled. He wouldn't pry further. She reached out to take the note as he tapped out a reply.

"Err… I need a computer for this." He rose from the table, bent over the screen.

Sanjana remained sitting in the breakfast nook. Once in the living room, he broke away from the screen to pick up the carry-on, striding up the stairs.

"Home-done pizza for dinner," she called after him. "Ready in five minutes." She shredded the note into strips and then each paper into smaller and smaller pieces, then she scooped them up and sprinkled them into the trash like snow. She shut the lid hard. Oh, to burn that paper, and the connections with that man. If only she could dismiss Sharif's problems as easily. She set out the circular placements, red dots of color against the blonde wood of the table, and went through the motions for dinner, her mind spinning.

She pressed the button for the intercom. "Dinner."

Daniel answered the upstairs extension. "Not hungry," he said.

She cupped her hand over the receiver. "Your father asking who drinking the alcohol," Sanjana hissed. "He's not drinking it any more. Selling it so that he can save enough money and get far away from his crazy parents after high school."

"Who he selling it to—that driver?"

"You mean your boyfriend?"

"*Chee!*" Her voice rose. "Why you say this dirty thing—and hide what you do? He not my friend. And you no friend to Sharif you let this continue."

"Hi, hi, hi." The kitchen door clanged behind Madam Cindy, her hands full of grocery bags.

"I'll handle it," Daniel said.

"Oh, more things in the car, Madam?" Sanjana hung up on Daniel.

"Yes, please. You know, it took three trips to different grocery stores to make the dish?" Cindy placed her load on the island.

Sanjana went into the garage to get the remaining bags and shoved a roll of paper towels under her elbow. Upstairs, Daniel gestured animatedly in the window, pacing back and forth on the phone.

"Pizza? I'm on a low-carb diet." Cindy eyed the contents of the oven.

"Ah." Sanjana set down the eggs, paper towels, and a bag of veggies. She smacked her forehead. "I am forgetting. I make salad, no problem."

Cindy straightened and pulled at her purple t-shirt.

"Sir is here." Sanjana put away the butter, Brussels sprouts and carrots.

Cindy brightened. "I'll say hi while you're getting the salad together."

Sanjana made quick work of settling in the other items and washed spinach leaves. She could relax when Sir and Madam were upstairs together.

Since the excitement with Manu, Madam did not speak with Sanjana at any length about any topic. Their sense of closeness after their near arrest evaporated once Manu moved in with them. Her brother wasn't the kind of guest for whom Madam maintained the guestroom.

Sanjana fingered the keyboard of her phone. No, she would have to come up with a solution on her own. One that didn't involve asking for help. Analyn, her one friend in the compound, Amira's former maid, was gone, shipped back to the Philippines. The only Filipina to be nice to her, sharing information about who needed extra babysitting on the weekends or villa cleaning on her day off. Her brother fought crime. Which left Sanjana to figure out how to avoid committing one.

Chapter Twenty Five

Ali stuck another passport photo on the wall of his office. Manu traced a line from that photo to a name. Basam Yusuf. There were fifteen women on the board, tied to six or so men. Creating the web took five days of work, with Ali depending on Manu for translation and hoping that these interviews weren't tipping off the male associates, one of whom was surely Lauren's killer. They developed a system. The principal brought the woman to the interview room, Ali's office. They dropped the sheet taped to the wall above the photos of the women they'd already spoken to.

A now-hoarse Manu translated the questions, running the interview mostly by himself, pausing now and then to reveal a new piece of information to Ali. Like a jigsaw puzzle, they'd found the pieces and begun putting them together. Fast enough for the media? No. Accurately enough for the family? Ali prayed yes.

"Lauren first found out about this through Sumitha," Manu repeated the story as they knew it to date. "On her birthday, sad to be away from her family. Her friend, Kamila, told her she knew someone who would take them out. Enter Basam."

Ali studied the photo, the now familiar tale washing over him like his heartbeat. Basam met the girls during set-up for major school events, like Hallowe'en and the international festival. He offered to take them out for their birthdays. And in return, he expected favors.

"This is prostitution," Manu exclaimed when the pieces came together, four interviews in.

"This is exploitation," Ali corrected. He searched for the word online and then showed Manu the spelling in his native script for the man to understand.

"They're exchanging money for sex. Same, same."

"We're looking for people who can't get out of what they do," Ali said.

"This is different."

Manu's wounded eyes said he disagreed.

Ali pushed back his 'agal. He agreed with Manu, but Khalifa saw things differently.

"Not your case," Khalifa wheezed. "Get this settled so you can focus on the task at hand."

The door banged shut.

"He's here." Now Manu wheezed, breathless from having run up the stairs instead of waiting for the elevator like a local.

Ali dropped the sheet and, with a scowl on his face, fixed his *ghutra*.

Basam entered. Manu indicated he should sit in the chair in the middle of the room. Ali remained standing.

"You know why you're here?"

Basam resembled a twig, thin as a tooth-cleaning stick, his suit hanging from his shoulders.

"I didn't do anything," he said, his voice high-pitched and wheedling.

Ali flashed a photo of Lauren, the one for the school website. Her gleaming smile shined whiter thanks to the white backdrop, and her hair curled over her shoulder. "You know this woman?"

"Yes, she came to dinner a few times. With friends. Friends from the school."

Basam's voice and the hours Ali spent in the room weighed on him. "She found out you were sleeping with the cleaners, and you killed her." Basam leapt from his chair. "No!" He tore at his hair. "No." He spread his arms out toward Manu, who looked out the window. "She knew—the American knew what happened. She said the girls could decide. I didn't sleep with them."

Ali stayed in the center of the room, eyes narrowed.

He wandered over to Manu to plead his case. "I swear—I swear to God. I mean, there were things—some things, but nothing like that. She said it was up to the girls."

"Dating is illegal," Ali said. "We're checking the workers to see if any are pregnant."

Basam took a shuddering breath. The left corner of his mouth lifted in a sly arc.

"Fornicating is illegal," Ali intoned.

Basam passed him a piece of paper in Arabic. Ali scanned it.

"You can't fornicate with your wife." He tapped his right hand over his heart and grinned.

Ali's hand trembled with the urge to crumple the piece of paper. A *misyar* contract. Temporary marriage. That declared Basam legally married to one of the cleaners.

Manu sent him a questioning look.

"You fought with Lauren?"

Basam took the contract back and tucked it into his jacket pocket. "No. She never talked to me."

"Any of your friends you introduced to the girls?"

Basam shook his head. "The only person I ever saw fighting with the American, that young cleaner, the one who refused all our deals."

"Sumitha," Manu said.

Basam snapped his fingers. "Yes, that's the one. They argued one day at school. Something—something about how Lauren needed to put more pressure. She needed to force the girls to stop going out."

Ali and Manu exchanged a look.

"Can I go now?"

"Go," Ali said curtly. The man made him embarrassed to be Arab. He'd taken advantage of women barely out of their teens, desperate for any happiness in their lives, precisely because they were Asians and vulnerable. "Where is she now?"

Manu paced the room. "She was leaving."

"The school?"

"The country."

Ali swore. This case was in a downward spiral from bad to worse. He called the back-up squad. They could get passenger manifests for the last few days and upcoming flights to cross-reference Sumitha's travel plans. The phone rang out. "Wait here," Ali said. He left Manu searching the Internet for departing flights from the capital to Kerala. The man used the computer as adeptly as Aisha. Ali strode through the office building, steam amassing. If he found the men of his detail reading the newspaper or drinking tea, he would give them a piece of his mind, no matter what the consequences might be. Ali burst onto the floor of their offices, to find the room full of men in plain clothes, poring over poster-size photos pinned to the all four walls.

"*Bismillah*," he said, taking a step back, and calling on the name of God. Surrounding them on all sides were images of charred human flesh. They were looking at the remains of Sandra Booth. The dozen or so men worked without speaking, aligning the photos together like a jigsaw puzzle. The burnt ends of her fingers curled like pieces of ribbon.

"Restricted area!" The stout guy from house investigation came forward, waving his arms at Ali.

Ali squinted, regretting not taking the time to learn the man's name. A badge read 'Ghanim'. "I'm sorry," he said. "I came to get a few guys to hunt down a suspect in the teacher case."

Ghanim passed a weary hand over his face. "I can't spare anyone. We are working round the clock to find the driver of the vehicle."

Ali listened as the details of the other case came tumbling forward. Dread filled him as he waited for someone to say Hassan's name or mention his involvement.

"So the three-digit plate traces to an important family."

Ali nodded. Vehicle plates with only three of the six required digits were reserved for the ultimately wealthy, the top tier of society. No wonder Khalifa kept this from the rest of them. If the international media got hold of this tidbit of information, there would be no silencing the questions about justice and fairness in their city-state.

"We have a lone driver, known to the deceased, not to her friend. Nothing after the moment they dropped her off. Nothing," Ghanim said with an ironic twist of his lips, "connected to your case."

Ali could only nod like a school child. Lauren's strangulation seemed like a playground incident gone wrong, compared with the effects of violence strewn across the room. "Okay," he said. "If I can help?"

"Get out the news about your suspect as soon as possible," Ghanim said in a weary voice. "Take some heat off this. Give them someone to hate. We won't have the luxury of transparency with ours."

Ali slowed his strides back to the office, almost like a meditation. Here he thought locating Sumitha could put him back in Khalifa's good graces and maybe earn him a little recognition. For all his girth, Ghanim's mind was nimble and, above all else, seemed fair.

"So when will they start?" Manu asked. "There are dozens of planes leaving every day for India. She could be on any one of them."

"Grab some water," Ali said. "We're to the airport." At his confused look, Ali began to fill the other man in, leaving out his concerns about Hassan's involvement. He felt queasy, saying nothing about his cousin's presence there that night, the fateful ride home. But until he spoke to him, Ali didn't, couldn't, find the heart to give Hassan up. After seeing the pictures, the conflict grew even stronger. Could the boy he grew up with have played a part in creating that kerosene-soaked corpse? Ali shuddered and hoped his instinct proved right, that Hassan was not involved.

They rode to the airport in silence, Ali lost in circular ruminations, his thoughts going from Ghanim, surely the shoe-in to be Khalifa's successor, to a half-baked strategy to find Sumitha in the newly-expanded airport.

Manu let out an appreciative whistle on the approach to the terminal, dusk alighting on the cascade of water gushing from a series of ceramic water jugs in the middle of a lake. "Haven't been back here since I arrived." His fingers clutched the door handle.

Ali swung the SUV into a parking slot designated for an official vehicle. Once inside the terminal, he strode straight to the internal criminal investigation desk, asking them to call in Sumitha's passport number and spelling of her name. They ushered Ali into the security office, a chrome-and-marble room filled with banks of giant monitors with scrolling green figures of flight numbers and departure times.

"Who's he? Family?" The officer asked Ali in Arabic and jerked his finger at Manu, who stood slack-jawed in front of a panoramic view of airport arrivals.

"He's with me," Ali mumbled. Manu's gaze locked on to the clump of men in slacks and button-down shirts, huddled in baggage claim, clutching their documents in one hand and pulling battered suitcases off with another.

"They know," Manu whispered, sidling up to Ali. "They know these guys are being taken by anybody. And they do nothing."

"Stay focused," Ali replied. "We find her, we help a lot of people."

Manu shook his head, trying to clear it.

The officer indicated Ali should take a seat. He sat in a bucket-shaped leather chair, head buzzing with all the information in front of them.

"There," the other man said with a satisfied grunt. A red four-digit number flashed on the middle screen. "She's at gate A8. You want us to go with you?" His fingers drummed his leg in excitement.

"We're good," Ali said. "They're boarding?"

"Last call," the officer confirmed.

"Let's go." Ali and Manu left the security room, the bright lights of the regular airport causing them to blink rapidly in contrast. They jogged through the security line, Ali flashing his pass at the screening officers, neither of them with their eyes on the screen. The escalator down into the belly of the airport spat them out into the duty-free area, where hundreds of people swarmed through kiosks selling overpriced toys, chocolate and cigarettes.

"There." Manu tapped his shoulder and they made a sharp right, causing a woman with a luggage cart to stop abruptly in order to avoid running them over.

Three main arteries branched off from the atrium: A, B and C. Terminal A arrows pointed to the left. They ran, Ali wheezing to keep up with the younger man's pace. Manu weaved through the passengers onto the people-movers. "Coming through!" he called. Ali followed suit, the two of them causing heads to turn. What sort of terminal started at number fifteen? He huffed, regretting not staying in shape after returning from military training. There, finally, a few minutes later. Number eight. A line of people snaked in front of the gate, documents in hand, waiting to board. A mother shushed a fidgeting baby, two teenagers shared a set of headphones. Ali scanned for the petite figure of the cleaner.

"Sir, you'll have to wait in line," the Asian woman with maroon lipstick said to Manu in a stinging voice.

"Police," Ali said, startling the check-in crew. "Stop this woman from boarding." He handed over an A4-size photo of Sumitha's school ID.

"We have to check, sir, we need your badge number," the woman stammered.

Ali didn't blame her, this kind of thing was rare in their airport, but she slowed them down. "Do it," he said. "Get on there and make sure she isn't on the plane." He waved at the walkie-talkie.

Behind them, the crowd grew restless.

"I hope this doesn't mean the flight will be delayed," the mother called, setting off other notes of worry among nearby passengers. As if in sympathy for his mother's plight, the baby let out a wail.

"We'll update everyone with information," the ground staff said over the growing disquiet.

"She's making a run for it!" Manu pointed at a figure speeding in the opposite direction.

"Now." They ran together, catching the woman, each with one arm.

"Come with us," Ali said stiffly, over her sobbing. Her arm felt as delicate as a bird's bone in his grasp. "Here." He ushered them past a staff-only door. "Out," Ali called to the janitors milling in the hallway. They looked at each other and back at Ali until Manu repeated the instruction in Hindi, adding a few phrases. They scattered like marbles.

"You killed Lauren Miller," Ali said without preamble. Without anywhere to run, Ali broke contact with the young woman.

Her eyeliner streaked across her face, giving her a cartoonish look. "No, no," she said. "Accident, it was accident."

Ali harrumphed, his heart hammering in his chest. The suggestion that this fragile creature hurt someone boggled his mind. He leaned against the opposite wall, allowing Manu to translate a series of questions. Ali caught his breath, impressed by the man's verbal dexterity in Arabic after a few months.

"She says she never meant to hurt Lauren. They were arguing, she wanted Lauren to be more active with the girls."

"And," Ali asked disbelievingly, "she ended up strangled in her own bathtub."

Manu's voice rose as he translated the question, complete with the derision in Ali's tone.

Sumitha shrank from their glares, turning her gaze to the marble floor.

"She said they argued, Lauren wouldn't listen. Sumitha got angry, she— hit her to make a point about the kinds of things men could do to the girls while they were out. She hit her too hard, caught Lauren unaware. She fell. Then when she stood up again, Lauren fought her."

Ali pressed his spine into the cool wall, letting the air-conditioning roll across his shoulders. His feet ached. "They fought," he repeated. "What, like school boys?"

"Like cats," Manu corrected after a few minutes of listening intently. "Lauren was angry. Sumitha was scared. She only wanted to get her attention but—"

Sumitha broke into a sob.

"She fell. She fell and pulled Sumitha down with her. They rolled. She strangled her trying to get Lauren off."

"And the clothes, the bathtub." Ali rubbed at his eyes. What a waste. A wretched use of two lives. For now, Sumitha would be locked up for a long time, having murdered an American woman.

"She panicked. She thought she could revive her. Maybe a head injury."

The door at the far end of the hallway opened, a janitor in the grey slacks and top of the airport cleaning staff wheeled in a cart. "Out," Ali called. The man left his cart and exited the hallway.

"Airport," Ali said into his phone. "We'll take her to internal security and then someone has to come get her."

Manu passed Sumitha a tissue as tears and snot mingled on the woman's chin.

Ali disconnected the phone. The two men contemplated the hunched woman in front of them. She made for a poor criminal figure—not the unrequited lover they suspected at the start of the case.

Ali started when his phone buzzed again. "Yes."

"Khalifa died an hour ago," Ghanim said. "Heart couldn't handle the chemo. Come to the hospital as soon as she's in custody." The call ended.

Ali leaned his head against the wall, closing his eyes. He felt as unmoored as the girl in front of him, overwhelmed by emotional vertigo. The remaining connections to his father were dwindling. His boss dangled the promise of redemption even as he assigned another officer to cover his tracks. *No one could cover two complicated cases at once,* reason said. Ali's heart wondered otherwise. An impossible assignment because Khalifa thought of Ali as half a man?

"Let's go." The officer from the security booth came forward, calling Manu and Sumitha by curling four of his fingers towards his palm. "You'll be lucky to pay blood money," he said in Arabic, which went unheard by both of them.

"The victim is a foreigner," Ali replied. The reminder brought him out of his daze. *Snap out of it,* Ali scolded himself, thinking of Martha, Lauren's mom. He had things to do besides wallow in self-pity. Like call Lauren's mother with a long-awaited update. He thought fleetingly of his sister offering her cleaner a bribe. Aisha's bribe called on the same need that Basam did. In principle, they were not that different. He knew Maryam would say so later when he told her everything. They were going to have a honeymoon like no one else.

Chapter Twenty Six

M aryam wrote and rewrote the last line of her piece on Lauren. The cursor taunted her like a winking eye. Middle-of-the-road coverage on her life, her untimely death. A few lines about the meager salaries of the cleaners, how their lives led them to take bribes from all sorts of people, for a variety of tasks. She stared at the blinking cursor. Common sense said she should take those lines out and keep those thoughts to herself. But when she cut them, the piece lacked any interest or vigor. A eulogy for a stranger. A set of words about yet another ex-pat in the sea of nearly a million-and-a-half in the city.

Leave it, or take it out? She chewed on her fingernail. Her phone rang. She answered it, despite the unknown number. "Hello?"

"Making trouble?"

"Nasser?" She fell back onto the headboard, relief rushing through her.

"What have you done now," he said, laughing, "to answer on the first ring?"

She twirled a piece of hair around her forefinger, wondering if she would keep it long after marriage. No haircuts for Maryam, besides trimming, after the age of eighteen.

"I don't care who says it's fashionable," her mother said each time she asked. "You're not married, so you listen to me, and I say no."

"I'm writing," Maryam admitted to Nasser. "About a woman who died."

"Oh, the American one." He sighed into the phone. "It's getting coverage here, even in America. They're saying it's not safe for young single women to live in the Gulf on their own."

"Hm." Maryam added a few lines to the opening of the piece. "Are you helping me?" she asked when Nasser didn't scold her for this line of reasoning.

"Maybe," he replied. "Though that's a no, if anyone asks officially."

She heard the strained notes then, his hoarse voice, the fatigue in the way his words strung together. "It's like five in the morning there. Are you okay?"

He grunted an assent. "Finishing rounds. Thought you'd be free."

Maryam ran her finger over the mouse pad under the keyboard.

"Have you seen *Ubooy*?"

She shook her head, though he couldn't see her. "He's been traveling. Italy, I think. Marble suppliers."

Nasser went silent for a few moments. "I should go... get some sleep."

"Okay." Her throat constricted with a million unspoken words.

"Follow your heart," Nasser said. "You won't regret it."

They ended the call with promises to make contact again soon. The phone fell from her hand onto the bed. Easy for him to say from the other side of the world.

Victory party! The phone danced on the duvet with the force of Daniel's message.

Mabrook, she replied, her mind far from the university elections. The gap between them widened with nothing she could do to stop it. She ran her fingers over the buttons on the Nokia.

"Maryam? Maryam, get ready." Her mother whipped into the room, her hands flapping like the wings of a bird.

"For what?" Maryam pulled the laptop toward her.

Her mother shut the lid. "Your in-laws are here."

She bolted off the bed. "All of them?"

"The sister." Her mother took a deep breath, at the end of which she seemed more agitated than before. "Maha."

Maryam ran a comb through her hair and swapped her leggings for a maxi skirt and a long-sleeved top.

Her mother jumped back through the door.

"I'm going," Maryam said in response to her wide-eyed stare. "Now."

"Maria put out some cakes," Fatma said, nodding her approval at the trim black skirt. "They're in the sitting room to the side."

Maryam made her way through the house, her steps muffled, then echoing, as she crossed marble and then carpet. "*Salaam alaikum.*"

Maha responded, offering her right cheek for the perfunctory air-kisses. She pulled away at two, an abrupt gesture. The more kisses and the longer the embrace lasted, the more one showed the other their high regard.

"You have to ask Ali for your own house," Maha said without preamble.

"Would you like to sit?" Maryam indicated the loveseat behind them.

Maha waved her words away as though they were mosquitoes in her ears. "You can't come to our house in the middle of the night and expect us to welcome you with open arms."

Maryam sat, though Maha showed no signs of joining her.

"You two do whatever you want." Maha gulped air. "Whatever they call it at your university. Islamically dating or whatever." She spat the word out. "I still have my sister to think of."

Maryam cursed inwardly, one of those long phrases Babu used when they were stuck in traffic and he thought she couldn't hear over the music blaring through her earphones. There were no notes for how to handle this situation. Nor could she ask her mother for advice; this would be enough to send her into hives. Calling Ali would show weakness or be a mean-spirited power move, neither of which she favored.

"You should tell your brother what you think." Amal burst out from behind the privacy screen in the corner. "Not come here lecture his wife."

Maha's mouth opened and closed several times in a row. "Who's this?"

"Her sister," Amal said, arms crossed.

Maryam raised her eyebrows.

"I mean so close we're like sisters."

Maryam bit the edge of her tongue to stifle the look of horror on Maha's face.

"Hello, hello, hello." Her mother entered, trailed by Maria, who set an ornate sliver tray with rows of bright colored juices on the glass-topped table. "So nice of you to come by, dear, and we can go over some of the particulars. I have some questions for you about the card. Oh, hello Amal dear." Fatma blinked at the three girls, standing in silence in the sitting room.

"You'll have to ask my mom," Maha said. "She's overseeing everything."

"Yes, but you know your mother best," Fatma said, beaming. She offered Maha a selection of pastel-colored parfaits in small plastic containers. "I can't stay, Auntie," Maha said.

"Oh?"

"Just wanted to share some news with Maryam. I'll come back another time."

"With your mother, then," Fatma said.

Maha offered a thin smile. "Goodbye." She swept out the side door and into the waiting SUV. "Not a word of our girl chat to Ali," Maha called back, her voice in a falsetto that fooled Maryam's mother.

"Ah, she told you about Ali? What he likes to eat, when he has lunch. Amal, did you hear everything? Sometimes brides are so nervous they need reminding."

Maryam didn't move a muscle for several moments.

"You're going to get those sisters you always wanted," her mother trilled. She poured herself a cup of red tea. Maria spooned in several heaps of sugar. "They'll help you adjust to your new life, and your in-laws will accept you as their own." Fatma sipped from the cup. "Have some."

Maryam took the brass handle of the glass teacup, cradling it in the palm of her hand. The liquid sloshed onto her leg, scalding her knee through her pants.

Maria yelped.

Maryam let her dab at the stain. She welcomed the sting as a reminder spilled tea would be the least of her worries in her life ahead.

"To your in-laws," her mother said with a smile, raising her glass of tea.

"In-laws," Amal echoed with a smile that stretched her full lips from end to end. Maryam raised hers, letting the liquid scald the tip of her tongue. Far too late to amend the signed marriage contract now filed with the civil authorities. Even if she could get her father to agree to any stipulations, Maryam couldn't answer the questions it would raise with Ali. No, she couldn't afford to reveal the animosity their unconventional relationship sparked with his family. Whatever his feelings, he would likely side with them. That's what most men did. They outnumbered her and, for now, outflanked.

"And you want to come to the mall with me?"

She started out of her reverie, her mother waiting for an answer. "Sorry, what?"

"Let's go look at some favors. I heard there's a new set of stalls in the that mall that just opened."

"We have to study," Maryam said. She placed the half-empty tea glass on the ceramic-topped table.

Fatma sipped at hers, the corners of her smile drooping. Maryam lacked spare energy to soothe her mother. She needed all her resources for the battles that lay ahead. She fled the room, racing down the hallway. If only she could so easily dodge Amal.

"What was that about?"

With her audience gone, Amal shrank against the dresser, her fingers following the circular gold pattern. "I came to say thanks," she said, fiddling with a fabric swatch of tablecloths.

"For?"

"Your help with the Ahmed thing. You're right, everyone who gave money can afford it. Better not to tell people and ruin it for someone who might really need help."

"Oh, good." Maryam stared at the girl who once been a frequent visitor in this room.

"Are you angry with me?"

"Angry?" Maryam squared off with her former friend, the frustration she couldn't unleash on Maha boiling to the surface. "Why wouldn't you lurk in the house and come to my rescue after a year of not speaking to me? Make that a year and a half. Completely normal." She threw up her hands in exasperation.

"You didn't tell me you were engaged." Amal batted her eyelashes.

"And now you know why," Maryam snapped. "Hardly the stuff of storybook dreams."

"Okay, so his sister doesn't like you but he took you to his house." Amal did a small squeal.

"This is not a book," Maryam said. "I am not Elizabeth Bennett. This is real life."

"No," Amal said. "But I might be."

"Now I have no idea what you're talking about."

"You're engaged. Off the market."

"So that you can go after—"

"Daniel," she mumbled.

"Daniel?" Maryam fell onto the corner of the bed, scattering pillows onto the floor. "All this time."

"Everyone said you two would get together." Amal gave a laugh that sounded like a sob. "I thought you were playing hard to get."

"But I never, I mean we're friends, yes. We never—I don't think he—he's not my type—" despite years of defending her friendship, words escaped Maryam. "Besides, he's American. No way. Not a chance."

"Yes." Amal nodded. Her sigh was like the air draining out of a punctured balloon. "Turns out I am Elizabeth Bennett," she said, chin quivering.

Maryam hugged her friend for the first time in years.

"Okay, so that's enough of that." Amal gave her a little shove.

Maryam let go with a shaky laugh.

"Our secret."

"Yes," Maryam agreed. This would be the easiest kept secret because sharing it would come to no fruition for either of them.

"I'm off. Good luck with that sister-in-law."

Maryam rolled her eyes. Amal's laugh floated along with her down the hallway. Alone in her room again, Maryam grabbed her laptop. Enough of this trivial drivel on manners and love. She sat cross-legged on the bed and hit 'send' on the report. Her days of freedom were numbered so she might as well use the ones left.

Within a few moments, her phone buzzed.

"You sure you want to do this?" Daniel's voice filled her ear.

"You think it's good," she said, Amal's face flashing before her. *A secret,* she reminded herself. *No good can come from this.* A local girl with a foreign boyfriend would be scandal enough. But a girl in love with a foreigner? Thinking she could marry him—cherishing hopes for lifelong love? In a region where only fathers, not mothers, gave children nationality, Amal's time would be better spent searching for the cure to cancer, rather than pining for a westerner.

"I mean it's the best thing you've ever written. Better even than the report on Manu. You should send it to my dad."

Maryam paused, her fingers tracing the computer keys.

"For the website launch. You'd get so many hits, people would post this to their friends in America and the UK."

Her heart clenched at the tantalizing idea of readers, her one obsession since applying to the university.

"I think they even pay a little, like by word. Maybe more when they get ads."

It's not about the money, she thought but didn't say. "What about a pseudonym?" she said. "Would they let me use a fake name?"

Daniel paused. Not standing by your material went against everything their American faculty were teaching them. "Probably not."

"Like 'Aisha on the Street'," she improvised. "A person that everyone can relate to – who could be anyone writing."

"You'll have to persuade my dad," Daniel said. "If anyone can do it, you can. He owes you."

They talked through some strategies to win Paul over. She would be the first local contributor, even if she did so anonymously. That would be a big selling point, given how marginalized locals were in the English outlets. She as a feminist Arab voice, represented a minority that checked major authenticity boxes for westerner journalists under pressure to show how their work was relevant to a national audience. Hope flooded Maryam for the first time in many months. If she could assume this new identity, then she could balance the demands of her two worlds and appease her heart. *Aisha from the Street*. Wouldn't translate well in Arabic – give the exact opposite impression - but this would do as a moniker for a mainly English-reading audience. *Aisha on the Street*. Her younger sister-in-law's rounded cheeks filled her vision. Aisha, the name of one of the wives of the prophet Mohammed, became one of the most popular girls' names. Aisha; someone's cousin, sister, wife, mother or grandmother. She would be the inspiration for Maryam's truth-telling alter ego. The question was, would she tell her husband?

Maryam typed a message to Professor Paul, outlining her terms and attaching the article that impressed Daniel. Knowing Ali, he would guess the writer's identity before anyone else. The question was whether or not he would allow his wife to keep it.

Chapter Twenty Seven

Sanjana stood on the curb, waiting for Reham. A white sedan with tan seats pulled up with Reham inside, her eyes obscured by wide sunglasses.

"Are you going somewhere?"

"We," Sanjana said. She thrust a piece of paper through the driver-side window.

Reham blinked. "Who's this?"

Sanjana took a deep breath to still the roaring of her heartbeat in her ears. "She run an agency. Bad people. They sell contracts, they promise people good work, and they send them somewhere else. If they complain, she make trouble."

Reham regarded the piece of paper and Sanjana's grave face. "You're who that article from last semester was about. Professor and Maryam's piece on labor abuses."

Sanjana bit her lip. "Not me."

Reham tilted her head. "You're going to have to give me more if you want my help."

"Not me," Sanjana managed. The panic, worry and rage bubbled back from memory. "My brother."

Reham took the piece of paper and slipped it into her pocket. "I don't know what we can do. I'll ask a few people. You'd probably have to make a report to the police."

Sanjana twisted her hands together. She wanted this all to go away. Sir Paul most certainly wouldn't appreciate her resurrecting these issues. The idea that Laxmi Pande lived her life undisturbed agitated her beyond the seconds that brought her ever closer to middle age. "I know where she works," she said.

"And your plan – to go there and call her out?"

"Yes," Sanjana said in a low voice.

Reham bent forward to catch the word over the idling engine.

"Yes," Sanjana repeated. "I'll tell everyone what I know."

Reham gave her hand a squeeze through the window. Sanjana wondered why she burdened such a young person with such a great task.

"Get in," Reham sighed with a sideways smile.

"Really?" Sanjana scurried around the car to the other side.

"Far be it from me to stand in the way of justice."

Sanjana clutched her purse in the front seat. They wound through the city streets, Sanjana pointing out the route she took with Vinay to the nursery. She relished silence. She needed this time to gather her thoughts. She couldn't file a formal complaint in the courts without revealing Manu's identity. This would compromise his assignment and the steady amount of money the government kept putting into his bank account.

"This one?"

Sanjana nodded. The white gate rose in front of them like a physical warning. This time an Indian guard stood outside. He gave her a friendly smile, called her Sister, and asked how he could help.

"Waiting for someone," she called back through the window.

The street behind them bustled with vans, trucks, and cars of all sizes, using the shortcut to make their way to the city's main arteries. She took deep breaths, rehearsing her speech in her mind.

"There," Sanjana said. "That's her."

Laxmi got out of an orange, box-like SUV, taking her daughter by the hand. The girl fussed, resisting her mother's attempts to smooth her hair. Sanjana gasped at the sight of the woman's rounded belly.

"Everything okay?"

"She's pregnant," she said.

They watched Laxmi waddle to the gate of the nursery, where the guard ushered her in with a wide sweep of his arm.

Money, husband, child, children. Sanjana saw red as fury pumped through her veins. She flung the door open.

"You wretched woman!" she shouted.

Laxmi kept talking to her daughter, not paying attention.

"You make your money on the backs of other people, and you spend it here." She flailed her arms in the direction of the nursery as the guard looked from one woman to the other.

Laxmi gawked at Sanjana and drew her daughter into the folds of her orange-and-white-striped skirt, then she turned away into the courtyard.

The guard started closing the gate, his frown deepening.

"You—you—*asshole!*" Daniel often used the word when one of his friends beat him at those video games.

"What's an asshole, Mama?" the daughter asked in Hindi.

Sanjana broke down in tearful laughter.

"A word for crazy." Laxmi held the girl more firmly, causing her to cry. "Come inside now."

"Why you causing trouble?" The guard asked Sanjana. "Ms. Betsy not take this lightly."

"No, she take money from this criminal."

"You get away from here," Laxmi spat. Her daughter went through the white gate on her own, backpack bobbing up and down. "I don't know what you're talking about."

Some of the other parents slowed in their morning routine, hauling children out of their strapped car seats and searching for lunchboxes.

"You promised my brother a job," Sanjana shouted. Manu's blistered hands and skeletal frame clouded her memory. "You sent him to work like a slave."

"We don't use that word lightly." A man with an accent like Sir's came between them.

"They not pay him for months. Little food. Too much work. That is word," Sanjana said. She blocked the path to Laxmi's car.

"You know this woman?" His son peered from behind his leg, brown eyes darting from one woman to the other.

"I never met her before."

"Liar!" Sanjana's voice broke on a sob. "You take money for a visa. And you not get him a good job."

"Daddy, let's go." The boy pulled at his father's pant leg.

"Just a minute."

"Potty!"

The exasperated father scooped the boy into his arms.

"You here, bringing up old matters," Laxmi said to Sanjana in Nepalese. "The police took away my company. I'm living on savings. And with the baby coming." Her voice broke. She rubbed her belly.

"You have savings," Sanjana sneered. "You're lucky you're not in jail."

At the sound of that word, Sanjana's ace card, Laxmi started. She darted around and into her car, starting it without putting on her seatbelt, and threw it in reverse. A car horn blasted as someone sped past.

The dam within Sanjana broke as Laxmi's taillights faded down the street.

Reham took her by the arm and ushered her back into the passenger seat of the car. "There, there." Reham passed her a tissue, reassuring Sanjana as though she were the child.

Sanjana sniffled like one. They nosed into traffic, and a horn blared as Reham cut in front of someone coming over a speed bump. "Want to catch her?"

Sanjana shook her head, then nodded. She ended with a shrug.

"I'm proud of you." Reham stomped on the brake, shaking her fist at the guy in front who swerved into her lane.

"Why?" Sanjana sniffed. "I do nothing. I go and yell at her, and nothing. She not even admit what she did."

Reham took her hand. "You confronted her. You said what you wanted to say. A great step."

Sanjana clutched at her fingers.

"That dad heard every word. You can bet he's asking some questions inside." Reham was older than Meena only by a few years. Yet she offered Sanjana counsel.

"I save no one, change nothing. Her company out of business, but she still here. She can find new papers to sell," Sanjana muttered. "She will take their lives."

"She'll know someone is watching." Reham held up a finger. "She'll know she's being held accountable. She'll be looking over her shoulder to see who it is."

Sanjana sat straighter. She wanted Laxmi to pay for what she did to her brother—what she still did to others. And she would pay, in time. Sanjana would see to it. They pulled into the compound. Reham flashed her ID at the guards in the booth, their returning smiles revealing rows of white teeth in contrast with their olive skin. They rushed to raise the security arm at the gate. Instead of turning left, counter to the directional arrows, but also the quickest path to the house, the car crawled forward at the advised fifteen kilometers-an-hour, over a series of speed bumps. Reham braked as a blonde girl darted in front of the car with a pink two-wheel bike.

"Watch out," Reham called.

The girl wheeled away, streamers blowing in her wake.

"Where is her nanny?" Reham muttered as they rounded the corner.

"Or her mother," Sanjana added.

"Right." Reham burst into laughter. "This place is starting to get to me." They pulled up in front of the house, each lost in her thoughts.

"Ugh, him." Sanjana jumped out of the car, recognizing Vinay's white sedan. She stormed into the house. Daniel, Sharif and Vinay turned to her in alarm, stacks of cardboard boxes spread across the living room.

"Out," Sanjana said. She pointed a finger at the man she thought could have been her future husband.

"Wait," Vinay said. "I can explain."

"Hmp," she snorted.

"Sanjana, baby—"

She blushed at the endearment. Long hoped for but never imagined in this scenario. All wrong. Daniel and Sharif stared slack-jawed as Vinay took her hands in his palms.

His eyes drew together in concentration, almost crossing. "I do this for us."

"Us?" She snatched her hands back.

"Yes. What you think—we get married. Then we live on my driver's salary. And we can't stay here together, after we get married. Where we will put children?"

A torrent of emotion ripped through her. All the words she wanted to hear streamed out of Vinay's mouth. *Marriage. Children. Together.* They resounded in her ears, her heartbeat quickening. Above Vinay's shoulder, Sharif continued gaping at them, his hair matted at the crown and nape, a stained t-shirt hanging from his shoulders. His skin was waxen as though he hid away from the desert sun. *He wants to be a doctor,* she reminded herself, *not an alcoholic.* "You not use these boys to build your money," she hissed. "You go now." He used her dreams to justify drawing teenage boys into an illegal ring of black market alcohol sales. Not much difference between Vinay and Laxmi Pande, if you got down to it. She whirled on her heel. She would haul the man out of the house herself.

"Uff." Sanjana bumped into Reham, stood behind her, listening to every word.

"Do you need help?"

"I—"

The peal of the doorbell interrupted them.

"What do you want—" At the sight of the local policeman on the doorstep, the question dried in her throat.

"Hello."

"Madam not here. Sir not here." Her voice shook. This man who enlisted her brother in undercover police work frightened and awed her. "My brother not call." *But there is this guy selling alcohol to kids.* Her throat convulsed with the urge to expose Vinay. But were there repercussions for it happening in this house? And would she have to share Daniel's involvement? Minimal, of course, but the hashish discovery a few months prior would not look good.

"Yes, I need to speak to the boy."

"Who is it, Sanjana?" Like Ali, Daniel towered over her. His cat-like emerald eyes shone as he gave Ali a once-over, taking in his black slacks, button-down shirt, and loafers.

"Can we help you?" He enunciated each syllable.

"I need to speak to you." Ali's English wasn't quite as smooth. "You're not in trouble. Business," he added. "May I come in?"

Daniel glanced from Ali to the maid and back.

"Only a few minutes."

Behind Ali, three kids streaked by on their bikes. Sanjana resisted the urge to tell them to slow down. Westerners didn't like strangers speaking to their children. And they put high confidence in police.

"Okay," Daniel said. "Come in."

Sanjana's mouth opened and closed in protest. She might be the adult, but she worked in Daniel's house. She stood aside and the boy escorted Ali to the three tan sofas encircled around a table in the middle, positioned so everyone seated could see one another, the largest one facing a mounted flat-screen television. She clenched and unclenched her hands. Now, she saw her chance to make sure Vinay paid for his negative influence.

"Would you like some water?" Daniel chewed on a fingernail and hovered to the left of the loveseat. His voice came out high and precise, like his mother's when forced into the role of host.

Ali shook his head. "You, and you, out," Ali said. He pointed at Vinay and Reham. Vinay headed for the door, the movement calling attention to the stack of boxes marked with the blue-and-white Tiger beer logo.

"I not mean harm," Vinay said, his hands raised at shoulder height. "They ask me and I do it."

"Not here for that," Ali said. "We'll deal with that later."

Vinay and Reham slid out the front door with relieved expressions.

"How is school?" Ali asked, the room at large. He sat on the edge of the sofa, and his knees hit the heavy wooden coffee table. A glass top covered the trellis that said it had previously been a door.

Daniel shrugged.

Sanjana trembled in frustration. Her chance to knock some sense into

Vinay slipped away. What could be worse than illegal alcohol sales?

"Going home," Sharif called to Daniel from the kitchen.

"You stay," Ali called into the kitchen. "You are Sharif?"

Sharif chewed at his lower lip. Sanjana and Daniel froze on the sofa.

Ali raised his hands, turning them one way then the next. They were empty. No weapons. No handcuffs. "Well." Ali cleared his throat. "We need to talk."

"Something happened to my brother?" Her voice rose in hysteria.

"No, no, no. He is fine."

Sanjana's eyebrows knit together.

"Which one of you took the video?" Ali blurted.

Sharif stiffened at the question.

Ali laid out the details of the footage showing the last few minutes of Sandra's life. Sanjana strained to follow the conversation, reading the tension in the boys' faces. He wanted to know who filmed a late-night video. Yes, the person would be protected. No, he or she was not under arrest. They would record the interview. Only for police records.

"Will I be made an accessory to the murder?" Sharif's voice shook.

"Not at the moment, no."

"How long will this take?" Sanjana asked.

Ali cleared his throat. "I'm not entirely sure. Maybe forty minutes."

The clock said they better move quickly or this conversation was not going to stay private for long. "Here or in the station?" Sanjana clasped and unclasped her hands.

"Here is fine." Ali said.

"This safe?"

"Yes," Ali said.

"I'm going for a swim later. Find Daniel and ask him to join me." Professor Paul strode into the house through the kitchen side door. "What is going on?"

Sanjana cursed her luck.

"Dad, this is Ali, the guy who rescued Manu."

Professor Paul's blue eyes flicked from Ali across his son, to Sanjana, and back to Ali. "Do you have a warrant to be in my house?"

Ali held his hands up again. "I'm not here to arrest anyone. Only to talk. To the boys."

Professor Paul turned to Ali. "You can't come into my house without my permission."

Ali cleared his throat. "This house is provided by your employer, I assume." Professor Paul gave a short nod.

"Then actually, this is the government's house because the Foundation is a government subsidiary." Ali whirled his hand, his English not keeping up with his thoughts. "I am here... A matter of national security."

Sanjana winced. That last part sounded like a phrase Professor Paul used often while ranting against the dissolution of life back home.

Professor Paul remained standing.

So did Ali.

"You all use that line here as well?"

Ali smiled.

"What is this 'urgent matter'?" Professor Paul's marked air quotes with his fingers.

"I'm sure you're aware, sir, that I cannot say." Ali crossed his arms.

Professor Paul ran his fingers through his hair. "Where's Cindy?"

"She's at an exercise class," Sanjana said, barely above a whisper.

"Of course she is."

"I'm not making trouble." Sharif jumped up, looking from Professor Paul to Ali and back. He nodded at Ali. "I'll go with you now."

For once that boy did the right thing.

"No, no you're not," Professor Paul offered a smile that didn't reach his eyes. "We're going to call your mother."

"No," Sharif protested. "She'll send me to live with my dad."

"You said you would interview him here," Daniel said, his chin jutting out.

"Whatever you have to say to him, he does have a choice, right?" Professor Paul said.

Ali studied the painting behind the man's head—the gates of Jerusalem, done in expensive oils. "Well, no. If he doesn't want to talk, I take him to the station."

"Alright." Paul stood, forming his hands into a T. "You need more time, anyone can understand that," he said to Sharif.

"I'm sorry," Sanjana croaked.

"There's nothing to apologize for." Rather than soothe Professor Paul, her vulnerability stoked his ire.

"No is not an option for either of us," Ali admitted in a low tone.

The three of them eyed him with raised eyebrows.

Ali shrugged. "This is not work I would have chosen. They chose me."

"And you're passing the buck," Professor Paul said.

"And I'm leaning on him," Ali agreed, "because I have no one else with video. This is the closest we get to answer of what happened that night." The tension in the room leaked out like used bathwater.

"I was there," Sharif blubbered. He handed over his phone. "At the hotel and I saw the women leave with those guys. They seemed like they knew each other."

"They?"

"Dr. Erin, her friend, and those two guys."

Sanjana tried to keep up, the words flowing over her head.

"There were two guys?" The police officer shifted in his seat.

"Yeah."

Everyone eyed the screen in silence. Two women giggled their way into the backseat of an SUV. Sanjana noted the three-digit license plate of a VIP.

"You were at Sandra's last known location. Perfect," Professor Paul muttered. "Just perfect."

"You took this video. And then?"

"And then I left," Sharif said.

"Were you there?" Ali peered over the phone at the other boy, the one quite friendly with Maryam.

Sanjana and Paul turned their attention to a now squirming Daniel.

"I'll run his ID number," Ali said. "If they scanned it that night, we'll know."

"I didn't go," Daniel exploded.

Paul gestured to the stack of beer in the middle of the living room. "You'll understand why I can't believe you."

Sanjana rubbed her temples. How dare Vinay leave her and Daniel in the lurch for his business interests? She rued the day the driver wormed his way into their lives. Lucky for them, Ali left in short order, illegal alcohol sales not even registering against a video of the murdered woman, telling a befuddled Sharif he needed to keep the phone. This was her life now, defending one person from other, and yet no one to defend her.

Chapter Twenty Eight

Manu contemplated the signed letter as if on the third time the Arabic letters would rearrange themselves into words he could read. A messenger held out the form, indicating he should sign to acknowledge receipt. He brushed droplets of sweat from his forehead, resting his weight against the paneled doorway.

"*Kalam*," Manu muttered in Hindi.

The older man pulled one out of the pocket of the sweat-stained yellow polo shirt. "You not read Arabic," he said, wiping his fist across his lips.

Manu pressed the limp paper against the wall, next to a painting of a pot of purple flowers. He scrawled his name in English letters Reham would not have approved. Manu shook his head, passing back the form.

The messenger wiggled four of his fingers, indicating he would take a look. "I read it for you. Come." Silver hair at his temples put him fifteen or twenty years older than Manu. He pulled the letter from Manu's grasp. He skimmed the contents, eyes flicking back to Manu every few lines. Clearing his throat twice, he began in a sonorous voice: "In the name of God, the merciful and benevolent, the department congratulates you on the occasion of service well performed in establishing the center for missing persons and successful resolving – you are police officer?" The messenger squinted at Manu, tilting his head as if a new angle would reveal super powers.

"Thank you," Manu mumbled. He snatched the letter back, shutting the door on the older man and his prying questions. The stillness in the apartment suffocated him like a wool blanket. He wandered the living room, his new living room, like one of the many stray cats, fingers alighting on the television console, loveseat, coffee table, bookshelf. *His*. All of it. Technically the landlord's, as the apartment came furnished, but leased to him. Sheer curtains deflected the sunlight spilling into the room twice the size of any of the bedrooms he slept in since arriving in his country, even that in Sanjana's house. With a few turns of the key, he swung the balcony door open and stood on the small landing, taking in the green spine of grass dotted with palm trees that stretched down the street in either direction. A woman in black pants and tank top walked her dog around the peninsula-shaped median. Another in a headscarf chatted on a mobile phone while pushing a child on a swing.

The shrill tone of his phone broke the reverie.

"All settled?" Ali's gruff voice came as a relief after hours of silence. "Everything to your liking?"

"Um, yes," Manu said. A cascade of water from the fountain in the pool shimmered up ahead. "Big," he said.

Ali laughed. "That's the smallest unit we could find."

"Two bedrooms," Manu said. "There's only one me."

"The others have three or four," Ali said. "In this country we only have one size. Big. I could put you in Al Saad. The traffic is terrible in that area."

"Sir, you sent me letter," Manu said. He couldn't ask for a roommate without sounding more ungrateful.

"Not me," Ali said.

"Came by messenger," Manu stammered.

"Not me," Ali repeated.

Manu repeated as much of the beginning as he could remember.

"Must be Ghanim. Don't know why he would send you something by courier," Ali muttered.

Manu chewed on the edge of his lip.

"Never mind, I'll ask. But yes, we owe you a huge thank you. The media, the mother, everyone is satisfied."

"Glad to help," Manu said, the praise making him squirm. His real question, *Sumitha?* went unspoken.

"You cracked a case the rest of us were spinning our wheels on, huge thank you is the least," Ali corrected. "And you're staying on. Hence the apartment."

Manu's eyes narrowed on the two-story structure rising in a semi-circle behind the pool. *Did they have those dance exercise classes there?*

"You sure you like it? We can look for something else. Something newer. HR says this one is ten years old."

"No, no, I am fine," Manu said hastily. Newer probably meant bigger. Getting used to being on his own would take some time, not to mention the opulence of a neighborhood with a pool, tennis court, and clubhouse.

A few units down on his left, the door opened on the balcony next door. A slender woman came out, dragging a white wicker chair and patterned bag. When she pulled her dark hair into a bun at the crown of her head, Manu realized with a jolt he knew this girl. His very own Reham. She sat back in the chair, long legs hanging out of floral print shorts. "I see you Sunday," Manu said in a rush into the phone.

"Yes, okay," Ali said. "I'll meet you at the station. We already have our next mess. Those burned remains——"

"Goodbye." He hung up, slipping the phone into the pocket of his borrowed shorts, pinned to his waist by one of Daniel's belts. He watched her from the periphery of his vision, trying not to stare as she surveyed the children fighting over a football in the garden below. Her gaze traveled up and down the street, coming to rest on Manu.

He raised a hand in greeting like in one of those television shows the American boy watched.

"Hi." She waved back.

"Hello," Manu said.

She squinted at him. "You seem familiar."

Behind her the door swung open and a woman with dusky skin carried out a tray with a soda can, two crustless sandwiches, and a plate with slices of green apple. She set the tray down next to Reham and also waved at Manu. "Moving in?"

"Yes," Manu squeaked.

"Welcome, neighbor." She bestowed on him a benevolent smile, one creased with more laugh lines than that of the younger woman beside her. "Time to write," she chided Reham.

"Mom, give me a second."

An ample bottom blocked Reham from Manu's view.

He slipped back into the apartment, curtains billowing in the gentle breeze. *Neighbor. Neighbor. Neighbor.* The word clamored in his mind.

Glossary

Abaya — a black robe, worn by women in the Arabian Gulf or Muslim women, designed to hide the curves of a woman's body.

'Agal — A black coiled circle of wool or cloth, used to keep a man's *ghutra* (worn over the head) from moving.

Allah barak feek — an Arabic expression that means from God comes the blessing, often said in response to 'congratulations'.

Bisht — black, transparent man's ceremonial robe, edged with gold cords.

Al salaam alaikum — Peace be upon you.

Enshallah — God willing.

Fajer — one of the five daily Muslim prayers, said before sunrise.

Ghutra — Soft cotton folded into triangular shape headdress worn by males in the Arabian Gulf along with a circular black cord to hold the ghutra in place.

Inshallah kheir — God willing, things go well.

Mabrook — Arabic for 'congratulations'.

Ma'a salama — a word used to say goodbye, literally means 'go with peace'.

Masha'allah — a word used to ward off the evil eye because of jealousy. Literally means from God comes a blessing or positive attribute.

Oud — scented oil.

Shabka — a set of jewelry, including necklace and earrings, given by the groom to his bride

Shayla — head covering worn by Muslim women.

Sheikh – name used in the Arabian Gulf for Muslim religious clergy.

Shawarma — Arab version of a chicken burrito, wrapped in pita bread with a spicy mayonnaise-like sauce, tomato, pickled vegetables and lettuce.

Tabouli — a type of salad made from chopped parsley, mint, bulgur, tomatoes, and onions served in the Middle East and North Africa.

Thobe — traditional men's clothing in the Arabian Gulf, a white starched robe with long sleeves.

Ubooy — traditional title for father in the Gulf dialect.

Ummi – traditional title for mother in the Gulf dialect.

Yella — slang Arabic expression meaning 'come on, hurry up, let's go'.

Yema — term used for mother when speaking to one's mother in the Gulf dialect.

Yuba — term used for father when speaking to one's father in the Gulf dialect.

Mohanalakshmi Rajakumar is a South Asian American who has lived in Qatar since 2005. Moving to the Arabian Desert was fortuitous in many ways since this is where she met her husband, had two sons, and became a writer. She has since published eight e-books, including a memoir for first time mothers, *Mommy But Still Me;* a guide for aspiring writers, *So You Want to Sell a Million Copies;* a short story collection, *Coloured and Other Stories;* and a novel about women's friendships, *Saving Peace.*

Her coming of age novel, *An Unlikely Goddess,* won the SheWrites New Novelist competition in 2011.

Her recent books have focused on various aspects of life in Qatar. *From Dunes to Dior,* named as a Best Indie book in 2013, is a collection of essays related to her experiences as a female South Asian American living in the Arabian Gulf. *Love Comes Later* was the winner of the Best Indie Book Award for Romance in 2013 and is a literary romance set in Qatar and London. *The Dohmestics* is an inside look into compound life, the day-to-day dynamics between housemaids and their employers.

After she joined the e-book revolution, Mohana dreams in plotlines. Learn more about her work on her website at www.mohadoha.com or follow her latest on Twitter: @moha_doha.

If you enjoyed this book and have a few minutes to leave a review, you'll help more readers find stories like these.

You can also receive a FREE copy of Mohana's short story collection, *Coloured and Other Stories,* by signing up for her email newsletter: http://www.mohadoha.com/newsletter/.

Mohanalakshmi Rajakumar
www.mohadoha.com
@moha_doha
www.facebook.com/themohadoha

Before you start reading, check out the book trailer for any of Mohana's titles!
www.youtube.com/themohadoha

The Migrant Report, Book One, Crimes in Arabia series

The penalty for stealing is losing your hand. No wonder Ali can leave his wallet overnight in his office. Yet crime hovers on the fringes of society, under the veneer of utopia.

Police captain Ali's hopes of joining the elite government forces are dashed when his childhood deformity is discovered. His demotion brings him face to face with the corruption of labor agencies and also Maryam, an aspiring journalism student, who is unlike any local girl he has ever met.

Ali and his unlikely sidekick must work together to find the reason so many laborers are dying. Against the glittery backdrop of the oil rich Arabian Gulf, Ali pursues a corrupt agency that will stop at nothing to keep their profits rising. As the body count rises, so does the pressure to settle the source. Can Ali settle the score before the agency strikes again?

The Opposite of Hate

"...this is a book which lingered in my imagination long after I finished it, and offered an invaluable insight into Lao culture and its recent history."
--Kate Cudahy

During the 1960s and 70s, more bombs were dropped on a landlocked part of Southeast Asia than in any other war - and it wasn't Vietnam. The turbulent history of the Land of a Thousand Elephants, the Kingdom of Laos, is the backdrop for this family saga, told as a historical novel. THE OPPOSITE OF HATE opens a window onto a forgotten corner of Southeast Asia and brings little known history to life through vivid characters and settings which explore the cultural heritage of Lao history.

This is a tale of intermingled violence, love and ambition. Seng and Neela embody the historic cultural struggle of thousands who fled the threats of communism only to face the challenges of democracy.

The Dohmestics

"On the surface, it appears to be about six women whose lives intertwine, three are privileged women and three are their servants. But, there is so much more to this book."

--Aya Walksfar

Edna, Amira, and Noof are neighbors but that doesn't mean they know what happens behind closed doors or that they have anything in common with their hired help.

Maria, Maya, and Lillie live in the same compound as their employers but that's where the similarities begin and end.

There's never a dull moment for anyone in this desert emirate.

The unending gossip and unrelenting competition may be business as usual for expatriate communities but the unspoken secrets threaten to destroy life as everyone knows it.

Love Comes Later

**Winner of the Best Indie Book Award 2013, Romance
Short listed for the New Talent Award, Festival of Romance
2012**

"*Love Comes Later* is about love, choices, culture, bigotry, family, tradition, religion, honesty, forgiveness and friendship, to name just a few. The story allows a Westerner to actually see and feel what it is like to be a Muslim, with strong family ties, living in Qatar."

--Diana Manos

Hind is granted a temporary reprieve from her impending marriage to Abdulla, her cousin. Little does anyone suspect that the presence of Sangita, her Indian roommate, may shake a carefully constructed future. Torn between loyalties to Hind and a growing attraction to Abdulla, Sangita must choose between friendship and love.

From Dunes to Dior

**Winner of Indie Book of the Day September 2013
Witty, Intriguing and full of stories and curiosities worth
reading.**

"Which country in the Middle East is safe and hip and quirky? How does an ex-pat survive in a world completely unlike anything they know? Mo is one of those rare joyful writers who will walk with you through these answers."

--Shariyousky

Called everything from the world's richest to fattest nation, Qatar has been on the breakneck path towards change for several decades. The capital city Doha, is where our family of three has lived since 2005.

Mommy But Still Me

Enjoyable, honest, very real and funny

"… a funny and entertaining journal that takes you inside the upcoming changes of a working women who is about to embark in one of the most important journeys of her life: becoming a mum!"

--Alejandra

Imagine a man volunteering to trade in his game nights for heart burn and back ache. Good thing there are women around to ensure the survival of the species. This hilarious look at the journey from high heels to high blood pressure, as a jet setter turns into a bed wetter, is what your doctor won't tell you and your own mother may have forgotten in the years since she was blessed by your arrival.

So, You Want to Sell a Million Copies?

Helpful, informative guide every author needs!

"This book is such a helpful guide and is chockfull of tips, exercises, humor, and practical advice for any writer, whether you are just starting out or finding yourself consumed with the minutiae of daily living and looking for a way to get your ideas down into some form of structure."

--Rachel Thompson

If you've had a story idea in your head for a day, year, (or longer) that it doesn't seem to be writing itself, you may want to take a closer look at this book. Designed as a concise guide for aspiring writers, you'll find here the key principles of how to get started, keep going, and finish a manuscript, all told by a fellow accidental writer who took the long way developing a writer's formula.

Coloured and Other Stories

5.0 out of 5 stars **Brilliant short stories**

"The stories in Coloured are instantly absorbing- which is a triumph with short stories where the writer only has a limited number of pages to win you over."

--Phoebe

What's it like being the ant in the ice cream? The characters in this short story collection will show you. Experience life as they know it as transplants from across the world into American suburbia.

An Unlikely Goddess

Winner of the SheWrites New Novelist Award 2011
4.5 out of 5 stars

"When a title fits the book in every way with everything within the tale, its like the sprinkles on top of a cake"

--Cabin Goddess

Sita is the firstborn, but since she is a female child, her birth makes life difficult for her mother who is expected to produce a son. From the start, Sita finds herself in a culture hostile to her, but her irrepressible personality won't be subdued. Born in India, she immigrates as a toddler to the U.S. with her parents after the birth of her much anticipated younger brother. Sita shifts between the vastly different worlds of her WASP dominated school and her father's insular traditional home. Her journey takes us beneath tales of successful middle class Indians who immigrated to the U.S. in the 1980s. The gap between positive stereotypes of South Asian immigrants and the reality of Sita's family, who are struggling to stay above the poverty line is a relatively new theme for Indian literature in English.

Sita's struggles to be American and yet herself, take us deeper into understanding the dilemmas of first generation children, and how religion and culture define women.

Saving Peace

4 out of 5 stars

"I do not know whether to laugh, cry or throw my Kindle because of how this book ended."

--Suzie Welker

You go to college to meet your bridesmaids," or so the saying goes in North Carolina, on the campus of the all female Peace College. But what happens when the friends you thought you were making for life, betray you? The same ones you'd be in the retirement home with aren't speaking not ten years later? The ups and downs of women's friendships are tested in SAVING PEACE. Thirty years intervene in the friendships begun at the all female Peace College.

Sib, the local news anchor with dreams of going national. Mary Beth, the capable, restless mother of three. Kim, the college president who admits male students.

SAVING PEACE is the story of promises made and broken, love found then lost, and redemption sought for the past. Three women. Two choices. One campus.

What if there's nothing worth saving?

Prologue

Abdulla's mind wasn't on Fatima, nor on his uncles or cousins. Not even when he drove through the wrought iron entry gate, oblivious to the sprawl of family cars parked haphazardly in the shared courtyard, did he give them a thought. Despite the holy season, his mind was still hard at work. Mentally he clicked through a final checklist for tomorrow's meetings. *I can squeeze in a few more hours if Fatima is nauseous and sleeps in tomorrow*, he thought, rubbing his chin. Instead of the stubble he had anticipated, his whiskers were turning soft. A trim was yet another thing he didn't have time for these days, though longer beards were out of fashion according to his younger brother Saad, who had been trying to grow one for years. Beard length. Just another change to keep up with.

Change was all around him, Abdulla thought. The cousins getting older, he himself soon to become a father. Abdulla felt the rise of his country's profile most immediately in the ballooning volume of requests by foreign governments for new trade agreements. By the day, it seemed, Qatar's international status was growing, which meant more discussions, more meetings.

He slid the car into a gap in the growing shadow between his father's and grandfather's houses. It would have to serve as a parking space. The Range Rover door clicked shut behind him as he walked briskly toward his father's house, BlackBerry in hand, scrolling through his messages. Only then did the sound of wailing reach him, women in pain or grief, emanating from his Uncle Ahmed's house across the courtyard. He jerked the hands-free device out of his ear and quickened his pace, jogging not toward the *majlis* where the rest of the men were gathering, but into the main living area of Uncle Ahmed's, straight toward those unearthly sounds.

The sight of Aunt Wadha stopped him short. Disheveled, her *shayla* slipping as she howled, she was smacking herself on the forehead. Then came his mother, reaching her arms out to him with a tender, pitying look he hadn't seen since his pet rabbits from the *souq* died. But it was Hessa, his other aunt – Fatima's mother, his own mother-in-law – who sent him into a panic. Ashen-faced, her lips bleeding, she was clutching the evil eye necklace he had bought Fatima on their honeymoon. At the sight of it, the delicate gold cord in Hessa's hands instead of around his wife's neck, Abdulla felt his knees buckle and the BlackBerry slip from his hand.

"What has happened?" he said. He looked from one stricken face to another.

Numbly, he saw his female cousins were there. At the sight of him, the older ones, glamorous Noor and bookish Hind, both now adult women in their own right, whom he hadn't seen in years, jerked their *shaylas* from their shoulders to cover their hair and went into the adjoining room. In his haste, he hadn't said "*Darb!*" to let them know he was entering the room.

"Abdulla, Abdulla…" his mother began, but she was thrust aside by Aunt Hessa. "Fatima," Hessa screamed, staring wildly at him. "Fatima!"

Rather than fall onto the floor in front of the women, Abdulla slumped heavily into the nearest overstuffed armchair. *Fatima…*

They left behind gangly nine-year-old Luluwa, Fatima's sister, who resisted when they tried to take her with them. His father, gray-faced and tired, entered. Abdulla slouched and waited, the growing dread like something chewing at his insides. His father began to talk, but on hearing "accident" and "the intersection at Al Waab" he remembered the Hukoomi traffic service SMS. Then he heard "Ahmed," and a shiver of horror ran up his back. The driver had been Ahmed, his uncle and father-in-law.

Later that night in the morgue, in the minutes or hours (he couldn't keep track) while he waited to receive her body, Abdulla flicked his Zippo lighter open and struck it alight. Holding it just so, he burned a small patch on his wrist just below his watchstrap. Even this couldn't contain his rage at the truck driver who came through without a scratch, at his uncle, or at himself.

The morgue was antiseptic, mercilessly public. The police advised against seeing her, insisting that he wouldn't be able to erase the memory of a face marked with innumerable shards of glass.

Surrounded by family and hospital staff, he couldn't hold her, talk to her, or stroke her slightly rounding stomach, the burial site of their unborn child. Any goodbyes he had hoped to say would have to be suppressed.

He would mourn the baby in secret. He hadn't wanted to tell relatives about the pregnancy too soon in case of a miscarriage. Now it could never happen: the need to visibly accept God's will in front of them would prevent him from crying it out—this woe upon woe that was too much to bear.

Fatima's body was washed and wrapped, and the prayers said before burial. His little wife with the round face and knowing eyes he'd grown up next to in the family compound, and the baby he would never see crawl, sleep or walk, were hidden from him now for all eternity. The secret she was carrying was wrapped with her in a gauzy white *kaffan,* her grave cloth, when he was finally allowed to see them. The child would have been named after Abdulla's grandfather if a boy, his grandmother if a girl, whose gender would now remain a mystery.

At the burial site, as was customary, he fell in line behind his father and uncles. Ahmed, the father, carried his daughter's slight form.

They placed her on her right side.

Men came to lay the concrete slabs that sealed the grave, so her frame would not rise up as it decomposed in the earth. Abdulla regretted not having been able to stroke the softness of her chin or the imperceptibly rounding curve of her belly. *I am burying my wife and our unborn child,* he thought, the taste of blood filling his mouth from the force with which he bit his cheek to stem the tears. Their secret would have to be lost within her lifeless womb. News of a *double* tragedy would spread with the sand under doors and into the ears of their larger circle of acquaintances. Someone would call someone to read the Qur'an over him. Someone would search out someone else for a bottle of *Zamzam* water from Mecca.

None of it would stop the acid from gnawing through his heart.

In swirls of conjecture and pity, his newly-assigned role as the widowed and grieving almost-father, would replace his role as the eldest grandchild in a fertile and happy extended family. His birth order had focused their marital intents on him. Caught between duty and tradition, he did the only thing he could do. He tried to forget that he had been too busy to drive Fatima that day, the day he lost a wife and a child because of his own selfishness. He had thought they had years ahead, decades, when they would have time to spend together. A chubby infant growing into a child who went to school, for whose school holidays they would have to wait to travel abroad, and eventually another child, maybe several more. Now none of this would ever be.

He should have died with them. But he kept on breathing—as if he had a right to air.

They returned from the funeral to gather at the home of the grieving parents for the 'azaa, the receiving of condolences. Abdulla rode in the back seat of the Land Cruiser, his father at the wheel, his cousins and brothers messaging friends on various applications. For him there was no sharing of grief. This was his burden to bear alone.

He was the last to climb out of the car, but the first to see Luluwa hunched on the marble steps of Uncle Ahmed's entryway. The lines around her mouth, pulling it downward, aging her face, drew his attention; the stooped shoulders spoke of a burden heavier than grief for her sister. His mother saw it at the same time and hurried over to the girl, concerned.

"*Yalla,* what is it?" she said, pulling her up.

Luluwa shook her head.

"Go inside, *habibti,*" said Abdulla's mother, but Luluwa shook free and drew back, panic in her wide eyes. Abdulla's mother turned her face back to the men. Then they heard the shouting.

"When? When did this all start?" Hessa's voice screamed, raw and startling, from inside the open door. "Leave this house."

The family halted in their tracks, exchanging uncertain glances.

Ahmed emerged, looking shaken but defiant, a weekender bag in one hand. Abdulla's father, the eldest of the brothers, stepped forward and took him by the arm.

"Everyone is upset," he whispered harshly. He was trying to lead him back inside, as his wife had done a moment ago with Luluwa, when Hessa burst forward into view, her face aflame with indignation.

"Tell them," she spat at her husband. "Tell them now, so when you don't come back here everyone will know why."

The words made no sense to Abdulla. His first thought was to speak up and still the voices. He had already forgiven Ahmed in his mind. The accident hadn't been his fault. "There's no reason to throw him out," he called out, half-climbing the steps. "It was my fault, not his. I should have been driving them."

Hessa turned towards him and laughed in a way that made the hairs on the back of his neck stand on end. "Who needs to throw him out when he's leaving?" she said. "Leaving his daughter to a house with no man to look after her. She might as well have died with her sister."

"*Yuba,* no," Luluwa cried, moving toward her father, but her mother grabbed a fistful of her *abaya* and spun the girl around by the shoulders.

Abdulla's mind whirred to compute what they were witnessing. A sudden white-hot rage stiffened his spine. His gaze narrowed on Ahmed. *So the rumors were true,* he thought.

"He doesn't want me and so he doesn't want you," Hessa hissed, nose to nose with her daughter.

The family froze in the entryway as understanding sluiced them like rainwater. Ahmed stood for a moment in the glare of their stares. He shifted the weekender bag into his opposite hand.

Saoud, the middle brother, stepped forward to question Ahmed, the baby of the family, but Hessa wasn't finished yet.

"Go," she screamed at her husband. "You'll never set foot in any house with me in it ever again." She collapsed onto the floor, her *abaya* billowing up around her like a mushroom, obscuring her face.

Saoud moved quickly to stand in front of his brother as his wife helped Hessa up. "Think of your daughter," she added pointedly. "The one that's still alive."

Abdulla brought Luluwa forward. Her face was tear-streaked and her body trembling so hard it was causing his hand to shake.

"Keep her, if you want," Ahmed said, his glance flickering over Luluwa's bent head. "My new wife will give me many sons." He sidestepped Mohammed and Saoud, continuing on down the stairs towards his car.

The look Hessa gave Luluwa was filled with loathing. She dissolved into another flood of tears.

The girl darted inside. Abdulla followed as his parents tried to deal with the aftermath of his uncle's leaving. His aunt looked as though she might faint. His cousins' faces were ashen. Mohammed and Saoud murmured in low voices about the best way to deal with their brother's child. She couldn't live in a house with boys; one of those boys, her cousins, might one day be her husband.

He followed Luluwa's wailings, sounds without any force, the bleating of a cat, like one of any number roaming the streets of the city. Without a male family member to look after her, she would be as abandoned as those animals. And, in the eyes of their society, as susceptible to straying. He found her on the sofa, typing away on her laptop, and hoped she wasn't posting their family's mess on the internet. Wedged next to her hip was an opaque paper bag stamped with their grandfather's name, the white tops of a few pill bottles visible.

Abdulla came and sat on the sofa next to her, unsure of what to do next. He was assaulted by her screensaver, a photo of Fatima and Luluwa on the evening of the wedding reception. He hadn't yet arrived with the male relatives; the bride and the rest of the women were still celebrating without *hijab*. His wife's eyes stared back at him even as her sister's now poured tears that showed no sign of stopping.

With trembling hands Luluwa wrenched open the bag of medicine and dug around for pills. She let the laptop slip and he caught it before it hit the floor. As he righted it, the heading of the minimized Google tab caught his attention: *suicide*. For one moment he allowed himself to admit that the idea she was apparently contemplating had begun to dance at the edge of his own mind.

"Don't," he said. "What will we do if both of you are gone?"

He put the laptop aside and, as if calming a wild colt, reached out slowly, deliberately, to take the bottle from her shaking hands. With little effort he wrenched it from her, and with it any remaining shred of strength. She dissolved into incoherent sobs, a raging reminder of what it meant to be alive, to be the one left behind.

Abdulla folded her into his arms, this slip of a girl who used to hide his car keys so that her weekend visits with her sister and brother-in-law wouldn't have to end, this girl who had already lost so much, a sister and now a father and mother. Instead of shriveling into himself, as he had felt like doing from the moment he saw his family in mourning, Abdulla's heart went out to Luluwa. He murmured reassurances, trying to reverse the mirror of his own loss that he saw reflected in her eyes.

"We can do this," he said. "She would want us to."

She pulled away to look at him.

"Together," he said. From deep in his own grief he recognized the despair that would haunt him for years, and made a pledge to keep the decay he felt growing inside him from tainting someone so young. He would bear the guilt. It was his alone to bear.

He would speak to his father. If nothing else, perhaps Luluwa might gain a new brother, and he a little sister. Small comfort, but tied together in the knowledge of the loved one they had lost, a bond that might see them through what was to come.

Made in the USA
Charleston, SC
07 July 2016